MW00830323

Digging Through Dirty Laundry

A Sharp Investigations Novel

Book Three

BY: E. N. CRANE

EDITED BY: A. O. NEAL &
SUE SCOTT

Dedication

Thank you to my dogs: Perry and Padfoot.

Their shenanigans, antics and behavior are the model for all things Winnie.

Thank you to my husband, because he knows how many "people" live in my head and he's never had me committed. He also keeps me in coffee and snacks when I start yelling at imaginary people.

Special thanks to Jeff Neal for lending me his artistic eye and military knowledge. Most of this is made up, but I strive for imaginative accuracy.

Chapter One: New Ride

"What the hell is that?" I stared in horror and simultaneously needed to blink repeatedly to stave off the brightness.

"It's your new Jeep," Larry responded without hesitation. Rubbing the sleep from my lavender eyes and shoving back my messy tangle of blonde hair, I tried to orient myself to what I was looking at. My eyes took in the Jeep, the sidewalk, and my feet in their yellow Crocs six feet below me... Everything was real... Real and...

"It's pink," I gawked as a group of middle school girls stopped in front of the car and took selfies with it. They threw up peace signs and tried to look cute but sexy, disturbing for pre-pubescent girls, but middle school was like that.

"You like pink," he countered, and I narrowed my eyes at the Jeep. I'd been happily sleeping in my own bed when Larry had let himself into my apartment, pulled me out of bed, and after a few inappropriate gropes, brought me outside. My apartment was on Main Street, a small single room affair that sat on a third of the library lot above a small office. The office and the apartment belonged to a couple of local senior citizens who let me live there in exchange for investigative services donated to the town.

"It has a giant Hello Kitty on the hood!"

"So does your underwear, Cyn," he smirked at his own joke. The middle school girls giggled, giving Larry sly glances. Hard to blame them, really. Dr. Larry Kirby was tall, leanly muscled with messy brown hair and flawless skin. Sometimes I just stared at him and giggled too.

Just not when he was talking about my underwear on a public street.

"Where did it come from? Why is it here? I *have* a vehicle."

"No, you were borrowing my truck. The insurance money from your Jeep came in, and you left it sitting there for two weeks. So I took it, bought you this Jeep, and now I need my truck keys back." He held out his hand and I rounded on him.

"Why can't I keep borrowing your truck? You stole my money? I'm sooo telling your brother!" I said, reminding both of us that his brother, Daniel Kirby, was local law enforcement. Incompetent law enforcement, but still technically tasked with upholding the law. He had been the hottest guy in high school with a reputation for nail and bail. Now he was married with way too many kids, and had the investigative skills of a toddler immediately after reading Sherlock Holmes.

He also had zero sense of humor, at least when it came to reminding him of his own stupidity.

"You would never willingly talk to Daniel. Not after his anniversary party!" Larry's wide smile reminded me of what happens when a bunch of children covered in food and food-like substances stand too close to a German Shepherd Malinois mix with an uncontrollable appetite. The child had been right at Winnie height, waving a hot dog around like a baton. Hilarious in retrospect, the incident may have taken years off her mother's life.

"Winnie didn't eat any fingers, so I think I'm good!" My eyes dropped to the fur monster in question. Sgt. Winifred Pupperson, Winnie for short, and I had been in the Army together. We had been military police and served four years with an impeccable record of chaos, destruction, snack theft and an occasional fire. The Army had been relieved when our contract expired, and they "accidentally" forgot to mention it so we couldn't re-up. Specialist Cynthia Sharp and Sgt. Winifred Pupperson retired to Cyn and Winnie, Ohio's most competent demolition experts.

Certified only to work at a farm maintaining livestock outputs for sale.

"Manda won't touch a hot dog if she's seen a dog in the last ten minutes!" Larry was now laughing, and I thought of the poor, messy child in her stained dress and muddy feet. She'd pet Winnie for twenty minutes once she stopped crying but it had been a long... however many minutes she'd been crying.

"Ugh, fine. I won't tell him you forged my name on a check, cashed it, and bought me a hideous pink Hello Kitty Jeep that is probably mechanically unsound and filled with bubblegum pop music. But why can't I keep borrowing your truck? I mean I fill it with gas, and I haven't hit anything!"

"Seriously? You don't know why?" I winced and shook my head. Innocent until proven guilty works in a court of law, maybe it works in the court of *your lover knows you took his truck mudding and spilled a two-liter bottle of Cherry Coke and a large McDonalds fries that Winnie ate and then barfed up into the upholstery.* "I saw that, you know what you did, young lady."

I moved really close to him and gave him sexy eyes.

"I could do you... in the truck. Doesn't that sound fun? Don't you want to... in your truck?"

"Yeah, I can hold out longer than you can. We've proved it. You can't have my truck, not after the gummy bears." He tapped a finger on my nose.

Damn, I'd forgotten about the gummy bears. Specifically, I'd forgotten that the gummy bears were now permanently adhered to the bottom of his glove compartment and one of the seatbelts in the back seat.

"Fine," I stepped back from him, and felt his eyes on my pajama shorts as I walked toward the pink abomination. For his benefit, I stuck my head through the window and pushed my butt in the air. It's important to remind a man that while he might be able to hold out longer, the world could see his affliction. With Herculean effort, I tried to execute a perfect Betty Boop sorority squat and hoped it looked sexier than it felt.

As expected, the seats were fluffy pink, the stereo lit up in shades of purple, and the steering wheel was covered in glitter. I picked at the wheel with a nail to remove the cover.

It wasn't a cover. Someone had silicone lacquered the steering wheel with pink glitter.

I shuddered as another group of girls came by and snapped selfies with it.

Larry had bought me Malibu Barbie's car, and he looked a little adorable for having done it. Hands in his pockets, nervously ruffled hair... he shifted.

"If you really hate it..."

Glancing at the front of his pants I had to smile and gesture to the door behind him.

I walked back to the front of my building and opened it, holding the door for the parade that followed behind me. First Winnie and then Larry came inside, the last locking the door to the office behind him. My apartment was accessible only via a rear fire door and a door in the back of my office. Both led to the same staircase, and at the top were cozy living quarters that were plenty for an ex-military working dog and her handler.

Larry just plugged himself in wherever there was space.

"How did you get that here?" I asked, walking into the kitchen. A full pot of coffee sat in the machine, and I furrowed my brows at it. Had I progressed to making coffee in my sleep? I know people did weird things on Ambien, but I was fairly certain I didn't take Ambien. Though if my sleepwalking meant I had coffee ready when I was awake walking, I was willing to keep taking drugs.

"I started the pot before I woke you up because I value my life," Dr. Kirby said from beside me where he set two mugs on the counter. "Also, I fed Winnie for the same reason. You're welcome."

I grabbed his butt in lieu of saying thank you, and he kissed my temple before bringing out milk, flavored syrup, and sauces. Eyes dropping, I just stared at his butt while he made two cups of coffee and passed me one in a delightful mug with a rainbow and a unicorn that declared I was "F***ing Magical".

"So, how did you get the pink Jeep here?" I asked again after half of the coffee was gone from my pink unicorn cup.

"I drove it." He left the kitchen to sit on the couch, and I stared. "What? Don't even pretend there's a no coffee on your couch policy. We both know that you would drink coffee while we had sex if your hand eye coordination could manage it."

As I had considered an option with a travel cup and straw, I decided to plead the fifth on that for now.

"You... Drove that? It's pink!"

"Yeah and?"

"You're... that!" I gestured the length of his body. Winnie cocked her head to the side on the couch beside him, and he mimicked her gesture. The man was wearing his glasses, sitting with a leg crossed over the other, in a hooded sweatshirt advertising his ridiculously named veterinary clinic. "Weren't you embarrassed?"

"Toxic masculinity is what's wrong with America, Cyn. Men can drive pink, glittery, Hello Kitty Jeeps without any loss of manliness," he patted the couch on his other side. I refilled my coffee and plopped on the couch beside him, being extra careful not to spill.

If the travel mug and straw option didn't work out, I was willing to work on my grace to have sex and coffee at the same time.

"First of all, toxic masculinity is an international problem. Second, I thought America was anti-vaxxers, systemic racism, lack of respect for nature, a disregard for science, the media..."

"Yeah... it might be a shorter list if we just listed all the things *not* wrong with the world... and America," he mused, following my train of thought. I clinked our coffee mugs in agreement and took a long drink.

"If only the Infinity Stones were real, Thanos could solve this problem."

"Would you snap away half of the population? Who would grow, harvest, and roast your coffee?" Larry wrapped his arm around me, and I leaned against him, drinking my hot bean water as though it could be snapped away at any moment. The question was a little too deep for morning hours, and I didn't have an answer.

"You know it's not staying pink, right?" My eyes drifted to the offending vehicle. It was still parked on Main in front of my building, and it had drawn the largest crowd of people not waiting in line for food in the history of Main Street. Almost on cue, my friend and local bakery owner, Mary O'Connor, appeared with themed cookies that she was selling to the gathered crowds.

"When do you think Mo made kitty cookies?" I asked, using her nickname and getting on my knees to look out at her artistry. Despite being too far away to actually see the cookies, I was certain they were as brilliant and adorable as everything she made.

"Do you think she'd bring me a kitty cookie if I asked?" My eyes drifted over my shoulder to Larry who licked his lips.

Larry was not looking at the cookies.

He also wasn't looking at the car.

"Some people are really into kitty... speaking of which?" he waggled his eyebrows suggestively, and my lower body flooded with warmth.

"Depends... Aren't you still allergic to cats?" I asked, studying him over my coffee cup. He took the cup, verified it was empty because he values his life, and put it on the table.

"I'm not allergic to this one," his mouth pressed against mine, parting my lips with his tongue while his hands slid up the pajama shorts I was wearing. "In fact, I think I want to adopt it so it's mine forever."

"Hello, kitty," he whispered.

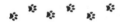

"What the hell is that?" Marvin asked, and I followed his gaze through the front window of the shop. Sitting in front was the pink Hello Kitty Jeep that now shimmered in the sun. The paint had just looked matte pink in the morning light, but at high noon, it was a beacon of mental and visual torture.

Also, the glitter steering wheel trapped heat and my hands had melted on the two-block drive despite the sixty-degree temps outside. I'd spent fifteen minutes I was waiting for Marvin's shop to open trying to buy a new steering wheel but kept getting outbid on eBay.

"It's apparently mine. Can you fix it?"

"With matches and lighter fluid." He couldn't take his eyes off the pink Jeep and I started to nod agreement but then remembered I didn't have any other money for cars. Not when I was constantly forking over money to repair Winnie catastrophes and keeping us in caffeine and snackage.

"I was more thinking about a paint job," I told him, and he shook his head. Apparently he really wanted to set something on fire.

"It'll take days for color to get delivered." He tapped into his computer. "Also, you gotta pick a color, and your dog ended my sample book."

I looked down at Winnie and she wagged her tail, a few crumbs and a smidge of mustard still on her muzzle.

"Sorry," I said to my shoes.

We'd walked into the body shop, and Winnie had been off-leash. Marvin had been eating a sandwich which we interrupted with our arrival. His shop hadn't opened yet, but lunch had arrived for the man. I was too distracted by the behemoth that was my car to notice he was eating. Marvin set the sandwich down on top of a book to help me, and Winnie had jumped onto the counter, devoured the sandwich, and picked up the book while holding half down with her paw, splitting the inventory from the ordering section. I'd jumped forward to get it back from her with a stern *no,* but that became a game of chase faster than Hello Kitty Pink Jeep could draw a crowd. A pursuit ensued, Winnie lunging and dancing just out of reach, straight into the workshop for vehicle restorations. She startled a man working with a caustic liquid that spilled when Winnie dropped the book to shove her snoot into his butt and give him what was likely his first proctology exam ever at the hands, or rather nose, of a canine.

The liquid spilled, missing the young man's shoes but dissolved the book in less than a minute.

"I'll pay for a new one," I glared at my partner, and she wagged her tail again. "Do you have any... left-overs from other jobs lying around? I'd like it to not be pink until I can pick what color it will be."

"Options are limited," he warned.

We watched a group of girls leave the pottery-painting place across the street and gush over my ride. They begged their moms to take their picture with the Jeep, throwing up peace signs and cupping their hands beneath their chins.

"Literally, any color," I confirmed, and he shook his head in disgust.

"Who would do that to a perfectly good automobile?"

"Who would do that to anything?"

We stared out of the window in silence as a bus of Asian tourists arrived, forming a line to take photos with the Jeep on their way into the restaurant next door. The nearest point of interest was an hour and forty-five minutes away, but the Noodle House must have paid someone a fortune to get their establishment added to a tourist itinerary.

A fortune they did not spend on ingredients since I found three-dozen packages of Top Ramen in their trash last week.

Finding the wrappers was unrelated to the reason I was looking in the trash, but they'd bought my silence with beef and broccoli. Silence and the gift of a bus boy to help me go through the trash looking for a purloined wedding band.

Marvin shook his head as the line slowly dwindled and the car sat alone once more. Both our phones dinged, and we looked to see we had been tagged in social media posts by every selfie taker that day.

"I'll see what I can do. Do you need it today?"

"No, I can walk everywhere I need to go today." A group of teenage boys took the place of the tourists and were now pretending to lick the character on the hood. "Seriously, what is wrong with this town?"

Marvin chuckled and shook his head.

"Let's be realistic, that Jeep is the most entertaining thing this town has seen since you blew up Roger's trailer." He pointed a finger at my chest and I felt my face burn. "Well, and when you managed to get Daniel Kirby stuck in that woman's cleavage."

"Can I blame the chickens?" I asked no one in particular. "The chickens and the rocks and... insufficient caffeination?"

"You can, but no one would believe you. We've all seen the delivery men going to your building with boxes upon boxes of coffee," Marvin tossed me a newspaper from a small stack beside his computer. "Catch up on current events, and I'll call you when it's done."

Nodding, I took Winnie's leash and we walked out onto Main St, carefully avoiding the Jeep. There was now a group of seniors, collectively muttering about the nerve of Millennials to ruin a perfectly good car. While I agreed with them, there was something insulting that they thought Millennials would do that to a Jeep. It was not a generational issue; it was a single person with issues that hopefully got help, which is why they sold the Pepto Bismol monstrosity.

To Larry, who arguably also needed help.

Who I was sleeping with so maybe the three of us could get a group rate.

Without anything to do on my Sunday, I took Winnie to the park, plopped on a bench, and opened the newspaper. A new column had appeared since I'd been back, Yvette Taylor's *Small-Town Scandals*. Last month, she'd taken down Amber Carter from Amber's Shoe Ambrosia with an expose on her life's failures that included trying to join the Army. While I hadn't known Amber had tried to join the Army shortly after I did, it was surprising that she failed the medical exam and aptitude tests.

Not surprising in that *she's so helpful and brilliant* kind of way. More surprising that she hadn't paid someone to make it go away.

There was also speculation she was adopted and not actually the daughter of Cartersville's Town Founder. While it was a stretch considering she was a carbon copy of the man but with breasts, watching her refute it for three days was delightful. Winnie and I had brought popcorn and lurked at the periphery of all of her public appearances.

It was weeks' worth of free entertainment between work and working Larry. Until Winnie tackled an old lady over some peanut butter, and we decided to make ourselves scarce before we ended up in Yvette's column. The article itself had been brilliant, but it borderline had made me want to defend Amber. Until I remembered she tormented me from Kindergarten through Twelfth grade, and I cut the article out to stick on the fridge.

Usually, I by-pass the front cover as it holds real news which I avoid, but the headline caught my attention.

GOSSIPER GOSSIPS INTO AN EARLY GRAVE

My eyes scanned the article, then I went back and read the whole thing. Yvette Taylor was dead, murdered in her office with a blunt instrument three days earlier. Many suspects, no leads, and a suspension of her column after this week as it had already been written. The article came off a little too light-hearted for murder, but Yvette wasn't exactly a pillar of politeness, and she'd exposed her own editor online before the Editor-in-Chief made the editor hire Yvette to raise sales numbers and increase online traffic to the dying paper's website. After a check of the by-line, I confirmed that the writer was one she'd ripped to shreds as a two-bit hack for hosting a Dear Abby column and accepting corporate sponsorships for advice answers. Coca Cola had paid big money for Mr. Fred Tannins to tell people soft drinks were the cure to depression and lack of energy.

He also liked to tell women that they would be prettier if they smiled more.

I flipped to page four, curious who Yvette's last victim would be. Though I'd never met her, the woman had made sarcasm and accusatory reporting an artform. While journalism was probably a little better off without her, I would miss the entertainment that came with her exaggerated ideas and her assertions into silence. Folding back the pages before, I smiled at her last headline.

LAW ENFORCEMENT'S BIGGEST LOSER: NEVER SOLVED A CRIME

Beneath the headline was Daniel Kirby in his police uniform, looking boyish and charming. A glance toward the shop showed the pink Jeep was gone, taken away to receive a makeover. My iced coffee was only three-quarters empty, so I smiled and settled in to read, delighted for once to enjoy a mystery and a scandal that did not concern me in the least.

Chapter Two: Big Brother

The sun filtered through the window and someone was using a sledgehammer nearby. I burrowed in deeper, pressing my face against the warm back of Larry. I inhaled his clean masculine scent and started to drift back to sleep...

A voice joined the jackhammer pounding and I realized someone was at the door.

"Larry! Where is your damn girlfriend?"

There was a very angry man on the other side of the door. Larry rolled over with half-closed eyes, looking at me with appreciation and satisfaction. We still weren't wearing clothes and the sheets were wrapped in a ball on the floor, damp and ready for a wash. It's hard to say for sure when the fun and games ended, but the big bad wolf looked pleased with himself. A scan of my body said I was pretty pleased with myself as well, and I gave him a smile that invited another round.

"Larry!" the man shouted again, and Winnie was startled awake. She jumped to her feet, claws clattering on the floor as she raced to the door barking loud enough to wake every one of Larry's neighbors.

"You have a visitor," I whispered to him and pulled a pillow over my head to block out Winnie's barking. He seized the opportunity to tickle my ribs until I released the pillow.

"No, *you* have a visitor," Larry countered, taking my pillow and putting it over his own head. I stole it back but before I could put it over my head, he tore it from my hands and threw it across the room. Heat filled his eyes and I looked down, noticing that mornings looked very good on him.

"If we ignore him, will he go away?" I asked, reaching a hand toward him and bringing his body closer.

"Probably not, but we can see how far we get before he remembers he has a key," Larry said, closing the distance so our mouths were joined. My heart hammered in my ears, effectively blocking out Winnie's barking. When I came up for air it was to see a man standing at the foot of the bed wearing angry eyes.

I screamed.

Winnie jumped on the bed, prepared to defend us from Daniel.

"I need to talk to your girlfriend, Larry." He crossed his arms over his chest. The move accentuated the fact he never missed arm day and tailored his shirts to prove it. I crossed my arms to emphasize the same, and Larry threw the sheet over my bare breasts.

Right... naked.

"Amber isn't here," I muttered, gripping the sheet and wrapping it around as much of myself as I could. Unfortunately for Larry, that left him hanging in the breeze. His brother decided it was a good time to turn around, and Larry stretched out his arms and legs, no intention of covering himself as his flag pole waved an invitation for fun and freedom.

"What the hell were you two doing?"

"Playing Twister," I answered at the same time Larry answered.

"Playing Hide-and- Seek, you can't be It."

Annoying Daniel was really a group activity for us.

"Will you put on some pants?" He growled at the wall.

"Nope," Larry and I answered in unison, and I could hear his eyes roll.

"Also I refuse to wear a bra in the house so it's just going to be the Garden of Eden in here!"

Larry snickered and gave me a small high-five.

"I brought chocolate doughnuts, but you can have them only if you get out of bed and put on pants." He walked back out of the room and Winnie followed. Poor fool was either going to give her some treats or take a headbutt to his genitals. Hard to say which I was rooting for.

I turned back to Larry, deciding to let Winnie and Daniel fight it out, but he wasn't in bed anymore.

"Let's go, time to be adults," he said at the door to the bathroom, clean clothes in hand. He was completely naked and I had no intention of letting him put on those clothes.

"Never, get back here!"

"No," he didn't look back at me.

"Why? Can't we just make him sit out there trying to keep Winnie from eating the doughnuts?" I whined. It had been such a promising morning until Daniel showed up.

"Nope," he threw a robe at me, and I tilted my head.

"What's wrong?"

"You'd know if you were my girlfriend," he said, and closed the door to the bathroom.

Twenty minutes later, I walked out of the guest bathroom showered and wearing my own clothes. I had built up quite the collection at Larry's house. Mostly, they were his clothes that I reappropriated as mine, and he politely kept them clean for me to wear in his house. It worked out well, because there weren't a lot of clothes in my apartment and he was much better at shopping than I was.

He also didn't own any bras so my breasts were free to annoy Daniel.

All of this and it still never occurred to me that we were dating.

Probably naked in bed wasn't the best time to bring that up. Probably not a great time to bring up his arranged marriage to a woman with more hair on her head than brains inside of it.

"Hey, Larry?" I said, hoping to talk to him before facing the accusations of his brother.

Daniel was in the kitchen, standing beside an open box of doughnuts. His hair was mussed, his face two days past needing a shave, and his eyes were drooping. I scanned the kitchen, but it was empty. No other sounds filled the house, and I had a sinking feeling in my gut.

"Larry took Satan's Minion for a walk," he raked his fingers through his hair again, and I slid into a chair at the counter across from him, grabbing a doughnut. "You owe me a new shoe."

He lifted his foot and I saw half of one of his laces had been chewed off.

"I only owe you a new shoelace," I countered and he nodded his agreement.

"Fine, but that dog is still a menace."

"OK." I took a bite and tried not to be concerned that my man had taken my best friend outside and left me alone with his brother. His brother, who I had punched in the face, gotten assaulted by a crazy-woman, and was occasionally armed.

I scanned his waist, and he shook his head.

"My gun is at home, and I don't share with my brother," I gagged at his implication and he smirked. "You want me, just admit it so I can let my brother down easy. He'll be so sad that his first real girlfriend likes me better."

"Why do you want Larry's girlfriend?" I asked, finishing off my first doughnut and noticing the full coffee pot beside him.

I reached for the pot and he moved it away.

"Do you have a death wish?" I narrowed my eyes, and he had the good sense to look concerned.

"I need your undivided attention," he shifted nervously from foot to foot. Whatever the look on my face, it might match the one I was wearing in Germany when I tackled a drunk for getting handsy with a barmaid. That man had the same look on his face right before I slammed him into the ground and took a glass bottle to the back of my head.

"If you want your body to remain undivided by knife wounds, you'll put that coffee pot back and keep your mouth shut until I've had some," my robotic deadpan voice said.

The man looked like his testicles had taken cover. Daniel passed me the pot, a coffee cup and a container in the fridge labeled *For Cyn's Coffee* in Larry's untidy doctor scrawl. Once it was assembled, I took a big drink.

That is when Daniel decided to speak.

"Why do you act like you aren't Larry's girlfriend?" he asked, and I choked. I was mid-swallow and he forced me to inhale in surprise. Coffee dribbled down my chin, burned my nostrils, and sloshed down the front of my shirt.

"What?" I sputtered, carefully setting down the cup and pulling a towel from the counter.

"Why do you act like you aren't a couple? I mean you spend more time in his bed than your own. You know that's how he thinks of you."

"We've... I never... you..." I stammered, hitting the cup and spilling the rest of its contents. This time, it had the decency to spill toward the sink, but I was too overwhelmed to be horrified at the criminal waste of magic bean water. Larry thought I was his girlfriend? Had he actually told people that?

"Never mind, I need your help," He shook his head, somehow appalled by my reaction. With a glance around the kitchen, he smoothly passed back to me everything needed to make a new cup and waited until it was assembled and I'd had a drink without choking to begin. "I've been suspended, and it's serious."

"From school? For the mono thing?" I asked, referencing the time I got to play on the basketball team in the finals when the entire rest of the starting team got mono three weeks after Daniel had it. That had ended with the gym needing repairs for fire damage and structural repair that was technically my fault and not his, but the verbal thrashing he'd received from his then girlfriend, now wife, was the stuff of legends.

Rumor was she'd bought him a cast iron chastity belt for which only she had the key.

He shifted awkwardly, and I smiled at his suffering.

"Do you think... can they take back my diploma?" he whispered, and I smacked myself in the face.

"I'm joking! You graduated; they can't kick you out or retroactively fail you. You're almost forty, man, let it go."

"I am not almost forty, I'm only thirty-four!" He fisted his hands and shoved them on his hips, and I decided it was safe to drink more coffee. We had reached the petulant, self-indulgent phase of the conversation, so probably we were done discussing my relationship with Larry and his past failures in that department.

Or mine for that matter, but Daniel had no insight into those, and I intended to keep my secrets.

"Your feet are on the ground, Daniel. What part of you is suspended?"

"I meant I've been suspended from my job on the force!" He was waving his hands in the air, and I was reminded of those car dealership inflatables. He looked one good gust of wind away from flopping over on the sidewalk. Despite his distress, I failed to see anything of concern to take seriously.

"Were you on the light side or the dark side?" I joked and he stole my coffee cup, threatening to dump the contents into the sink.

"This is serious!"

"Give me back my coffee!" There wasn't much left in the pot, not a single additional drop could be wasted.

"Not until you shut up, listen, and help me!" His eyes were in full panic mode, and the humor drained from my body. He was being serious. Daniel Kirby had lost his job and he wanted my help. With a nod, I made the key locking gesture by my lips.

Serious Cyn had arrived.

I got my coffee back and sat quietly waiting for his story. Disproving the popular belief that I could neither shut up nor take anything seriously, I waited him out. He gathered himself, pacing the kitchen twice. First he leaned his palms against the counter, and then he stood up, leaned against the fridge and walked back.

If Winnie were here, she'd have nipped his ankles already.

"Did you see that article yesterday?" He finally spoke, and I nearly leapt out of my skin as my brain registered that I hadn't actually stunned him into a permanent silence.

I nodded.

"Yvette had been hounding me for a story. After the incident on Roger's farm, she'd taken to cataloging every case you solved that I hadn't. Even cases that weren't really cases, she kept a score card that she brandished while she demanded answers. The Town Council launched an investigation, and while they are quoted as saying they support the police department and my work, they dug deep into my qualifications."

I laughed.

"Yeah, the article said you were too stupid to pass a spelling test. I thought it was hilarious, but everyone knows she stretches the truth. It's almost as bad as claiming Amber was adopted. As if Amber could have been born anything but a Carter," I nearly laughed coffee out of my nose.

Daniel was not laughing.

He shifted uncomfortably, rolling onto his toes and then back to his heels. His fingers tapped restlessly on his legs and he didn't quite meet my gaze.

"Did you fail a spelling test?"

"Just one!" he declared, and his face washed over with relief. It had apparently been weighing on him to keep this secret. "Just one and I had been up all night in the hospital because my wife was in labor and the next day at the academy was an academic day. The only word on that test I really didn't know how to spell was 'vacuum', and I know how to spell it now!"

My mouth opened, and then shut again.

A grown adult had actually failed a spelling test.

What does someone say when an adult fails a spelling test? You'll do better next time?

Geez, hopefully there won't be a next time.

"So... Do you want me to investigate how to get it removed from your record? Do you want a re-test?" I rotated my finger around the rim of the coffee cup. Daniel was an idiot, but he'd never broken the law or been anything other than obnoxious. If they suspended him for failing a spelling test in the academy, something they would have known before hiring him, it was probably just for show. Easy enough to clear up if you tried.

"No, it's not about the spelling test. It's about Yvette," he picked up a coffee cup, set it back down. He picked up the saltshaker, then set it back down, and then back to the coffee cup. I placed my hand over his to stop the fidgeting. Though the cup he was picking up was empty, I had horrific visions of him putting coffee in it and sloshing the contents over the rim.

"What about her?" I prompted, not nearly as interested as I should be in watching the man squirm and spill imaginary coffee. My time would be better spent with Larry, trying to figure out if we were in a relationship and hopefully climbing back into bed. My clothes on his floor said yes, but the casual invites to come over and no real dates since the one I got drunk and passed out on his couch said no.

"They think I killed her," Daniel said, and everything else fell out of my mind.

"Who... what?" I stammered, setting my coffee down before I spilled it again. "How?"

"The council and the committee think I killed her to keep that story from getting published. I'm their prime suspect because I was the last person she was pursuing, I was near the building

24

the night in question, I'm strong enough to bludgeon her, and I didn't want to look like an idiot who couldn't spell vacuum!"

"They told you all of that? Kinda stupid to tell your suspect all the evidence against him, and it's pretty damning, but do you own whatever the weapon is?" I speculated, maintaining eye contact. Now that he confessed to failing a spelling test, he was relaxed. He was still stressed, but he was no longer uncomfortable, leading me to believe he *probably* hadn't killed her.

"No, I went to the Chief when she was killed and told him everything. No one has identified the weapon yet, not to me. He'd already known about the spelling test but I was sworn to secrecy. He didn't want the town to think poorly of me," he walked around the counter and flopped into a chair beside me. I snorted at Chief David Jones' hope, as anyone who'd met Daniel would think poorly of him.

"So, he'll probably clear you then?" I offered, taking another doughnut from the box as Larry and Winnie came in. She made a beeline toward me and the food, forcing Larry to drop the leash.

"Winnie, no!" I ordered and she tried to stop, but there was too much momentum and not enough rug on the laminate floor. She slid three feet, crashed into the back of Daniel's chair, and toppled it. The suspended deputy landed face to the floor, butt in the air, and then Winnie sat on him.

"Seriously? Could this get any worse?" His muffled voice came from beneath her tail, and he swatted her butt so he could get up.

"Hey!" Larry and I said together, and he held his hands up in defense.

25

"I was just moving her off my face, you two need to chill. I thought getting some would make both of you more mellow." His cocky swagger was back, and I rolled my eyes. Maybe for fun I'd prove he was the murderer just so he could go to jail. The man could use a time out to check back into reality.

Sweet Pea jail was a half underground cinder block without AC or heat. The upcoming summer was the perfect time-out for the man with more sex-drive than ambition and looks that made his brain shrivel in despair. I started to imagine really creative ways to prove him guilty when I noticed everyone watching me.

"The Chief, David Jones? What does he say?" I prompted him, looking at Larry. He'd probably stop doing that thing I like if I put his brother in jail. I really like that thing... I really like all of his things.

"Dave's retiring next week. There won't be a Chief until they hire a new one," he dropped his head into his hands after righting his chair and settling in. "There's no one to investigate until a new person is hired, so the Sheriff's department is taking over, and the Chief of the Sheriff's Department hates me because of this incident with his daughter at homecoming..."

Larry and I held up our hands for him to stop.

"Don't you mean Sheriff? I thought you were a sheriff... what's the difference?" I looked around the room and Larry shrugged, shifting his rug back where it had been before taking the seat beside mine. He borrowed my empty coffee cup, poured some for himself, and took a doughnut.

"You have bigger problems than that right now," Larry said, taking a bite. It wasn't lost on me that he'd left space between us. He usually liked as little space between us as possible within the laws of physics, but there was a brisk four inches between our bodies that the Colorado River could travel in.

"Bigger problems than your brother maybe being a murderer?" I said, leaning in and stealing a bite with my hand splayed on his thigh. His eyes flashed heat, and I decided maybe I'd been hasty in comparing four inches to the Grand Canyon. It was probably a ravine that could be filled with open and honest conversation.

Crap.

Talking was probably my least favorite thing he did with his mouth, and I'm fairly certain the feeling was mutual. It wasn't that we weren't capable communicators, it's just that talking reminded me of all the times he'd let me down in our lives. What it reminded him was that I was petty, held a grudge, and was better company when there was something in my mouth.

Preferably coffee, but I accepted other possibilities.

My eyes stared at his lips, and I forgot his brother was sitting behind me. I leaned in and licked a crumb from the corner of his mouth, he tilted his head, and our lips met.

Everything else faded away as I tasted coffee and doughnuts on his tongue.

"Seriously, what could be worse?" Daniel said, and I jumped, smacking Larry's hand. He dropped a piece of old-fashioned cake doughnut that Winnie ran over and devoured in a second. Laughing, he pulled me up against him, so I was in his lap. Daniel made a gagging face, and Larry gave him the finger.

"Should you be that nice to her before you've had *the talk*?" His sneer made me want to punch him again.

"Should you be messing with her while asking her to prove you're not a murderer?" he countered, and I poked him in the ribs.

"You said there was something worse. What's worse?" I asked and he hugged me tight, pinning my arms to my side.

"For him, not much. For you... there are ten people outside Sharp Investigations, and they all want you to prove they didn't kill Yvette," he winced before finishing. "Including Amber."

Chapter Three:
Bribes and
Debauchery

L arry had not been joking.

Mo called five minutes later and said if I didn't arrive soon, she would run out of coffee and pastries to keep them happy. Her tone indicated that while she was doing killer business, she didn't doubt for a second she would be the business of a killer should she run out before I got there.

"You never run out of coffee!" I whined into the phone as I hooked Winnie to her leash to walk home. "Which one do you think is the killer and I'll have Daniel arrest them."

"They'll all kill me if I run out of coffee. I'm serious, Cyn. This is new Star Wars movie level anxiety in a line," and she hung up.

"Guess I'm going to do unpaid work first." I shrugged into my jacket. It hadn't been a warm January, but rain had been replaced with snow in February that kept going into March. Winnie needed little shoes to walk outside with the road salt, and I saw Larry had left them on after their morning walk. My heart did a gooey little flip of appreciation and I mentally smacked myself.

The man was a veterinarian; of course he cared for her paws. If he didn't he'd have to fix them.

"Smoke's coming out of your ears," Larry spoke right beside me and I felt myself go soft again.

"Thanks for putting her shoes on," I leaned in to give him a kiss and he pulled back. "What?"

"You know we need to talk, right?"

"About how I'm going to frame your brother for murder?" I asked, glancing over his shoulder at the idiot in question. He was losing a fight to a jar of pickles and even Larry rolled his eyes. When he turned back, I held up a finger.

"I know what we need to talk about, and we will... later," he nodded but I couldn't delay later forever, and we both knew it. He kissed my cheek and opened the door. "What was that?"

"We'll talk about it... later," he replied, and I considered punching him.

"Fine, but if I am murdered by a swarm of supposedly inno-cent townspeople, I want you to remember you didn't give me a proper goodbye," I walked out the front door in a frustrated state. Why was he pushing this? Why did we need a label? Why couldn't I have a damn kiss goodbye?

"This is stupid, Winnie. We're almost thirty. Who calls someone their girlfriend at thirty?" she wiggled her brows and peed on a mailbox. "Exactly!"

She pooped dangerously close to my shoe, and I cleaned it.

"You weren't agreeing with me, were you?"

Winnie wagged her tail and I sighed.

"What if he changes his mind? What if he discovers we think brushing our teeth is optional if we're really, really tired?" She leaned against my leg and I looked beside me at Mo's. Mary O'Connor had been working with Teach for America when I joined the Army. She came back, bought Margaret's Muffins, and turned it into a must-see boutique bakery. A week after I got home, there was an incident where she was taken hostage in the bakery and I was brought in to negotiate. I shot off a man's hand, and she went home with an EMT because she was "shocky". Last-ish month I wore a hideous dress to the party she insisted they have to prove to the world they were exclusive. Mo was the biggest commitment-phobe I knew, and she could do it.

Though as far as I was aware, Chris hadn't asked for a label as much as reassurance they were exclusive. Which was pretty reasonable from a physical and mental hygiene perspective.

Maybe Larry would be satisfied with a promise I'd only be with him... then we could both orgasm worry free. That would be good... no worries, no labels.

My phone pinged and I looked down at the screen.

An email from Ian Cruz sat in my inbox.

My stomach fluttered and I walked into a light pole.

"Shit!" I grabbed my head and Winnie wagged her tail. "You did that on purpose."

The dog did not deny it, and my eyes drifted from my phone to the front of my building.

"What the hell?" I stared at the line of over a dozen people. They all had coffee cups from Mo and various wrappers from her baked goods. The creator herself had wild hair and a sweat stained brow as she fought to keep up with demand. I waved to get her attention, hoping to score a coffee on my way into auditory hell, but Stephanie saw me first and screamed.

"She's here!" I expected her to finish it with "*get her*" and the whole line to surge toward me angrily. Part of me shifted my weight to run, but the other part decided Winnie probably wasn't suited to live life on the lam. Cautiously, we walked toward the office door, my hand wrapped around the doughnut in my hoodie pocket for support.

"Please don't murder me," I asked the assembled crowd, and the group shuffled into a single-file line. I felt like a first grade teacher walking toward her students on the first day of school except there was probably a murderer in my class.

I unlocked the door, carefully avoiding eye contact with Stephanie at the front of the line. Despite having known her for years, if I made eye contact she would start talking. If she started talking, I expected they all would. If they all started talking, I wasn't going to make it to the coffee machine.

Stephanie owned the local nursery and her plants grew larger and faster than anyone else in the state. I tried to place where and how someone would place a woman with the greenest thumb in Ohio as a suspect in the murderer column. People came from all around to buy her roses because they somehow defied logic and never died. Even if being tended to by a moron like Daniel Kirby, those roses would not die.

We marched into the office and I went straight to the coffee pot, adding water, grounds and pressing the on button. The line moved forward but remained mostly orderly, and I made eye contact at last.

"How are the... flowers?" I asked her and she rolled her eyes.

"Look, we're all here for the same reason, can we just get in and get on with it?" Her matter-of-fact condescending manner reminded me why I never felt the urge to buy a plant.

The woman was scary with her wild curls, gardening boots, and propensity to carry sharp objects.

"Right..." I sat in my chair and grabbed a tablet of paper, noticing the entire group had come in at once. Every one of them had an expectant look on their face, and none of them could contain the indignation radiating off of them. "So I'm guessing you are all here to tell me why you aren't murderers?"

Everyone surged forward to talk at the same time and my eye twitched.

There may not be enough coffee in the world for this.

Two hours later, I was standing in front of Marvin's shop with a raging headache and a desire to start drinking at ten in the morning. Despite two whole pots of coffee, the urge to hit the Bailey's and the Kahlua was stronger than my sense of responsibility to go to work sober.

Though with my typical lightweight rate of intoxication, if I started drinking now, I wouldn't be going anywhere but to bed. Alone.

Because I doubted Larry would take anything I said drunk at face value.

"Bad night?" Marvin joked and my eye twitched.

"Do you know how many people in this town might be murderers?" I grumbled, and he shook his head. I sniffed his breath as he popped his gum. Tobacco, spearmint, onions... the man would not be able to help me with booze.

"A lot?" he guessed, and I plopped into the guest chair, dropping my head into my palms.

"Just give me a minute," I said, as he held up a set of keys. He looked like he might toss them but thought better of it and set them on the counter.

"When you're ready, it's out back."

My head hurt too much to nod so I offered a weak thumbs up. His feet shuffled and I heard the door to the garage open. When it clicked shut, I let the ambient sounds of an oscillating fan, an ancient computer and a leaky sink soothe my frazzled and raw nerves.

So far this morning, in addition to learning way too much about the citizens of this town, I'd been offered services I not only never wanted but couldn't imagine needing. Jacob Weissman, a man four years my junior who worked at Pickles, an all-male review that leaves nothing to the imagination, offered me a lap dance. There was also an offer of a box of sex toys from the owners of The Glass Stump Shop to keep their secret of how exactly they made their incomes, especially from their family members, in addition to proving they were not murderers.

I'd also been offered a full sheep's worth of wool, a no-questions-asked favor from the undertaker, free beef and broccoli for life, and a pair of slightly used handcuffs.

The last was disturbing only in that the offer came from Daniel Kirby's one coworker, Barney Fife. Despite his insistence that there was no relation to the fictional character, I had a feeling his mom knew what she was doing when she named him. His life and personality had been predicted at birth and I often wondered if she was horrified or proud.

I rubbed my temples, trying to unlearn the dirty secrets of this town. Not only was I convinced every person I'd spoken to today could have murdered Yvette, I knew exactly how they had planned to do it. The bells on the front door jingled, and I winced at the auditory intrusion.

"Uh! There you are!"

"No," I didn't lift my head out of my hands. There was no need. The high-pitched, nasally voice was unmistakable, as was the two gallons of body spray that accompanied it and the return of my eye twitch.

Amber Carter had come to prove this day could actually get worse.

"You have to!" she simpered, and Winnie let out a fart in protest. I choked on the smell and started coughing. Winnie's cold wet nose pressed against my neck and the sensation sent shivers down my back.

"OK, OK," I said to the canine, and she wagged her tail. "When did you turn against me?"

"Are you talking to your dog?" Her voice grated my already raw nerves. "You know it doesn't understand you, right?"

"What do you want, Amber?"

It was definitely a "tequila before noon" day. Forget Bailey's, that was for amateurs.

"Hmph, obviously I need you to investigate something. Not like I'd ask you for fashion tips." I considered telling Winnie to bite her, but the toxic quantities of body spray would probably kill the fluff monster and I'd grown quite fond of her. "They think I murdered that gossiper, or whatever."

"Did you?" I asked, wondering if I could find a way to make it look like she and Daniel did it together.

"No! I wanted to, but I sooo wouldn't have hit her on the head. That's so messy." My eyes trailed up to her noodle arms. Probably she didn't have the strength anyway. Stephanie had reason to want her dead, but her plan involved burying the body and planting an endangered species on top so it would be illegal to dig her up. She also hadn't known about the bludgeoning, and she seemed a little slicey and dicey.

The local home improvement store owner had planned to dig a twelve-foot hole, put her in the bottom, add six feet of dirt, put a deer carcass in and then finish filling the hole so even if cadaver dogs were used, they'd only find the deer. Bludgeoning seemed in his wheelhouse, but his plan showed a little too much forethought to leave the body in her office.

Though I'd seen all of these as memes on the Internet, both had gone so far as to get an endangered plant and a hunting license. Not to mention the references to killers I'd never heard of and how they learned from the "mistakes" that had gotten those killers caught.

I'd be locking all of my doors and sleeping with a gun under my pillow from now on.

Also I needed to write a strongly worded letter to true crime podcasters because they were not helping the population of this town.

"I was going to push that woman in front of a bus so it would look like an accident. I even looked up bus schedules!" The last had an emphasis that suggested such things were beneath her, and I added buses to my list of things to avoid... right next to Amber Carter herself.

"What do you want me to do?" I asked, knowing the answer but curious what she thought I'd do and what she'd offer in exchange. Couldn't be better than Kyle the chicken farmer who offered me free eggs for the rest of his life.

"Prove that I didn't kill her! Obvs that's what everyone wants!"

"How would you like me to prove that you didn't kill Yvette?" I asked Winnie's toe beans. She had her paws in the air and was taking a nap. Apparently, this was not interesting enough to stay awake for.

"Tell the cops I wanted to push her in front of a bus and that *I looked up bus schedules*," she shuddered, and I suddenly knew how she failed the ASVAB.

"To be clear, you want me to go find whoever is investigating this and tell them that while yes, you wanted to murder her, you didn't because that's not how you planned to do it?" She nodded emphatically, and I couldn't help but wonder how she'd made it to twenty-nine without being arrested before.

Something must have clicked because she stopped nodding.

"No, don't do that. How did you get Maggie arrested?"

"I didn't 'get her arrested'. I got drugged and she confessed all her crimes like an idiot and then some stuff blew up. It was a whole thing." It was also a waste of effort to explain to her. The story was more well-known than just about anything Amber had ever done, and she still refused to remember.

Or was incapable, but either way I was better off saving my air for cellular respiration.

"So, arrest the person who killed her! That way they'll know it wasn't me!"

She wasn't as stupid as I thought, but I shook my head.

"I'm not a cop, I can't arrest people."

"But you *were* a cop. Can't you call that super-hot guy and have him arrest someone?" She was referring to Ian Cruz, my training sergeant at K-9 school while I was in the Army. My phone thrummed in my pocket, and I remembered he sent me an email. Cruz had switched from training K-9 handlers to solving crimes with the Army's Criminal Investigations Command, CIC. He'd come to Ohio to get a program that never existed made by Maggie's brother. Maggie wanted to kill everyone because she was an arms dealer and people were digging around where they didn't belong.

Probably she was also crazy.

Cruz had shown up when I was in Afghanistan and helped me drive a truck through a wall and kissed me in an alley. While he was in Sweet Pea, I nearly ripped his clothes off in a cemetery. Both times, he'd disappeared after.

Both times, I'd waited for him to come back.

Both times... nothing.

"Who would you like him to arrest?" I rubbed my temples. Thinking about Cruz was as painful as listening to and smelling Amber. Thinking about Cruz with the impending "talk" with Larry coming up made my stomach churn and I needed fresh air ASAP.

Also, possibly the aforementioned tequila.

"He can arrest me," she said as she ran her hands on her hips and I wanted to smash my head into a wall.

"Great, so you did kill her and I can tell the authorities?" I stood up. If she wanted Cruz to arrest her, I'd arrange for *someone* to arrest her. Barney did have those slightly used handcuffs to offer and that would be it. The End. No more "innocent" customers and she'd be in jail... or prison. Wherever murderers went, she would be with them.

Hallelujah there was a God... maybe more than one if you count Anubis, who I personally worshipped exclusively for his resemblance to a dog... maybe also his sense of obligation to weigh the hearts of man and pass judgement on them.

Not that I was judgey... much.

"No! That's not... I'll *give* you Larry!" She grabbed my arm and dug her pointed manicure into my arm. "If you find and

39

arrest the person who actually killed her and prove I didn't do it, I'll give you Larry."

"He doesn't belong to you!"

A fire filled my belly and I needed to take a long inhale before I said or did something stupid. Except the air was polluted and my heart was thudding in my chest preventing airflow. That she thought she had a say in his life was one thing, but to act like she could get and deserved better sent a new rage coursing through me that I didn't want to look at too closely.

"His mom and my dad still want us to get married if we're single at thirty. I'll tell my dad I don't want him, and then you can have him!"

She looked pretty satisfied with herself.

"Amber, I already have him." Kind of. Right after I told him that I wanted him for more than orgasms. Which I was definitely pretty sure I probably did.

Just after I got over the fear of rejection he'd heaped on me for all of our childhood.

"Do you?" she jutted a hip and I hesitated.

"What do you mean?" It was a ridiculous question; she was trying to get to me. Smart Cyn knew not to listen to my childhood bully, but insecure and needy Cyn wanted to be fed something to turn tail and run.

"Guess you didn't read Yvette's blog, I suggest you start there," Turning on her heel, Amber flounced out of the office, the bell tied to the door jingling behind her. Winnie laid her head on my shoe.

"What the hell, Winnie?" She nosed up my pants and licked my ankle.

Sighing, I took out my phone and was once again met with the email from Cruz. Just sitting there, waiting for me to open it and let him back in to ruin my life.

Ruin my life and or fill it with fun and adventure or both.

Skipping the email, I opened Yvette's old blog, searching for Larry and expecting there would be some hopelessly devoted fluff piece. When his name popped up, it was on the last post she'd made before getting her column. It featured a petite redhead with a body like a back road, she was all curves and voluptuous magic. I scrolled through the article, looking for Larry's name and instead found a picture of him, taken through a window in the woman's house and neither he nor her were wearing many clothes. The picture was captioned; Larry Kirby has a strategy for keeping his practice's misdeeds out of the press.

My stomach clenched and I scrolled back up to the top, checking the date.

Mid-January... I went on my first date with Larry in mid-January... my brain throbbed harder, and tears threatened to spill from the corners of my eyes. Closing the app, I walked out of the garage and searched for Marvin. He was standing by an open bay door offering advice to a man beneath a hideous yellow SUV that was two black stripes away from being a bumblebee.

"Make sure there are no gaps or peeling."

"Who wanted that?" I asked, walking up beside him.

"Who wanted what?" he asked, double-checking the tech's work.

"A yellow Jeep..." my eyes scanned the area just outside the garage.

"No," I begged, even as he opened the door for me. "Why? This isn't better!"

"You said any color I have, Cynthia. This is the color I had," he patted my shoulder, nudged his tech inside and left me standing there next to the mobile embodiment of sunshine.

With an enamel glitter steering wheel and the outline of Hello Kitty on the hood.

Chapter Four:
Missing Pieces

"**S**eriously, Joseph, you can't be serious?" I was glaring at him as he blocked my entrance to the barn.

"I can and I am Cynthia. You are on paid leave until this case is resolved," the old, paunchy man stood blocking my path with his arms crossed. He had on too-clean cowboy boots, slightly better worn-in jeans, and a flannel covered in tapioca pudding and what might have been steamed spinach or cow manure.

It was a little depressing to admit it might have been there before the mob of people had arrived.

"But..." He just shook his head and pointed stiff-armed to the parking lot where five people loitered beside my car to speak with me "in private". Except, I didn't need to speak to them in private because they were all loudly pleading their cases to each other. Based on what I could overhear before a woman's bored teenager stole pudding from a toddler and sent it flying in Joseph's direction, their alibi was the same as all the others. Yes, they had wanted to kill her, but not *that* way.

"Come on! You were in my office doing the same thing yesterday! I need to spend time in a place where no one else is allowed!" Like the back forty on an ATV with my Angry Chick playlist, scooping up cow dung, and collecting temperature samples.

"Cynthia, this is a farm," he stated, as though the smell and animals were not a dead giveaway. "And on this farm we have..."

"A cow, ee ai ee ai oh," I sang and tried to move past him.

"Rules, damn it!" He kicked at the ground and I snickered.

I was totally wearing him down and I would be back at work in no time.

Larry appeared behind Joseph, lab coat over his usual jeans and T-shirt. He gave me a wide smile, humming the old MacDonald tune but I couldn't quite meet his eyes.

Was I his consolation prize when he lost the redhead? Had he been seeing both of us at the same time?

Joseph recovered before I could launch another assault on his good sense.

"Get," he said, and I glanced at Larry. His face... near hers...

Anger flamed through me, and I threw my hands in the air.

"Fine! Just fine! I'll solve the stupid murder, get no credit, and come back to stick my arms into cow uteruses!"

Still not looking at Larry, I turned on my heel and flounced back to my car in an impersonation of Amber. The waiting mob tried to descend but I put Winnie on alert and she growled until they all went silent.

"Look, I heard all of the reasons all of you are innocent. Whoever donated DNA to the pudding thrower owes Joseph a new flannel shirt. The rest of you are dismissed. If I have questions for anyone in this town, I'll seek them out. Anyone interrupting my day with a sudden appearance will become the new top suspect!" My speech was loud, but I wasn't dedicated to it. While they all tried to work through my declaration, I climbed into my Jeep with Winnie riding shotgun, Larry trotting to get to the window before I left. Pretending I couldn't see him, I threw the car in reverse and pulled away, watching his lab coat billow behind him like a cape as he stood in the dust we kicked up.

Winnie let out a whimper, looking out the window behind the truck.

"Don't you dare! You peed on him," I warned and she showed me her teeth. "He might have been cheating on us..."

Winnie let out an exasperated sigh.

"What? I don't want to be anyone's second choice!" I declared as the email from Cruz still sat in my inbox.

Knowingly, the dog nudged my phone and I rolled my eyes.

"Larry wasn't my second choice. He was never even a choice until he was..."

She wiggled her eyebrows at me, and I pulled over to bang my head on the steering wheel. That wasn't true. I'd had a stupid crush on him all through school and he never once returned it.

I was just waiting for him to ditch me again, and that picture reaffirmed my insecurities. If I kept Cruz in my inbox, I had an out. He could be the reason Larry left me *and* he could be the reason I didn't commit.

"I'm not running scared, I'm hedging my bets!"

Winnie let out a burp and put her paw on my shoulder.

"I hate Amber," I muttered, and she replaced her paw with a cold wet nose beneath my ear. I wrapped my arm around her neck and cuddled her close. "I know... let's get this over with."

Opening the phone, I bypassed Cruz's email again and pulled up the article related to Yvette's death. Died in her office, based... in Yellow Springs. I Googled the address and entered it into the navigation of the car. I would arrive in twenty-three minutes. I traced the route with my finger. Google knew geographic distances, but it did not know the traffic delays caused by livestock.

Only four farms, so I added fifteen minutes. Not bad, I decided when the phone pinged a text message. I glanced at the screen and it displayed the message of the text.

Ian: You can't avoid me forever, Cyn.

Rolling my eyes, I challenged his statement to no one in particular.

"I can do whatever I want, cuz I'm a big girl."

I put the car in drive when the phone went off again. I glanced at the device in the cup holder.

Larry: You can't avoid this, Cyn.

"Shut up, both of you! You don't know me!" Winnie let out a long howl, and I wisely took her advice to consider everything. "Alright, fine, but I'm only avoiding Larry. I'm just ignoring Ian. You can't argue in his favor!"

Winnie licked my face and I pulled back onto the road.

"As long as we have an understanding," I said and she let out a fart.

Yup, same page, she and I.

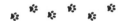

"Ma'am, this is a crime scene!"

We'd arrived at the red brick newspaper office and were slowly circling the building when a short squat woman appeared in a security guard uniform.

"I'm aware," I said, letting Winnie scent the door and the parking lot. She paused on a few spots that looked like areas where someone had spilled something. One of the areas looked like the aftermath of a ketchup packet being placed under someone's tire. The red gunk sprayed the ground and Winnie sniffed at it intently before raising her head to look at me.

"What are you doing at a crime scene, ma'am?"

While the security guard was arguably doing her job, I elected to ignore her. My brain was a pint short on coffee, and there was one too many men in my inbox who thought I owed them something. Following Winnie's nose, I studied the splattered ketchup and paused.

Not ketchup.

I took a photo and then a few more. Winnie followed me, the security guard speaking into her two-way radio while I followed the widest part of the pattern in search of the narrowest. The splatter was in a parking space on the edge of the parking lot. Standing, I studied the lot for a source.

In front was the red brick building, a large picture window with a closed curtain sat beside a metal fire door, and the parking space where we stood was directly in front of the door. Curious, I backtracked toward the door, but there were no red droplets on the sidewalk. Winnie and I went back to the parking space and stared.

To the side of the spot was a planter full of rocks and a couple of succulents. It wasn't much, but closer inspection showed it was clean.

"What are we looking at?"

"Blood, I think." I didn't look at the man. Based on the noise of his car and the racket he made walking up, he was some sort of law enforcement. I heard a cat stuck in a tree call come over his car radio and rolled my eyes. "Are you kidding me?"

"What? The fire department is busy, and we have a couple of really tall cops." My eyes drifted to the officer, and I fought a grimace. He was six inches shorter than me, rail thin, and had more equipment on his belt than he had waist to accommodate it. The sandy brown hair and acne-scarred face coupled with an Opie Griffith haircut put his age anywhere between twelve and seventy-five.

"Did the evidence techs collect a sample of this?" I asked him and he shrugged.

"Dunno, it was a Sheriff's Department call. Locals not invited," he gestured over his shoulder to the additional black and white pulling up. "I was just supposed to make sure you didn't steal evidence until the guy from the Sheriff's Department got here."

"Why would I 'steal evidence'? Also, if it was evidence, wouldn't you have collected it?"

"Didn't collect anything, it was the Sheriff's Department's call," he repeated himself, and I was worried he was broken.

"Do you need help?" I asked, referencing his mental health.

"Not my call, ask him."

Opie jerked his thumb over his shoulder and my eyes looked at the deputy behind the wheel. Backlit by the sun, I couldn't see squat, but the square shoulders hinted at a larger man than the one in front of me. With a shrug, I turned back to the blood spatter and crouched beside it. What had looked like a backward spray had a hollow circle at the apex, and I tried to imagine how the pattern was created.

"Looks like the time I hit my baseball bat on the ground after smashing watermelons," the kid said, stuffing a stick of gum into his mouth. I turned to him, tilting my head while Winnie ventured into the planter.

"Explain," I prompted, and he shrugged, stuffing the gum wrapper in his pocket.

"The school had a garden and in the summer no one tended it. We had baseball practice, and we walked by to see it was full of watermelons. The gate was unlocked and we went in. I wanted a snack but they had gotten moldy, and Chester thought it would be fun to use them for batting practice." He paused to chew contemplatively on his gum, and I heard a car door shut behind me. "We lined them up on fence posts and swung. My bat hit a soft spot and the melon guts got all over the bat. I smacked it on the ground and it made something like that."

Officer Melon Killer used his toe to point to the circular shape at the front of the spray.

"Baseball bats have a hollow at the top," I crouched low again and studied it when a familiar tingle slithered down my spine and my nipples stood at attention.

Winnie let out a low *woof* and took off behind me. I heard a grunt, the jingle of her collar, and a lot of doggy kisses happening.

"Your dog sure likes the new deputy," Opie commented, and I felt my eye twitch as the tingle in my spine sank to my lady parts and I tried not to moan when his scent reached my nostrils. Heat flashed through my whole body, and I needed an iced coffee more than I wanted to take another breath.

I needed something cold.

I needed spare underwear for when mine dissolved at the sound of his voice.

"Hey, Chica ," Ian Cruz said, and I shivered when he trailed his fingers along my neck and moved my hair off my ear. "I wondered when you'd show up to help. You've been ignoring me."

With a glance over my shoulder for confirmation, I spun around and sucker punched him in the gut.

Chapter Five:
Instigating Arrest

I rested my head against the window in the back seat of Officer Opie's police car while Ian Cruz tried to explain that getting punched in the gut was a friendly gesture. Winnie was on the seat beside me, and though neither of us was handcuffed, the door was still locked and we were detained at the very least.

Most likely we were arrested.

My phone went off in my pocket and I pulled it out.

Larry was calling me.

"Hey," I said into the phone, Winnie butting my elbow with her head when he answered.

"Hey." There was silence over the line, and Opie's radio crackled requesting assistance with livestock traffic control. "Where are you?"

"Back of a police car in Yellow Springs," I answered, closing my eyes and fighting tears. His voice was distant, indifferent. He'd already changed his mind about us, and we hadn't even had "the talk".

"You OK?" he asked, guarded.

"Don't know... might need to be bailed out," I answered as a single tear trailed down my cheek. It was one thing to be arrested, it was quite another to only get to punch the jerk once before getting arrested *and* have to talk to the man who proved in photographic evidence he could do better. "Can you ask Mo to be ready?"

He scoffed into the line.

"Mo? Seriously?" I could hear the vinegar in his voice, and I found my mad.

"What? Wouldn't want to keep you from your date with the red head," I spat, and I could hear him rubbing his face and counting slowly.

"Care to explain?" He spoke calmly, and I hated his mature and calm reaction after I just punched a guy.

Once.

And was freaking arrested.

"Amber showed me the picture," I snarled and he sighed. "Don't sigh! I was just minding my own business when she walks in, telling me to prove she isn't a murderer. Her noodle arms are enough proof, but apparently the only acceptable way to murder people is to throw them in front of a bus, and I can 'have you' if I get the *real* murderer arrested and..."

"First, stop talking to Amber. Just on principle." My brain agreed with him but my mouth couldn't be trusted, so I closed it to avoid another rant. "Second, Carla was... before you."

"Not much before me," I challenged, and he let out another breath.

"Not exactly... She was before you came back and a while after you got back. It's... complicated. Hand the phone to Daniel so I can demand he let you out and I'll pick you up. We can have our talk and if it goes well, I'll give you a cookie and an orgasm."

My stomach fluttered, and I realized I really wanted both of those things.

Bad body, I scolded myself, *we are mad at him.*

"It's not Daniel."

"Barney?" His voice raised a quarter octave in concern.

"Nope, Opie," I stared through the windshield and watched the young officer swinging an imaginary bat toward an imaginary ball. He was apparently either sharing the watermelon story or batting advice.

"We don't have an Opie, Cyn." The concern became more prominent.

"We don't. Yellow Springs does."

"His name is seriously Opie?"

"No, he just looks like Opie Griffith."

"Opie Taylor," Larry corrected, and I scrunched my face. "What?"

"The actor was Andy Griffith, the character's last name was Taylor. Sheriff Taylor, Opie Taylor, Aunt Bee..."

"Then why wasn't it The Andy Taylor show?"

"Why is it The Mindy Project but the character's name isn't Mindy?" he countered, and I had no answers.

"Hollywood is stupid," I grumbled but he didn't respond. Probably he was working on figuring out how to spring me from the cop car or keep me here forever.

I watched the two men in front of my temporary residence. Cruz was gesturing, not a flattering gesture, Opie was looking at his shoes, nodded once in agreement, and shook Ian's hand. Opie looked disappointed, but it would seem the other man had convinced him. Ian had a smirk that promised revenge, and I couldn't decide if I really even wanted out of the car.

"New deputy is coming over," I spoke into the phone, but I wasn't sure whether I was talking to Larry or just talking.

"Who's the new deputy?" Larry asked just as Ian opened the door.

"Hang up the phone, chica, we have work to do." He took the device from my hand and hung up as I heard Larry shouting.

"What the hell-"

"If you just cost me my cookie, I'm going to be pissed," I glared at him.

"Cookies?"

"Yes! I was promised a cookie and if you cost me my cookie, I'm going to rip you limb from limb and use those limbs to..."

Cruz pressed his hand against my lips and I huffed out a breath, shoving away his hand.

"What do you want?"

"Aren't you going to ask why I'm here?" He passed my phone back and I stuffed it in my pocket.

"No," I looked at Winnie's tail. She was wagging just the tip of her tail and I captured it. "What do you want?"

"No?"

"No. It's just part of your MO. Show up, make out with me, disappear for a few years, and then reappear as though everything is normal and fine." I crossed my arms and stared at my dog. She never disappeared... except briefly to chase bad guys or snack men but she always came back and she always came through.

"It wasn't years this time," he said, taking my hand and tugging me out of the car, pulling me flush against him. I tried to move away but he locked his arm at my waist.

"You're right. Go away so hopefully enough time passes I won't want to hit you." I glared at him and he booped my nose.

"You always want to hit me. Besides, now that you've hit me it's out of your system. I want you to help me with this. Let's get to work."

"Fine, whatever. Sooner I get away from you, the sooner I get a cookie."

"I'll give you something better than a cookie," he spoke against my ear, and I had a whole-body shiver.

"He promised me one of those too, and based on experience, only one of you can be depended on to follow through." I side-stepped him and went back to the parking space. Cruz followed quietly behind me, Winnie bringing up the rear with her nose working.

The lot hadn't changed since I'd been in the police car. Nothing near the possible blood had sprouted any more blood. I looked to Winnie who was scenting the fire door into the building again.

"Can we go inside?"

"Inside where?" Opie asked, and I looked around for a hidden camera... or maybe an anvil that had recently landed on his head and knocked his brain clean out.

"The building where the lady was murdered, genius."

The kid blinked and scanned the lot.

"In how many of these buildings has a woman been murdered?" It wasn't really a question, but he took me seriously.

"I mean, just that one as far as I know..." Opie gestured to the newspaper office. Then he looked to Ian, who nodded, and pulled a key from his pocket.

"How many people have that key?" I asked as he inserted it into the fire door and propped it open with a rock from the planter.

"Everyone in the police and fire department, couple of hospital people," he shrugged and gestured to the dark stairwell. A motion light activated and the depressing fluorescent glow revealed nothing new of interest. "Might be a shorter list to ask who doesn't have a key, given the rate at which some of those folks lose them."

"Are you kidding? I can't tell if you're kidding. Why do you all have a key to the news office, on purpose or otherwise?"

Opie hitched a thumb toward the front of the building, and I walked out of the stairwell to read the sign... which was obscured by a giant shrub, and I glared at the small man who didn't seem to notice.

"It's not just the news office. Our police administration works out of here, and the coroners have offices here to get away from the hospital." Opie spit his gum out in the trash can just inside the door and I studied his hands. They were clean, no dirt under his nails. I switched to looking at Cruz's hands... also clean but he had callouses on the pads of his fingers. I looked down at mine, dirt under my nails, dog slobber residue, and something that might be a crushed candy cane sprinkle.

"Do you have gloves?" I asked either of them, and Cruz pulled out a pair of black latex. I slid them on, trying and failing to make them snap theatrically, and lifted the lid off the trash can. Beside the young officer's gum were numerous other pairs of black gloves, paper shoe boots, and cheap plastic tarps. Pawing through to the bottom, I found a puddle of dark liquid that might be coffee.

"What are you looking for?" Cruz asked from right beside me, and I resisted the urge to inhale his scent... and punch him.

"Is this can always here?" I asked the kid, and he nodded.

"Yeah, bag is new, came in with the techs and stuff," he opened another fire door, propping it open with the metal stopper at the top. More motion activated lights showed an off-white hallway with off-white tile floors and a pock marked ceiling. Just through the door, Opie stopped at the crime scene tape on the first office to the left.

"Why is it interesting that the techs put the bag in the trash can? Isn't that why trash cans exist?"

"They usually just bring a bag, but the can was empty when they got here, and since no one is supposed to be in or out, they've left it."

He shook the scotch tape free from the yellow tape and reached for the doorknob.

"Shouldn't you wear gloves?" I asked him, suspicious.

"Nah, already dusted. Wasn't a thing here which I know because I was standing next to that damn trash can with the scene log for six hours," he shrugged and turned the handle, letting the door move inward without his guidance. It bounced off the back wall with a hollow thud, and I peeked around to see an indent from the handle.

"If you had the scene log, then you were here." He nodded confirmation, and I rolled my eyes. "So then you knew they got all the evidence because you were holding the log!"

Cruz nudged me further into the room and gave me a warning look to leave the little guy alone.

"Leave it." He gave the same command we were trained to use with the canines, and I elbowed him in the gut. "Feel better, Cyn the Determined?"

"Call me that again, and I'll take up batting practice on something a little smaller and more round watermelons."

Opie snickered at the open door, and my eyes took in the dimly lit office for the first time.

While I'd expected it to look like a TV PI office with a frosted glass window and a wooden desk all in sepia tones, it wasn't a surprise that it was sleek and modern. My imagination never came up with realistic ideas, so not looking like a flashback in a film reel meant I wasn't dead or hallucinating. Everything was stainless steel and grey, the fake white flowers pristine in a spot by the window. Yvette had a glass-topped desk and beneath the dried blood, it had a small crack.

"She was hit on the head and then hit her head on the desk?" I asked no one in particular and Ian shrugged.

"It's a theory."

With that vague statement, I walked to the window and stared at the parking space with the blood spatter. Her office chair sat perpendicular to it.

"If she'd been sitting, wouldn't she have seen the car that pulled up?" I asked and Ian pulled out his phone, opening a video and passing me the device. Pressing play, I watched the camera from the bank across the way show four wheels pull into the spot, shoes get out of the car and walk in the direction of the red brick building and the fire door. A few stalled frames passed and the feet reappeared, climbed into the car, and drove off through the lot.

I pressed pause on the video and restarted it from the beginning. There was nothing being tapped against the ground, but there was an odd light trick. After I watched it a third time, trying to place the familiarity, it clicked.

"Reflective tape," I said, when my eyes tracked to the same material on my running shoes and the police car outside.

"Yes," Cruz answered, and I studied him with a sense of curiosity. He'd already known. With a nod toward his phone, I handed it back and he tapped a few buttons. Satisfied, he turned the device to me, and I pressed play.

A new camera angle filled his screen. This one a traffic light camera from the driveway beside the office that offered an angled overhead view of the cars, including a black and white with 93 on the roof. Just as it turned left, I pressed pause and tried to zoom in.

"Is that..." but the grainy image wasn't especially helpful.

"We think it's Daniel Kirby," Cruz said, and I tried to make the image somehow more visibly accessible.

"He admitted to being in the area, but right outside?" I looked at Cruz, his deep brown eyes were attached to my face, and I studied him for a sign that something else was happening. That this was a joke or a game, but he was just staring, waiting for me to offer an explanation, a solution... something. "Have you tested the blood in the parking spot?"

He nodded.

"Not a match," he clarified, and I chewed on my cheek.

"Is it blood?" I asked and he tilted his head to the side like Winnie.

"Is it... blood?"

"Yeah, did it pass a Heme test? Did you get a blood type? Is it *blood*?" He was studying my face, and after thinking for a minute, stepped away to make a call. I walked around the office, ignoring the blood-soaked desk and chair. That area would have been thoroughly searched and all the technology had been removed.

I ran my gloved finger along the edge of her bookcase, reading the spines of books and looking for something out of place. There was no dust, she'd kept it clean, but the books looked more for show than reading. She had an old, gold-leaf volume of

Huck Finn beside a battered hardcover copy of Harry Potter. At random, I pulled one out and was surprised by the weight. It was four inches thick but weighed next to nothing.

Flipping it open, a hinge creaked and a dozen photos fell out.

"What the..." I picked them up and saw a man and a woman in compromising positions. Neither looked familiar, and I grabbed another book. Flipping back the cover, I found it was also filled with pictures of people in compromising positions. This time instead of sex, it looked to be a secret meeting where items were transferred in a handshake.

"Chica," Cruz said from behind me, and I handed him the book boxes.

"All of these..." I kept plucking books at random and none of them were anything more than a storage place for photos that, regardless of context, looked pretty damning. "They're all people she spied on."

Cruz studied the shelf, finding a well-worn volume and opening the lid, eyes narrowing at what was inside.

"This... isn't looking good for Larry," he said softly.

I leaned over his shoulder and saw him bent over the busty redhead, completely naked.

"What do you mean? Larry said he had a thing with the redhead... Sex isn't really a crime, Cruz. Taking photos of it without permission is..."

"That's Yvette's editor, Carla." I tried not to look murderous, but something niggled in my mind. Did he know she worked here? Was he planning on saying anything?

"Outside... is animal blood," he continued, and my heart stuttered. Had he killed an animal for her? Larry rarely had blood on him. Why did animal blood place him at fault?

"What kind of animal?" I asked and he stared.

"Why does it matter?"

"Because Larry's allergic to cats," I picked up a few more books and looked at the pictures inside. The question was ridiculous, but this whole thing was ridiculous. Larry would have told me he was a potential murder suspect when Daniel did... wouldn't he?

"They haven't identified species yet," he said.

"So, you're grasping at straws," I said, patting him on the shoulder while acknowledging that the reference was to both of us. Hesitating, Cruz pulled out his phone and showed me a grainy video of a hallway. Larry looked to be getting yelled at by the short bombshell, Carla, if you believed Ian. She was waving her hands in anger and he leaned against the wall. Nodding, looking passive and unconcerned. She moved toward him and pressed her hands to his abs, sliding up to his chest, wrapping them around his neck...

I looked away.

"What does that have to do with this?" I gestured to the bloody mess, not feeling steady. The time stamp had been five days earlier. The date of the murder and he hadn't mentioned it. He'd been here, with her, the day a woman was murdered in a neighboring office. Larry let the woman touch him. She'd...

My eyes drilled a hole into Cruz's head, watching him study me for a reaction.

"Chica..."

I held up my hand for him to be quiet.

"His brother was here, was he in the car with his brother?" Cruz shook his head. "Do you have a video of where he parked? How he got here? What direction he traveled after he left? Time of day?"

More head shaking and I shrugged.

"Were there any other vehicles that showed up or left in the 24 hours before or after the murder?"

"It has a six hour limit, and no. Just the employee cars and Daniel's coming and going."

"Then we have nothing new. There's blood in the parking lot that belongs to an unknown animal, an angry woman in a hallway the day Yvette died, an incompetent deputy also here that day, and..."

I stared at all of the books filled with compromising photos.

"...a whole lot of people who wanted the victim dead."

Chapter Six: Dirty Little Secret

"**M**a, why are you yelling?" I shouted into the cab as we headed home. Night had fallen, and despite hundreds of potential suspects, and hundreds more victims of Yvette's voyeurism, there was nothing new to find in the office or around it. Thankfully, the sun set early because darkness was a perfect excuse to go to bed.

"Where are you?" Her shrill voice filled the cab and I felt the stabbing sensation return behind my left eye. It had shown up just after Cruz showed me the video and was just starting to lessen as I left the village of Yellow Springs proper and hit the open road.

"I'm driving," I sighed, looking wistfully at Winnie in the rearview mirror. She had four paws in the air and was snoring softly, even through the nightmare that was this phone call. Winnie could sleep through anything, lucky dog.

"When will you get here?"

Some background noise filtered through the line and I shuddered.

"Why, ma?" I asked cautiously. The last time I'd been to her house and people were over, she and my sister were selling sex toys to the men and women of Sweet Pea. The rumors of how the night ended are spoken about only in hushed tones, but my parents now had a reputation as the town's party house. Not the fun kind where teenagers learned the lessons of moderate consumption, there was no alcohol, drugs or guests who hadn't suffered the downfalls of gravity and benefits of Viagra.

"Larry is here," she shouted. "So are Seth and the kids."

My eye twitched again and I weighed my options.

Her house would have food, and I missed my brother, Seth.

Her house also had Larry and a cave of wonders that even Aladdin would decline to enter.

"Cynthia! When are you getting here?"

If I told her I was sick, she'd ask for a note.

If I told her I died, she'd demand custody of Winnie.

"Twenty minutes, Ma," I sighed into the phone.

"What?" she shouted as what was either a child pretending to be a racecar or an air raid siren went off in the background.

"I said twenty minutes, Ma!" I shouted, and her voice turned clipped.

"There's no reason to yell," she announced and hung up on me.

"What do you think, girl, could we turn around and disappear to Canada?" I asked Winnie in the rearview mirror. She remained paws in the air, napping. "It wasn't too bad last time. I mean... gravy and cheese on French fries..."

She let out a fart and I rolled the window down an inch.

"Right, you are on a diet that doesn't include any of those things," I muttered, dropping my head to the steering wheel at the stop light that marked the end of Yellow Springs and the beginning of Sweet Pea. My phone started ringing again through my car, and I answered without checking the display.

"It hasn't been twenty minutes, Ma!"

The other end of the line remained quiet and I glanced at the screen.

"So, you're coming?" Larry practically gave me frostbite through the phone.

"Yeah, so you should probably leave. I'd rather not have the 'Are you a murderer, you filthy lying asshole' conversation in front of my family," I spat back at him and silence filled the line.

"I can..." he started but the light went green and I "accidentally" pressed the end call button.

Winnie's head appeared on my shoulder and I squished her head against my neck.

"Don't rat me out, OK?" I asked her and she licked my cheek. "I promise I'll talk to him... eventually. After the cops... if he isn't arrested... or a murderer."

Winnie let out a soft whimper, and one bitter tear trickled down my cheek.

"We'll have some ice cream and reassess later," I decided and she wagged her tail.

Forget diamonds, a dog is a girl's best friend.

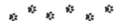

Larry had the good sense to fake an emergency and be gone when I arrived. My mom, on the other hand, decided it meant we were breaking up.

"I saw Jacob Weissman at your office today. He's quite the looker now, if you don't mind them a little young and inexperienced." I choked on the sip of wine I was drinking and the alcohol burned my nostrils.

"Ma, Jake is a stripper!"

"That doesn't mean he has experience, Cynthia. It just means he's good with his hips and has a sense of rhythm. You could do worse." She took a long drink of her wine, and I looked for something, anything, that would derail this conversation. "All I'm saying is that I've seen him at work, and I've seen his pleasure toy preference. You two could be a good match if you'd let go of your foolish hang-ups and he'd stop worrying what his mother thought."

I gave up on a distraction, grabbed the bottle of red, and chugged until Seth tugged it from my hand and took a hit for himself.

"Thank God it's someone else's turn." He gave me a wink and I shoved him in the arm.

"Kaylee has been gone for two years. You know Ma already has a list for you," I hissed and he let out a small smile.

Seth was the closest to me in age, at forty-one. He'd been handsome and outgoing his whole life, with a steady stream of women in and out, most of whom were biding their time to swoop in. When his wife got sick and passed, he jumped back into the self-destructive dating pool with both feet. The internet had offered him an unlimited pool of options, and he hadn't bothered with names, occupations, or protection until he woke up in a strange place with a man threatening his kidney.

Stumbling home that day, his kids and mother-in-law staged an intervention. He decided he'd punished himself enough and focused on being there for them. Them, sleeping and not needing medication for syphilis and an ointment for his...

"I think I met someone..." he started, shifting excitedly. "It's just... she's not available yet..."

I opened my mouth to ask more but whipped my head around at a sound of strangled breathing.

"Stop!" I shouted, pointing squarely at my niece. She had her brother in a headlock, peanut butter on his cheek that she was shoving toward Winnie's mouth.

"But Aunt Cyn..." she wailed and I shook my head.

"You know the rules, Sylvia. You cannot feed your brother, cousins, or cheese to Winnie. I signed a legally binding document with the Army. Let him go," I warned and she sighed as though I had just informed her the bra and panties prom dress she was wearing would not leave the house uncovered. I marveled at the sass of an eight-year-old and tried to ignore the sinking feeling that I was now a responsible adult.

Worse, a responsible adult that kids listened to instead of laughing at.

Definitely going to need to eat Oreos for dinner the rest of this week and go to bed at an unreasonable hour just to wash away the shame.

"Fine! But I'm giving her cheese!" Sylvia shouted and took off toward the kitchen.

"Winnie," I warned, but she was gently cleaning Erich's face of peanut butter while he giggled.

Her brother was almost eleven and had thirty pounds on her, but he was stuck in the "don't fight girls" notion that was probably going to get him a lot of dates and a lot of keyed scratches in his car. He was likely to end up in a Norbit situation with an aggressive, violent woman who cheated on him because he was too "nice" to walk away.

Then I would have to murder her and let Winnie drag the remains cross-country.

"Her tongue tickles!" Erich laughed and I smiled despite myself.

"Don't forget to wash your face later, I think I saw her eating cow poop earlier," he laughed harder and I shrugged. "Your kids are gross. I don't really know how or why anyone would have or want them."

My eyes softened staring at the little boy, and Seth poked me, offering a toothy grin.

"You want one!" His glee grated my raw nerves. I rolled my eyes.

"Don't."

"But you'd be so good with…"

"Shut it Sethany, or you're going on my shit list." I raised a finger in warning and used the nickname my two sisters had given him to deny they had a brother in any and all social situations. He made a baby rocking cradle arm gesture at me and I threw a green bean at his face. It slapped against his glasses with a wet *fwap*, fell to the floor, and my dog ate it.

He mouthed "you'll pay for that" and I motioned for him to bring it on.

Worst idea ever.

"Hey, Ma!" Seth had a wicked gleam in his eyes and I started to sweat.

"Yes, Seth," she said and his sneer had me raising my hands in surrender. I would not throw any more vegetables if he stopped.

"Didn't you say there was a new product you wanted Cyn to test for your club?" he asked, and I kicked him under the table.

"You asshole," I hissed and my mom's face lit up.

"Yes! It simulates oral sex with air! I'll just go grab it!"

"No!" But she was gone up the stairs. My dad had been sitting quietly, reading a paperback. Indifferent to the chaos around him, he glanced up for a moment to make eye contact.

"It has a lot of really excellent reviews online. Your mom thinks it'll help you relax more," and he went back to his book.

"You know this is not normal dinner conversation, right?" I said to no one in particular and threw out an arm to catch Sylvia as she tried to rocket past me with cheddar. "Give it, you little gremlin. Or I'm putting her farts in a glass jar and mailing them to you."

"Eww!!!" She squealed and dropped the cheese. Winnie lurched toward it, I dropped the child and scooped it up, stuffing it into my mouth with direct eye contact at my partner.

"Mine," I growled and she flattened her ears.

"Cynthia, did you just pick up and eat food off the ground?"

My eyes met my mother's. She was appalled, lips pressed into a thick line as she tapped what looked like a pink ear scope against her thigh.

"What's that?" I stammered and she frowned.

"Cynthia, you just ate food off my floor. There have been children, dogs, and god knows what on this floor. Didn't I raise you better? You need to go brush your teeth."

"Seriously? You give your kids sex toys, but eating food off the floor is on par with a Geneva Convention violation?" I banged my head against the table before looking back at her. "Cheese is delicious mom! No one should waste cheese! Or wine... or... mashed potatoes!"

I scooped up some mashed potatoes from my plate to eat and Winnie bumped my arm. Potatoes smashed into my face and down the front of my shirt.

"Dear, you wouldn't be eating cheese off the floor or be so grouchy about mashed potatoes if you had more orgasms. Now, take this and here are a few spare batteries. If you're going to keep Larry, I'll have to send him some articles. He's clearly not on his game."

I smashed my face into the table and screamed into the cloth table cover.

"Honestly, Cynthia," she grumbled, tucking the toy into my bag. "You are so dramatic."

We pulled up behind my building and I stared at the light coming out of the windows.

"Damn," I muttered, Winnie licking mashed potatoes from my cheek. "He's up there."

The curtain to my back window twitched and Larry's face filled the window, staring at my sunshine yellow Jeep.

"We could still make a run for it..." I said and my phone chimed.

Larry: *Get your ass up here.*

Me: *Go to hell and get out of my house.*

Larry: *No.*

"He just told me no. I can have him charged with trespassing," I muttered. Wrenching open the door I climbed out and watched Winnie leap to the ground and lead the way to the back door. Without a good reason not to, I followed her. She nudged it with her nose and the door opened to reveal... Ian Cruz.

"What the hell?" I asked and he grabbed my arm, tugging me up the stairs where Larry stood beside a pot of coffee, a chocolate bar, and a bag of Winnie's treats.

"We need to talk," Ian said and Larry's solemn face smirked.

"What the hell is that about?" My voice was too loud but I couldn't get it quieter.

"Nothing," Larry said, rubbing his hands over his face before passing me a mug of coffee. For the first time in my life, I didn't want it. My brain flashed to the woman, yelling at him, running her hands up his body, around his neck...

I ignored the cup and turned to Cruz.

"You want to talk, talk," I crossed my arms and leaned against the counter, letting Winnie have the couch.

"You aren't going to take the coffee?" Cruz asked, brow raised in amusement and concern.

"I don't want coffee," I hissed. "I don't want coffee, I don't want you two in my apartment, and I don't want to use the sex toy my mom stuck in my purse. No one asked what I wanted though. So, get with the talking or get the hell out."

The men exchanged a look over my shoulder and I rolled my eyes.

"Cyn, drink the coffee," Larry said quietly behind me and I flipped him off over my shoulder. "Please, it's not what you think."

I heard the door at the bottom of my staircase open and a slow set of delicate footsteps climbing my stairs.

"Who's in my house?" I asked, loud enough for whomever it was to hear. Cruz remained perfectly still, and Larry squirmed behind me. "Answer me or I'm getting my gun."

"It's Carla Herrera," Cruz answered just as the curvy redhead appeared at the top of my staircase with her hands raised. Despite the jeans and sweater, it was still very clear that she had a lot of curves in all the good places.

Betty Boop would be proud.

I tried not to feel inadequate and failed.

"Get out," I growled, and Winnie lifted her head to let out one of her own.

"I can't... I need your help," her voice was Jessica Rabbit sultry. "Ian said..."

She gestured toward Cruz, giving him the once over with her eyes. He didn't so much as blink in her direction.

Point for him, but he was so far in the red with me it hardly mattered.

"I'm not helping anyone at the moment," I turned around to look at Larry, bumping the coffee cup he'd placed on the counter.

"Please?" he asked, eyes pleading.

He moved the coffee cup a little closer and I chugged it one gulp, while considering chucking the cup at his head. First I have to see pictures of him screwing her, watch her kiss him on surveillance, mere hours after his mouth had been on mine, and now he wanted me to help her. I swiped an angry tear from my cheek and watched his face crumble.

"If I help her, you leave and never come back," I spoke quietly, voice threatening. He hesitated, just a moment, and nodded.

Another tear followed the first. He'd picked her.

He'd picked her over me and I had no other choice but to turn around and face the woman beside my couch.

"What do you want?" I asked, voice sharp enough to cut glass.

"My husband received all the pictures Yvette took of me. He... Larry wasn't my first... or even my last. I'm in more of those photo boxes, Cyn. He..." she looked at the floor, arms trembling. "He said that if I was stupid enough to get caught screwing half the men in the area, then I deserved to be accused of murder. Then he stormed out of the house and..."

My face remained hard. This woman wanted me to help her? After she cheated on her husband a whole bunch of times.

"He's gone, Cynthia," Larry said from behind me and I shivered.

"They think he's dead and I'm responsible," her tremors turned into hiccups as she swayed in small circles on the spot. It was impressive, but there was something about the way she glanced at each man that was cool and calculated. "They... the real killer, left this note."

I met Cruz's eyes. He tilted his head minutely. Either he wasn't the "they" who thought her responsible or he wasn't sold on the note. Either way, this was staged. It just wasn't clear who the intended audience was.

"What does it say?" I asked, too angry to be curious but wanting the woman out of my house so I could have an emotional breakdown.

"It says, 'Hope you enjoyed playtime, there's no dick in jail'..." her voice stuck and I watched her mouth move, but no words came out. With a look at Larry over my shoulder, she tentatively pulled the paper out of her purse and held it out to me. I crossed my arms under my chest.

"There's more, Cyn," Ian said softly and I rolled my eyes.

"So... you want me to prove that you aren't a murderer just like no one else is?" I clenched my jaw around the words and she shook her head no. She passed the note to Cruz who walked it over to me so that I could read the rest.

TOO BAD YOUR LYING ASS WON'T LIVE LONG
ENOUGH TO MAKE IT THERE

Beneath that was a crudely drawn picture of a hanging man in heels. I glanced at Carla's feet.

She was wearing heels.

Chapter Seven: Disappearances

I woke up cold and alone for the first time in weeks.

"Ughn," I grumbled into my pillow while Winnie took a flying leap onto my back. "Ger roff."

She decided that my garbled get off was an invitation to lick my face and nip at my ears. When her cold wet nose nudged the back of my neck, I cried out and felt her wagging her tail.

"Just for that, breakfast is cancelled!" I growled and she let out a whimper. The heavy metal fire door at the bottom of the stairs opened and she scrambled on the wooden floor like Scooby Doo, desperate for traction but in too much of a hurry.

My heart skipped a beat. Maybe he wouldn't listen to me... Maybe Larry would walk in and...

"Hey, Chica. You decent?" I flopped back on my bed and covered my head with a blanket. I listened to Winnie scramble at the sound of his voice and figured her momentum might send him tumbling down the stairs and I can listen to Adele in my pajamas.

"You are not invisible under the blanket," he said and I pulled it off my face to offer him a death glare with my middle finger. The man laughed, holding a box of doughnuts with two of Mo's paper coffee cups. He left the bakery box on the counter and carried the two cups toward me.

"Rise and shine, Cyn," he said, sitting on the edge of the bed. He was wearing jeans and a t-shirt today, nothing special, but I marveled at how easily he dropped his cop and Army personas. The blue shirt hugged his abs and biceps, the jeans showing off an ass that was just as tasty to look at as it was to touch.

Too bad I wasn't hungry.

"No," I ignored him and the coffee and pulled the comforter back over my head.

His weight shifted off the bed and my whole body jerked as he ripped my blanket away.

"Hey!" I squealed, trying to cover myself against the cold and my lack of pajama fabric. The short shorts and tank top left nothing to the imagination, and his imagination of me was the only thing he could have after the last time.

"I've showered with you, Cyn," he said easily and tugged me to a seated position and forced coffee into my hand. Reluctantly, I drank deeply from the plastic lid opening and let out a small sigh. Mo had added chocolate and marshmallows to my coffee with a sprinkling of cinnamon. "You didn't look half as in love with me naked as you do with that coffee."

"This coffee has never made out with me and then disappeared to never be seen or heard from again. Twice," I snapped, finishing the cup and pulling the second one from his hand. With an amused smile, he watched me down the cup he'd gotten for himself, though he remained quiet on the subject of his abandonment. "This one didn't force me to watch a guy I'm sleeping with make out with another woman and then pick her over me in my own house."

Once the second cup was empty, I decided I wasn't nearly caffeinated enough for this and shoved to standing. I stumbled into the kitchen, popping a single serve pod into the machine and sticking a mug that read, "Bitch, I will kill you" beneath the coffee maker's spout. It had an image of an Army woman, and I tried not to sob when I remembered Larry gave it to me.

"None of this coffee came in uninvited to demand I do something other than eat ice cream and listen to Evanescence."

A single tear rolled down my cheek and I let a small sob escape.

Then I pulled my shit together because he was just a man and they were unreliable, replaceable and...

Warmth filled me as Ian moved into my kitchen, grabbed the twelve-cup pot and started working on making sure caffeination levels remained elevated. We moved around each other quietly, neither of us unfamiliar with the operating patterns of the other. Cup in hand, I grabbed Winnie's bowl and prepared her breakfast while Cruz took her leash off the hook by the door. She pranced, he clipped it on, and they went out for her morning business.

I stared blankly at a wall, absently picking up my phone when it rang.

"Hello?"

"Why is he walking her?" Larry growled and I sighed.

"You made your choice last night, buddy. You chose Carla," I hung up and it rang again.

"What?"

"Cyn, it's Marvin. Who pissed in your Cheerios?"

Call waiting beeped and I ignored it.

"That phrase is disgusting. What's up?"

"Got a new paint sample book in. Want to come in tomorrow and have a look?" I relaxed. Soon, my Jeep wouldn't be sunshine yellow. I couldn't put a new coat of paint on the rest of my problems, but this I could do.

"Sure! What time?"

We agreed I'd be there around noon and I hung up. The phone rang immediately and I saw Larry's name flash on the screen.

"Ugh."

I switched it to mute before tossing it on my bed. Checking out the box Cruz brought, I was surprised to discover all of the doughnuts were glazed and frosted with sprinkles. Mo had tucked a little note inside stating that it would all be OK.

After bawling into the phone to her for an hour last night, I strongly doubted it.

She drew a little flame with a question mark... probably wondering about Ian, but I didn't have an answer to that. At least I thought it was a flame. Could have been the poop emoji... or a hat? Ian's footsteps joined Winnie's claws as he climbed the stairs and peeked at me around the wall.

"Are you feeling more human?" Cruz asked, setting Winnie free. I swallowed my last bite of doughnut while Winnie scrambled to her food dish and tried to gobble every last morsel in a single breath.

"Go away," I muttered, carrying my coffee toward the couch. Cruz held out an arm and pulled me into a hug. I tried to shove him off but he held tight.

"You can change your mind, chica. You can call him and tell him that while you are upset with everything, you don't want to kick him out of your life," his lips brushed the side of my neck as he spoke and I felt the first stirrings of the heat he used to generate within me by smiling.

"No, I can't," I sighed, gently pushing him away. He conceded and took a step back. "He made a choice."

"He chose to give you up to keep someone else alive," Cruz studied my face and I shrugged. "Are you really not even going to talk to him about it?"

"Didn't look that hard for him. Maybe now that her husband is dead and he kept her out of jail he can get back into her pants." The bitterness shocked even me, and I mentally face palmed.

Just a guy, Cyn. Larry is just a guy, I repeated to myself even as I felt the stinging in my eyes.

"He's not dead," Cruz said and that got my mind off Larry. The man was leaning against my kitchen counter, arms crossed

81

and bulging his biceps beneath his shirt. I studied him, but he didn't keep speaking.

I gestured for him to speak more.

"We have no body or evidence that anything bad has happened to him. The locals wanted to make her believe he was dead to see what she would do. At the Sheriff's Department, they think he might be the killer and the one to leave the note."

I scanned his face for more but he was curiously blank. He hadn't referenced himself as part of the Sheriff's Department. He hadn't said what he believed.

Which meant he was following a different lead that I wasn't invited on.

"So, what am I supposed to do? Keep looking for the killer?"

He pulled his lower lip into his mouth thoughtfully and I involuntarily licked my own lips... and then wanted to kick my own ass. Twenty-four hours solo and I was attracted to lip chewing. Worse, he was holding back, again, and I was bumbling around in the dark with a broken heart.

He is hot though, my lady parts acknowledged. My brain tried to fathom a nail and bail scenario that didn't leave me wanting and came up blank. *Larry would be crushed.*

Great, now I'm worried about hurting a man who rejected me.

"We want you to find the husband... well, I want you to find the husband," he corrected and I tilted my head to the side. "You have a talent for tracking the living."

"It's not a talent, or an it, her name is Winnie," I muttered and after stomping into the kitchen for more coffee, I walked over to the couch and plopped onto it. The finder of people climbed on the couch beside me and I stroked her fur, studying the man across the room. "So, his last known location was the house?"

Ian shook his head.

"He was last seen at a gas station between Yellow Springs and Sweet Pea. He filled up, bought snacks, a hat, sunglasses and a travel blanket."

"What kind of car?" I asked and he pulled out his phone to check.

"Lexus E Class sedan," he said, and I pulled out my phone to look up estimated gas mileage. It would give me a radius he'd have to stay within or refuel. If he refueled, I'd have a direction of travel. If I found him, I could get back to my actual job at the dairy.

If I found him, Carla would still be married and Larry... didn't care the first time so he would do nothing differently.

Nothing except choose her over me.

"Why do you look like someone stole your cookies?" Ian asked, voice closer and I jumped. He was seated beside me. Very, very close beside me, and I could smell his woodsy soap mixed with residual bakery smell and coffee. My eyes drifted closed and I just inhaled him. His hand moved to my thigh, massaging the muscle gently, waiting.

The fire door opened downstairs and a shrill voice carried.

"Cynthia! I'm coming upstairs so if Larry is here, tell him to put on pants because I knew that boy in diapers and I don't need to see his growth a second time!"

I exhaled and dropped my head to Cruz's shoulder, feeling him shake with laughter beneath me. When the landing creaked, my mother shouted.

"Cynthia! That is not Lawrence Kirby!"

"Good eyes, Ma. You remember Ian Cruz?"

I could feel her scowling at us and decided if I couldn't bury my head in the sand, I'd settle for Ian's chest.

"Where is Larry?" she demanded and I shrugged.

"Probably mounting and riding a red-head with a better body," I grumbled and my mom tutted.

Actually said "tut" four times in a row.

"What, Ma?"

"Have you used the product I gave you? You look tense, and pleasure is a necessity for any woman." It came out like she'd lectured a college course, and I lifted my head to drop it back onto Ian's chest. Once, twice, then he put his hand in the way and I met his gaze, filled with heat and humor. "This man is still wearing all of his clothes so clearly you aren't getting anywhere with him."

"Can I see this product?" He asked quietly.

"Right after you cut off my ears so I can never hear this again," I sighed and my mom tutted again.

"Really, Cynthia, if you can't tell your man about your pleasure ..." I held up my hand, and she blissfully complied with my request to end the sentence early. Cruz was laughing quietly beneath me and I slid my hand up his leg and under his shirt to pinch his skin between my fingernails.

His breath caught and he stopped laughing. Mission accomplished.

"What do you need, Ma?" I said, flopping backward and picking up my coffee.

"It's your brother," she sighed, pulling out my stool and propping herself on it daintily. Despite her nearly below average height, she never came off as short. "I think he's planning something."

"Seth is over forty. He can plan whatever he wants," I muttered and her sharp gaze pinned me to the couch.

"Don't sass me, Cynthia." Again, I got frostbite in seventy-degree air. "You know that since his wife passed he hasn't made the best choices. Now, I think..."

She wrung her hands nervously and glanced at the window as though Seth could be floating outside of it like Casper.

"Spit it out, ma," I grumbled, ready for her to finish so I could tell her to mind her own damn business.

"I think he's sleeping with a married woman," she hissed and pulled out her phone. With an eye roll, I accepted the device and stared at the image that had been texted to her. Seth was at an outdoor café, somewhere outside the immediate area based on the height of buildings, sitting across from...

"Are you kidding me?" I moaned and Cruz looked over my shoulder.

"Chica..."

I exited the photo and looked at the message that accompanied it.

Unknown: I tried to warn him. Now only you can save your son.

My face got sweaty and I re-read the words again and again.

"What the hell, Cruz?" I glared at him and he took the phone, pulling up the number and taking a picture of the image and the number before passing the phone back to my mom. Cruz scrubbed his hands over his face and leaned forward, elbows propped on his knees.

"Where is Seth?" His voice was eerily calm.

"I don't know. He went out last night, taking the kids to their other grandparents, and hasn't been back," she said, and I felt my stomach start to hollow out. "He said he might go out of town, but then... his car..."

"Did he drive himself?" I prompted when she just stood there silently.

"Yes, but they found his car outside a bar with his cell phone, wallet, and keys." My world swam. My brother might be an asshole, but he loves his kids. He wouldn't just leave his life behind... would he?

"What bar?" I asked, pulling up maps while Cruz started making calls.

"Derby's in Yellow Springs. It's in the same parking lot where that news woman was murdered."

Chapter Eight: Surveillance Secrets

"**M**a'am! We went over this yesterday!" Cruz badged the security guard who moved away without a word. Cruz made a sweeping "after you" gesture, beckoning me forward.

I rolled my eyes.

"I could have taken her," I grumbled and he rubbed a hand on my back as we approached the car. It was sitting in the parking lot surrounded by crime scene workers, looky-loos, and a few reporters trying to give traction to a slow Tuesday morning news cycle. Each person I passed was catastrophizing the incident, offering conspiracy theories, and suggesting that organized crime was to blame.

Cruz covered my ears and got us to the car.

My brother drove a three-year-old Toyota Corolla. The back seat was filled with doll accessories, smashed French fries, and something that was either poison or melted crayons. The front seat was tidy, a cup holder organizer kept pens and post-its. Seth kept a sketchpad and rulers in his car, all of which were still there.

Just sitting beside his wallet, keys, and cellphone.

My heart stopped and I felt lightheaded.

"You OK, chica?" Cruz said, rubbing his hand in small circles along my back. Without meaning to, I leaned into his touch and felt my eyes burn with tears.

"I'm going to kill whoever did this," I whispered, and Winnie let out a rumbly growl of agreement.

Cruz gave us a tight smile and moved into the foray of police activity while I scanned the area. We were halfway between the building that housed the newspaper and some government offices, a bar, and a chain restaurant that smelled like greasy onions and magic. Winnie sniffed in a wide circle around the assembled spectacle and caught a scent that piqued her interest.

Her nose led us closer to the newspaper office where a green older model Jaguar sat. Still scenting, she kept going just beside it, sniffing the driver's side door handle, then the passenger side. Winnie walked to the front of the car, back toward the passenger side and turned sharply toward the newspaper building. She fixated on something in a shrub just in front of the car and let out a low bark.

"What's that?" My eyes spared a glance at the man wearing a suit that had spoken. He had the build of an athlete gone soft, bleached blonde hair, dark eyes, and leathery skin. While he looked like a man who spent time outside, the tan was paid for and the hair was either plugged, a piece, or he had unlucky genetics. The smile and clothes said if his genetics were unlucky, it didn't concern him because the world was his for the taking.

Freaking white men.

Disinterested, I turned back to where Winnie waited and picked up a small key on a ring. The only other thing on the ring was a keychain shaped like a fountain pen, engraved with CRH.

The blonde man came closer and I moved away from the item.

"What is that?" He asked again, and I looked around for something out of the ordinary.

"What's what?" I asked, Winnie sitting to my left.

"That," he pointed at my dog and I tilted my head to the side. Winnie also tilted her head to the side and we stared at him. We kept staring and he repeated his statement, waving his hand up and down.

"It's a Velociraptor," I crossed my arms under my chest and his mouth fell open. Despite the idiotic look on his face, the eyes were sharp and tracking every subtle movement Winnie made. Had he been looking for something or just looking?

"Why is it by Carla's car?" He asked and my eyes went to the Jaguar.

"That's hers? And my dog is not an it." I asked, peering into the windows. The interior was beige, spotless, and looked like it had never been driven before.

"Yeah, though I haven't seen her today," he scratched his belly and searched around him. I got the impression he was hoping to speak to a manager... emphasis on the man. With my most charming smile, I extended a hand.

"I'm Cynthia Sharp. I work as a private investigator in Sweet Pea. How do you know Carla?" His hand looked soft and clammy when he held it out, and I considered closing mine for a fist bump. I started to close my hand, changed my mind to reopen it and just gave him a thumb up.

He didn't seem to notice as his hand redirected to rub the stubble on his jaw.

"I'm the Editor-in-Chief here, Elliot Maize. Carla works for me... worked for me... not really sure where she stands on the employment list. Haven't seen her since Yvette turned up..." He made the slicing gesture across his throat. Despite the serious and morbid topic, his two-thousand-watt smile didn't so much as dim. I studied his flawless teeth, bright white and perfectly straight.

He either got them bleached or bought them with his tan, and I waited for him to continue. In the silence, he scratched his belly, sucked on his teeth, and picked at something on the ground with the toe of his loafer.

"Have you seen her?" His attempt at casual fell short.

"That was almost a week ago," I redirected and he shrugged.

"Guess so."

"Has this car been here all that time?"

He rubbed his chin in false thoughtfulness.

"Don't recall," he said and I saw Cruz walking over. "Definitely saw it this morning."

"Saw what this morning?" Cruz said, flashing his badge. The sharp brown eyes went wide before sliding back to blank. I studied his hairline and watched a single bead of sweat run down his temple.

Badges made him nervous.

"You uh... new around here?" He extended his hand, and Cruz stared until it fell away.

I needed to ask him to teach me how to do that.

"Been here my whole life, never seen you," he drawled. Again, Cruz remained silent. "You do sports?"

"I thought you looked familiar, what did you play?" I asked, drawing attention away from Cruz and back on me. With a casual head nod, I signaled Winnie to lead Cruz to her discovery.

Winnie took the newly deputized man by the wrist, tugging him gently. With a glance of confirmation in my direction, he followed the dog to her treasure.

"Yeah, probably saw me play. I was a pitcher and darn near everyone came out to the games. I had a line of ladies though you might have been a little young then... I played through college. Got a scholarship and everything." He puffed out his chest and I tried not to look as bored as I was about to be.

Or gag at the insinuation I would wait in line for any man... except maybe Chris Evans.

If it wasn't too long, my attention span wasn't great.

Geez, Elliot the player of sportball was still talking.

"I nearly played semi-pro. My fastball was stuff of legend."

My brain tried to relate fastball to a sportball game but nothing came to mind.

My eyes took in the area, trying in vain to see something I might have missed... like a neon sign declaring my brother was fine and Cheetos were on special. I caught more words, pitcher and plate... something about bats. Normally I would ask Seth about sports... my chest tightened and I glanced back at his car.

Please let my brother be OK, I begged.

The man was still speaking, my brother was still missing... this day sucked.

"... Could have gone to the World Series if they hadn't benched me. Council Member Burt Kielder played on the same team with me. Now he works right across the street. Like we're still a team."

The man gestured toward a federal building, and I gave him a half-hearted smile.

"Cyn," Cruz said, interrupting a recount of Elliot's most famous pitch in college. Pitchers... catchers... bases... Baseball, maybe? He didn't so much as take a breath when Cruz spoke.

"Can you tell me if anything is missing from your brother's car?" He interrupted him louder this time and I turned around without offering a "nice to meet you" in parting.

It would have been a lie anyway.

Elliot puffed his chest, clearly offended, but I followed Ian back to Seth's car. Laid out across the trunk were all of the personal effects that would normally be on his person. A tech handed me a pair of gloves and I pulled them on, starting with the keys. The car key was obvious by the emblem, a mail key, something that looked like it went to a padlock and...

"What's this tiny key for?" I asked no one, and everyone around me shrugged. It looked the size of the tiny diary padlock I used to keep on my Lisa Frank Sand Castle Puppies diary. It hadn't needed a lock, my siblings were already gone, but I needed it locked to feel like a normal pre-teen girl.

Seth wasn't a pre-teen girl. He wouldn't need a diary key.

Setting the keys aside for now, I moved onto his phone. Lifting it, the screen illuminated a picture of his kids and asked for a passcode. Given that my brother was nearly as childish as I was, I had a decent idea what it would be but I wasn't ready to give strangers access to his phone. Last was his wallet and I peeled back the Velcro flap.

"Are you sure that's his wallet?" Opie asked, and my eyes trailed to him. His name badge said Gibson, but I was fairly certain someone had misspelled Griffith.

Or Taylor if you believed Larry.

"Yes," I answered, opening it and looking at the contents. Two access cards, his debit and one credit, a membership card to a gym that may be older than his daughter, and... a condom.

I blanched and dropped it like it burned me.

"Seriously? That bothers you after your mother gave you..."

"Shut up, Cruz," I growled, checking the area dedicated to paper money. There was none and I tried to think if that was weird or normal. "Do you have cash?"

"Right now?" Cruz asked and I nodded. He shook his head. I glanced at the tech who also said no.

Lack of cash was not weird for a man of his age.

"Anything you would expect to be there that isn't?"

"Pictures," I answered, checking the pockets and seeing the outline of what had once been the interior flap of a picture insert.

"People just keep those on their phone now," Opie said and I gave him a death glare.

"My brother is a structural engineer. He draws shit on paper and likes hard copy. He carries actual prints, you..." a hand came over my mouth and I felt myself being pulled backward and away from the young officer.

"That's it for Cyn's talking time," Cruz said against my ear and I tried to elbow him in the gut. He easily avoided me and used his second arm to pin both of my arms to my body. "You need to breathe and compartmentalize."

"Fu oo," I said into his hand and he tugged me farther from the scene until we were once again beside the Jaguar and he let me go. I spun around and charged at him, trying to tackle him to the ground. Instead, he caught me and pulled me against him, eyes pure fire.

"If you want to fight me, we can arrange a time and place for you to fight me. But right now, I need you to calm down and use your skills. You know your brother, you know Carla's keys were in the planter, and this is her Jaguar. Your brother left everything in his car but pictures of his kids. What does that mean to you, Cyn?"

"He left willingly." I sagged against him and just let him hold me as the sob I'd been choking on finally escaped. "Whomever he went with, they knew each other and he left everything behind on purpose."

"Why would he agree to leave it behind, Cyn?" His hand was moving up and down my back and tears creeped out of my eyes before I could stop them.

I only had the one brother and I wanted him back so I could get him psychiatric help for boinking Carla.

"I don't know," I swiped at my cheeks, letting the last of the useless emotions go. I shoved Cruz away from me to get to work. He chose to move but kept a hand on me. My eyes scanned the plaza. It wasn't exactly a commercial complex or an office complex. Despite being near the hospital and government buildings, it also held the bar, restaurant, and a coffee shop. My eyes traveled up, looking at the trim of every building.

"Guess we should find out."

I started walking, Cruz taking my hand and following me. He searched eye level and I kept my gaze up. Seth's car was just out of view of the cameras at the news office and too far out for the traffic cameras. Starbucks probably wouldn't have cameras. The restaurant wasn't open yet, but strangely the bar had a sign stating it was.

"Has anyone been in there yet?" I asked and Cruz tilted his head.

"No idea. But they probably didn't ask the same questions you would." He led the way to the establishment and I followed without stopping my search of the upper eaves.

"There," I said, stopping short on the small walkway just to the front. There was a small wraparound patio at street level separated by a wooden railing with a latched gate. In the upper corner, facing the door and patio area was a small bubble camera. Cruz studied it, but I elected to go inside without him.

My eyes were instantly met with darkness and I was blind.

"Shit!" I shouted, walking into something that was either an umbrella stand or a coat rack. Winnie let out a soft bark and I reached down for her collar. She guided me forward and after four steps we stopped because the dog was not good for more than four steps of seeing eye dog work. Opening my eyes, we were beside a podium with a pimple-faced kid standing beside it.

"Hi," I said, rubbing my shin and trying to look badass and non-threatening. An impossible feat on my best day, which today definitely was not so when the kid went owl-eyed I rubbed my face to get it soft and blank. "Can you access the surveillance cameras?"

He shook his head no.

"Is there someone on site who can?"

The kid nodded.

"Can I speak to them?"

His eyes were pure panic and Cruz came up behind me with a badge. The bastard managed to not run into or trip on a damn thing, and then I remembered he didn't *need* coffee in the morning either. He'd sold his soul to the devil and there was no comparing my life to his... but I punched him in the arm anyway. He gave me a brow raise and turned back to the kid, who was already walking to an employee's only area.

"I hate you," I pouted, distracting myself from worry by cataloging all the things wrong with Ian Cruz... starting with his name, face, scent...

"That's not hate, Cyn," he said quietly, leaning in to brush a kiss on my cheek and whisper in my ear. "I imagine it's how your mom expects you to look when you try out that toy."

I punched him again and he laughed, wrapping me in a hug that pinned my arms to the sides of my body.

"Later, chica," he said, brushing his lips on my neck, and my legs trembled.

"Do I even want to know what that's about?"

The kid had returned with a blonde sporting spiked up hair, soft features, a baggy button down, jeans, and boots.

"Hitting him or..." I asked and the blonde laughed.

"Pat," the manager offered a hand and we shook.

"Cyn," I identified myself and Ian offered his hand next.

"Cruz," he said and Pat nodded.

"You want to see the camera footage?"

We nodded and Pat gestured for us to follow toward the back. Passing the kid who had worked at the entrance, I couldn't help notice the sudden flush he was sporting.

"How old is that kid?" I whispered to Pat and got another laugh.

"No idea. I'm not in charge of hiring, but let's just say we don't let him work the busy hours... or the themed nights," another laugh slid out and I felt some of the tension in my body leave.

"Probably I should have asked, M..." I hesitated.

"Just Pat is good," was the response and I nodded.

"Are dogs OK in here?"

Pat looked down at Winnie and the dog offered a paw. They shook and we continued into a neat office area.

"Don't see why not. What do you want to see?"

"Can you open all the current views?" I asked and Pat tapped a few keys, opening a split screen view of ten cameras. "Can you filter just outside?"

A few more key taps and I had five outside views.

I leaned close, trying to find one that had any of the police activity in the parking lot in frame. A few caught glimpses of the periphery, none had a direct line of sight.

"Could you go back to... after ten last night on these two?" I pointed to views six and nine that had the most glimpses of my brother's car. Pat was smooth and efficient, having just the two camera frames fill the monitor and queuing up to ten minutes after ten PM.

"Real time or a little faster?"

"A little faster, please." I asked and Pat complied, the three of us watching the screen. People went in, people went out, I saw Elliot scouring the area, shaking hands with a suit man and taking an outdoor table. They shifted a lot, left, and it was nearly eleven fifteen before the first glimpse of a car in the spot my brother parked appeared.

"Slow down," I asked and the frames began moving in real time. The lights shifted around and cut out. A second car came in, full frame and left the headlights on. I held my breath watching the driver's door opening, not daring to blink and miss whoever had taken my brother.

A short curvy figure moved around the car and my brother appeared beside her. They hugged, kissed... really kissed and then broke apart to scan the area.

"Pause it?" I requested, just as the driver of the second car turned toward the camera. "Mother fu-"

Winnie whimpered mid-swear and I closed my mouth. I rubbed her ears, seething. First Larry and now Seth? I hated this woman, hated her so much.

"Carla abducted your brother?" Cruz asked and Pat let out a laugh.

"If she abducted him, she's been abducting him for months to make out in this bar."

"Are you kidding me? Months?" Was Larry banging this woman at the same time as my brother? I paled and started to choke.

"Yeah, never seen them actually kiss though, so don't get your panties in a bunch. Usually they just hug and hold hands. She'd always move in and he'd take a step back. Classy guy, most of her conquests would take her up on the blow job in the bathroom offer," Pat waggled brows and I tried not to gag.

"Did Carla come here often? With dates?" I asked, still watching the two figures on the screen as they went back out of frame to his car, reappeared and got into hers.

"I don't know if I'd call them dates, except him and that doctor," Pat shrugged and Cruz clamped his hands on the back of my neck to keep me from smashing my face against the desk. "Not that I blame her. Her husband has been in here on theme nights with his share of other dates. Hard to believe they thought she'd work as his beard when they're both getting jiggy in the same bathroom with men."

Chapter Nine: Doughnuts and Don'ts

I left Cruz to police matters, unclear if the scene was even still considered a crime scene.

If one believed the video, he wasn't taken. If one were to use common sense and thinking, anyone who left behind their cell phone, keys, and wallet was being abducted. When I called my mom, she was in favor of the latter, but admitted that Seth had once shacked up with an older woman at nineteen for two-weeks and he hadn't had any of those things either.

When I asked whether or not cell phones had even been invented then, she hung up on me.

On the way back to Sweet Pea, I detoured to visit Sylvia and Erich's other grandparents. The kids were behaving like little angels and I suspected it was an act. There was something green smeared on the wall and either the adults hadn't noticed yet or they'd been a part of it.

"Oh, we haven't heard from Seth but we don't expect to. He said he was going to an off the grid retreat to re-find his spark," Mrs. Peony nodded sagely and I looked over her shoulder at the pictures of my brother and her daughter gracing every wall.

"Did he mention if he was going... alone?" I felt awkward asking in front of framed photos of the child they lost.

"Did he tell you he thinks he met someone?" She was speaking quietly, mischief in her eyes. Apparently she wanted my brother to be happy. I wanted him not to get an STD, but I guess results may vary.

"Yeah..." I said, recalling dinner and almost immediately wanted to gag. He'd been talking about Carla. Carla the beard with more men than a monastery, yuck.

OK, it was only yuck because my brother and my not-boyfriend may have been doing the same woman at the same time. No one wants to be twice removed screwing his or her brother. At least not outside of banjo country but I didn't live in banjo country, I lived in farmland and the only freaky sex thing people did here was sell sex toys and molest livestock.

Maybe join my parent's "circle", but that was definitely emotionally scarring territory.

I shuddered and went back to thinking about Carla. The rest of her choices were her right and within the rules of her own marriage. If I looked like Carla, I'd probably have a harem. Though I'd probably never take advantage of having more than one man at once just for the logistics of it.

"Have you met her?" Mrs. Peony asked and I was wondering if I'd spoken or there was something on my face because her mischief shifted to concern.

I was just thinking about harems in front of my niece and nephew's grandmother, I thought and went red.

"Maybe... I'm sure he just forgot to tell my mom about the retreat. She was just a little worried. What's on your wall?" I pointed to the green smear and her face filled with glee.

Thank dog, she will never know about the harems.

"Radioactive waste. We were becoming ninja turtles earlier," she swiped the smear and stuck it in her mouth. I reflexively heaved and she shook her head at me.

"It's just Jell-O dear. Your mom is right; you need more sex so you'll be less uptight. Maybe he could do the job," she pointed behind me and I didn't need to turn around. The flutter in my stomach, anger in my chest and warmth in my good spots told me who it was. "Based on his face, he's gotten the job done before."

I looked for a light socket to stick my finger in, but coming up snake eyes, I just blinked at her.

"Yes, well, if you need help with the little demons," I said and she reached in to hug me.

"I'll call you. Have a good night, Cyn," Mrs. Peony whispered in my ear and I could swear she winked before she closed the door.

"It's not even three in the afternoon," I said to no one in particular and a cup of coffee floated in front of my face. The smell combined with the pine trees, apples, and hay had me grabbing the cup and drinking deeply as though it could satisfy every one of my needs.

As though I even knew the complete list of my needs.

When the cup was empty, I turned around to see Larry standing there with a pink doughnut box.

"Is Mo running a Cyn delivery special?" I asked, noticing her business name on the box. I lifted the lid, but before I could get a peek inside, he pushed it closed again.

"Can we talk?" He asked and I felt my face flush. This was the second time a man had shown up with coffee and doughnuts to "talk" to me. Except this time, I probably wasn't going to be saved by the news my brother was missing.

"If I say no, are you going to refuse to share those doughnuts?" I asked, knowing that despite having had some this morning, there was no such thing as too many doughnuts. Not when men kept insisting you talk to them.

"If you say no, I'll resort to Plan B," he shrugged, and my eyes studied his face.

"What's Plan B?" I asked and he smiled, passing me the box. I opened it and saw they were all glazed and with sprinkles again.

Mo must have been working mental overtime to give two different guys a clue into my doughnut preferences. Maybe she was of the same school of thought as my mom and my brother's mother-in-law. If one more person started expressing concerns about my orgasm level I was going to have to move... to a brothel.

I plucked a doughnut from the box and put it in my mouth. Larry moved, but the sugar on my tongue made me indifferent to him until he scooped me up and carried me to my Jeep, putting me in the passenger side before I could even process the fact I was airborne.

He'd managed to swipe my keys, activate the child locks, and secure the car so I couldn't get out.

"Plan B is I take you hostage," he said, walking around the car, climbing in and sitting behind the wheel. "It wasn't really Plan B, it was Plan A. Distract you with doughnuts and lock you in a room with me. I didn't have a Plan B."

"Plan A is pretty convoluted, but..." I shrugged and picked another doughnut out of the box. I still had an iced coffee in my cup holder, and I drank that while Winnie snoozed in the back seat. My mind tried to focus on the crunch of the sprinkles, the hit from the frosting, and the perfectly crisp doughnut dough.

My body said Larry and I were wearing too many clothes, and I decided this whole thing was her fault. Life was so much easier when we only thought about coffee and doughnuts. I dragged my eyes to him, feeling a magnetic pull I refused to give into with more than my eyes.

Larry looked like crap. His face was overdue for a shave, he had circles under his eyes, his clothes were wrinkled and didn't look like they had been washed. He stared at me. I ate another bite of doughnut and sipped coffee. He reached for a doughnut and I said nothing. He took his hand back without getting one and still I said nothing.

He booped my nose and I took another bite.

A long, exasperated sigh escaped his mouth.

"You... don't want to yell at me?" He asked, and I shook my head. "Hit me?"

I just ate another bite and sat quietly.

"Do you..." he chewed his cheek and even Winnie lifted her head to absently stare at the man in front of me. His body shifted, and he was clearly uncomfortable. Good, he should be uncomfortable. I had to watch him get felt up by a woman who was dating my brother.

If I was forced to endure that image, he could endure my silence.

I drank more coffee and watched him.

"Damn it," he said, dropping his head against the steering wheel and bouncing it a few times. "Damn it, Cyn. What the hell is going on?"

I watched him, his frustration and pain evident in the lines of his face.

"Going on with what?" I asked, trying to remain blank and indifferent.

"Everything! You, me, Ian, your mom calling me and telling me that you might need both of us to meet your needs, and Mo threatening to murder me if I screwed this up and saying if I didn't bring you doughnuts Cruz would have one up on me. What the hell is going on?"

With a long slow exhale, I tried to push past my pain, fear, and disgust at the twice removed brother sex to answer him. At the memory of him picking Carla over me, agreeing to never come back to my house... for her.

"Seth is with Carla. Mo is... being a super-nosey friend. My mom... probably best you don't think too much on what my mom says."

He lifted his head to look at me.

"Seth... is with... Carla?" His mouth gaped, and I wondered if he was making the same connection I did.

"They've been dating for months, apparently, mostly at Derby's. That's where she takes all her playthings."

He nodded but said nothing.

"Apparently, it's not really cheating," I continued and then backtracked in my mind. What had her husband said? *If you're dumb enough to get caught, you deserve to be accused of murder?* "He was seeing men there as well."

How had Carla gotten caught, but her husband didn't? Such a strange disconnect between the scene and the outcome. Why would a person watch the place, catch Carla and not catch her husband? Or had they and he paid to keep their silence?

Why wouldn't he pay to keep everyone silent and protected?

"Who is Carla's husband?" I asked, and Larry shrugged.

"I'm just a plaything," he said without any heat or emotion. Apparently he'd been fine with that, mildly comforting for me. I grabbed my phone and called Cruz.

"Who's Carla's husband?" I asked without any preamble.

"Jessop Rockwaller," he said and my frontal lobe pinged.

"Why do I know that name?" I asked and he laughed into the phone.

"Everyone knows that name. He inherited Rockwaller Quarries and Mines, and is on the Forbes list," he said easily and I stared at Larry.

"Wasn't her last name Herrera?" I asked both men and Larry nodded but Ian corrected.

"Rockwaller-Herrera, that's why the initials on the keychain are CRH. Looks like they belong to the newspaper office. We found some sort of gizmo in the key chain, don't know what it does just yet," he paused and a female voice said something in the background about cleaning everything up. "Pat agreed to give us copies of every video with Carla or her husband that is still on the server. It's a lot of files, what do you hope to find?"

"I'm not sure, but I'll take what I can get. Tell Pat thanks," I said and hung up on him.

"Who's Pat?" Larry asked and I tilted my head in surprise.

"Works at Derby's, the bar where Carla takes all her playthings. Blonde, short spiky hair, fond of blue jeans and flannel?" But he just shook his head.

"Never saw a person like that... but we usually met in the parking lot and got a room. Don't know if I ever actually made it inside the bar," he stroked his chin and my brows furrowed. If he wasn't the doctor Pat had referenced, who was the other man she'd actually dated?

"Did she ever tell you about... the others?" I asked and tried to stem the green slimy monster clawing up my throat. Hard to figure out where to rank awkward conversations, but this was probably up there with the eighty-year-old man asking to just slip me his key directly at my mom's house. She'd asked me to pick something up, but apparently she wanted me to be picked up.

"We... didn't talk much," he said to his hands in his lap and I lifted a brow at him.

"How come she got out of talking and conversations?" I crossed my arms and tried not to look smug. If I looked smug, he'd know I wanted to be special, wanted to be better than her.

"Because she was just for fun. You're not just for fun, you're..." he switched from looking at his hands to looking out the window. "Look, I only hooked up with Carla two, maybe four times. I met her at an event hosted and sponsored by Amber Carter's dad. She was supposed to be there as the press, but she ended up being there as a visual treat to Mr. Carter and many of the other men she shamelessly solicited. At the end of the night, she was wasted and this guy was looking at her like Winnie looks at unattended food on the counter. I grabbed her and pulled her out of the building, tried to take her home but she refused to tell me where she lived. Instead, I took her to the newspaper office and helped her crash on the floor by her desk."

"How did that turn into..." I mimed thrusting my hips and he groaned in annoyance.

"Could you not do that while you're mad at me?"

I shook my head no, but motioned for him to keep going.

"Honestly, I don't know. I don't even know how she got my number, but she called and she was lonely. I was lonely..." he seemed to be counting back months. "The party was in July, so the first time was July. Then October and January I think... We didn't do anything regularly. She was married, and though she said it didn't matter, it bothered me. Daniel said it's because I'm a little bitch. I said I'd rather be a bitch than knock one up... then he tried to punch me..."

"Daniel knew?" I asked, wondering if that was what caused him to become the target of Yvette's terror.

"Yeah... I mean he knew after. Yvette sent him pictures to try and blackmail him. He laughed and said I could, and this is a direct quote, 'put my dick anywhere I want'." He looked pained at the statement but I laughed.

"Did he say that when he found out about me, too?" Just picturing it had me doubled over and gasping for air until I felt Larry's hand on mine, lacing our fingers together.

"It's probably best I never tell you what he said about you," Larry answered smiling and I shook my head.

"Not if you want me to prove him innocent."

"Why is Ian back, Cyn?" he asked the spot two inches above my head.

"No idea."

"He didn't tell you?"

"I didn't ask," I shrugged and watched a white and red ball roll across the street. It was too big to be a baseball but too small to be a colorful soccer ball. "What was Daniel's sport in High School?"

Larry opened his mouth to protest the subject change but followed my gaze to the ball. When he looked back my face must have registered something because he answered.

"Football, wrestling, and cross-country. Why?"

I shrugged. It had been a long shot he'd played baseball. Just like it was a long shot the blood in the parking lot was even related at this point. I watched the ball bounce off of the neighboring curb and sit in the gutter. I glanced around, but whatever person or child that had sent it that direction wasn't looking for it.

"Just... thinking out loud..." I stared at the ball for a minute. Yvette had been murdered, but no one seemed to be looking that hard for her murderer. Mostly, everyone just wanted to declare that it wasn't them... loudly. What did it say about your victim that enough people wanted her dead that it was more work proving who didn't kill her than who did?

Sure, she had a thing for blackmailing people... that was a little rude... including Daniel.

But... Daniel? Daniel had way too many kids to have money. Did she only blackmail for money?

"What was she blackmailing Daniel for?"

"What do you mean?" Larry asked and I tilted my head to look at Winnie.

"Daniel has more kids than income, and it doesn't seem like she tried to leverage anything from you. What did she want from Daniel?"

Larry rubbed his chin, the stubble scratching against his calloused palms. The sound tickled my ears and I shivered.

"I don't think he ever told me... hang on," Larry got out of my Jeep and went to his truck. Despite a sense that we were beyond childish issues, it wasn't lost on me that he took the keys and locked the door. I watched him climb across the seat, grab something and shimmy back out.

Cell phone, I decided as he manipulated it in his hand before pressing it to his face.

My phone buzzed an incoming file and I glanced at the sender.

It was a massive video file from Cruz and I opened the message to see a note from Pat: *I pulled what I could remember, but I think the 19th may be of most interest to you.*

Because the bar worker had never steered me wrong, I went straight to the file in question. It took awhile to load, but when the image came in it was sharper than the one from the newspaper office. A lone figure was seated at one of the outdoor tables, the light making it look to be early evening. There was no zoom on recordings, but the frame was familiar. I watched, finger tapping against my thigh to the same rhythm the person in the picture was tapping.

Pop goes the Weasel, maybe.

The gate opened at the edge of the frame and another person entered the patio, glancing around. Much shorter, the person walked to the table and stood beside it, eyes glancing at the camera. Yvette I think, but the figure at the table didn't stand. The shorter person tossed something on the table, tapping the cover.

Seated figure shrugged, neutral and indifferent, as Yvette became more and more agitated until another person appeared. Short, curvy, and she dropped into the lap of the seated man, wrapping arms around his neck. Yvette looked prepared to punch her and she tossed her head back, laughing.

Carla.

Yvette pointed at Carla, then the man before she smacked the folder and stomped off the back patio, leaving behind the folder with Carla and the man. The two figures put their heads and faces together, the seated man sliding his hands up her thighs. When he leaned back, his eyes strayed to the camera, and I paused it. There was something too familiar in the face, but I couldn't figure out how or why I knew him.

The door opened behind me and I fell onto Larry.

"Ew," he said and shuddered.

"What? You know him?" My eyes went back to Larry who was very, very close and smelled like warmed apples and hay.

"That's Amber's dad," Larry said, making a gagging gesture.

"Are you serious? Wasn't it bad enough I twice removed may have had sex with my brother, but now Amber's dad?" I squeaked and he rubbed my back.

"I promise I always used protection. No directly indirect contamination occurred," he smiled but I still felt sick.

"What did she try and get from Daniel?"

"Looks like what Yvette wanted in exchange for silence was information and a no documentation investigation," he wrapped his arms around my torso to keep me in the car... and pressed against him.

"About or... into what?" I asked, closing my eyes and enjoying the feel of his hands on me. Just for a moment. He was still a traitor who picked another woman.

"Senator Tim Thomas," he declared, releasing me to grab his phone. He pulled open a picture on his phone, handed it to me and went back to rubbing my shoulders.

"Hey! I know..." my brain tried to catch up with my mouth and I stared again at the glamour shot. "He was in Yvette's boxes."

"Doing what?" Larry dug his thumbs into my scapula and I let out a moan.

"Not a what..." I sighed. "A who and he didn't look familiar either."

"What did he look like?" Larry asked, still massaging my shoulders. The video kept going, and I was half-watching Carla and Mr. Carter leave. Another minute passed, maybe ten, and a new man poked his head out of the bar while a second came in from a swinging gate. They embraced and each took a seat at a two-top table. Both men wore fitted suits, tailored to their exact body with haircuts straight out of GQ. Even in the surveillance video, both men screamed money and breeding, moving together in familiarity and ease. They held hands across the table, knees touching and I wanted to sigh at the cuteness.

Just a couple out on a date, and I considered skipping past it when one turned to the camera, just as my phone rang.

"Yeah?" I asked and heard Ian come through the line.

"We have a problem, Chica," he said and I squeezed my eyes shut.

"*Afghanistan landmine problem* or *you need more room in the front of your pants* problem?" I asked and felt Larry stiffen behind me.

"A *Winnie peed on the shoe of a visiting colonel problem*," he said and I watched the dog wiggle her eyebrows. "We've been served with a cease and desist. An order has been placed to forbid sharing of any and all data from the Derby."

"By who?" I asked, wondering if Pat had told him I already had the footage or if he was in the clear legally as far as knowing I had it.

"Senator Tim Thomas. Pat said he's on there," I closed the call screen and stared at the video, trying to make out the men.

"You there, chica?"

"Yeah, have you seen the footage of who he's with?" I asked, thinking at least one of the suits looked a little senator-y.

"Yeah, Carla's husband."

Chapter Ten:
Spinning Wheels

"What the hell is that?"

I was standing in Marvin's auto body shop and we were once again staring through his glass window at my jeep. It was still sunshine yellow, but that wasn't what he was staring at.

"Vandalism," I muttered.

Larry had left Mrs. Peony's house for an emergency birthing at the farm that I was strictly forbidden from attending. Apparently, despite the town no longer following me around to prove their innocence, Joseph was still pissed about getting hit with pudding, and it was somehow my fault. Winnie and I had spent the night eating pizza and binge watching The Good Place, contemplating our own mortality in melancholy.

Cruz had called, Larry had called, my mom had called, but we ignored all of them. If ignoring phone calls got me sent to the bad place, so be it.

"It was like that when I woke up this morning," Marvin was still staring at the hood of my Jeep where someone had painted an x-eye smiley face with the tongue sticking out. While arguably it would have been cute, what Marvin couldn't see smeared in the paint was a hangman's noose.

Frankly, whoever was leaving these messages had a little too much free time or an artistic passion that had yet to find a positive outlet. Like taxidermy, or picking up trash on the side of the road in an orange jumpsuit.

"Is that a death threat?" he took a step back from me as though an anvil would fall on my head like Wile E. Coyote.

"I thought it was a comment on how I look when I'm sleeping," I shrugged and turned my back to the Jeep and the mysterious image. Cruz had been pissed when I texted him the picture, telling me to call Daniel. Larry had been pissed, also telling me to call Daniel.

Daniel... was a pain in my ass so I didn't call or text him and elected to turn off my phone. Sure, Larry and Cruz would be pissed, but they'd have to find my vandalized sunshine yellow ass and I had no intention of spending any more time off my couch until someone told me otherwise. Someone being Joseph letting me go back to work at the job I was actually paid for.

Marvin still stood transfixed, and I tapped the counter impatiently.

"You have the color sample book?" I asked and he tore his gaze from the automotive terror.

"Yeah, I marked the pages in your price range." Again, a look of pain.

"That bad, huh?" I asked, flicking it open to the first post-it. Shades of red that didn't look half-bad. Blues that would blind other drivers, greens that reminded me of *MASH* and a burnt orange color.

"Why?" I showed him the book and he shrugged.

"Why the hell did I have yellow paint?"

I nodded in agreement.

He did have a point. There was no accounting for taste.

I flipped back through the blues, considering the sky blue. If I painted puffy white clouds, I could pretend I was part of the sky on surveillance. My eyes trailed to the window and the grey overcast day outside. Probably wouldn't be useful for another month or so. Orange was a definite no, so I looked at the reds. A deep Merlot shade caught my eye and a glance at Winnie had me thinking she'd look good in a burgundy jeep.

"This one please." He made a face.

"What?"

"It's just a little... girly," he scoffed and I rolled my eyes.

"I'm a girl! Well, a woman. She's also a girl," I pointed to Winnie who was considering whether or not she could get anything good out of the trash can before I stopped her.

"Not really," he grumbled, jotting down the color number on a blue sticky note. My eyes drifted back to Winnie. She'd already gone poop so I didn't have anything to threaten him with. The trash was beside his coffee maker that probably hadn't been washed since I joined the Army, no way would anyone be putting that in their mouth. Knocking over the man's coffee was a crime...

With a sigh, I moved on.

"When do you think it will be here?"

He shrugged and stuck the note to the counter.

"Rough estimate?" he winced as a bro took a flexing selfie with the Jeep.

"I'll call you when it shows up, for now get your photo prop out from in front of my store!"

"It's not..." But he had walked through the door into the shop and I stuck my tongue out at his back. Winnie sniffed his trash can again and peed on it, so I decided it was a great time to leave... and get her a pup cup.

On principle, we did not move the Jeep for another twenty minutes. We got ice cream, took a stroll, and ignored Marvin's death glares at the sun worshippers. Muscle tank clad men and bikini women were acting as though they were at the Jersey Shore and not in the middle of nowhere Ohio, posing across the hood. Winnie and I watched in fascination as more just appeared, climbing out of dune buggies and sports cars.

"Where are they coming from?" I asked Winnie, scanning the sky for a mother ship. While this looked too unintelligent for aliens to consider worth their time, April Fool's was less than a month away. "Maybe traveling across the galaxy threw off their math?"

"Excuse me, Ms. Sharp?"

I nearly dropped my ice cream, turning toward the woman who'd suddenly appeared. She'd made no noise, and Winnie hadn't even been alerted to the presence of another human.

Definitely a corporeal ghost.

"Y-yes?" I asked, and she knotted her fingers.

"I... need your help. It's..."

I held up my hand and shook my head.

"If I need to know why you're innocent of Yvette's murder, I will call you. I'm no longer taking requests. Also, I'm not qualified to help you cross over either, but I can offer you a book?"

"Cross over?"

"To the other side, because you're a ghost?" I hazarded speaking my mind and her eyes went wide.

"N-no. It's my baby. I need your help finding my baby. I let him out to stretch his legs and now I can't find him. I've looked under everything and..." her eyes misted and I took a small step back.

"Babies aren't really my thing. Also, I think if you wait long enough it will wake up and make noise?" I offered, hastily eating my ice cream in case the kid appeared and demanded I hand it over. It's not that I'd really give a kid espresso ice cream, but I don't negotiate with terrorists, and after seeing my niece with the peanut butter, they are not above torture.

"No, it's my Arnie. He's my pet, just a little friend who keeps me company and in comfort. He has a terrarium, it's just sometimes I feel bad that he's always in there..."

"Arnie isn't a snake is he?" I asked, nervous again.

"No," she shook her head, eyes wide. "Will you help me?"

My Jeep now had a line and a few of the Kirby kids were selling rocks to the chumps who were waiting.

"Yeah, OK. Do you live far?"

She shook her head and I followed her through the center of town to an outer area of small duplexes. They were newer builds, still sporting their original paint colors but in a matter of time I imagined the left and right sides would cease matching. Unless there was an HOA, then they would probably insist on coordinating colors or levying a hefty fine.

"Which one..." we walked up to a duplex still completely decked out in Christmas filigree. The lights were on, there were singing inflatable trees, and a Santa on the roof.

"What..." I checked my wrist. Nope, it was definitely still March. I hadn't lost a year.

"I just... really like Christmas," the woman sighed. The side of her mailbox said Birch, so either it was her name or instructions for her decorator.

"It's uh.... Certainly festive, Ms. Birch."

"Please, call me Noelle."

"Your name is Noelle Birch?" I asked, hoping to get it written on paper somewhere before my body was found trussed up in boughs of holly.

"No, it's Cassie. I just really want it to be Noelle," she looked wistfully at the Santa on the roof, and I took a step back.

"I think we need to..." I started but she turned back to me in panic.

"Please! What about Arnie?" she begged and I let out a long breath staring at my shoes. Whatever this woman's issues, it probably wasn't the animal's fault. I'd been in more dangerous situations for animals. I scanned the woman once more.

I could take her if she tried anything... probably. Except maybe if she weaponized fruitcake.

"Yeah, OK," I said and gestured for her to lead the way into her house. The overboard decorations continued inside, sound being joined by smells to really capture the insanity. Immediately on the other side of the door was the kitchen. Peppermint sugar cookies were cooling on the counter, and beside them an incense warmer made more peppermint scent.

Straight from there was a living room and then hallways leading off to bedrooms. A terrarium sat on top of the coffee table, and I directed Winnie to scent it. Her eyes went wide, but she put her nose to the ground and got to work.

"Have you... lived here long?" I asked, keeping an eye on Winnie as she moved in an erratic pattern around the rooms. Though I was confident she wouldn't eat whatever lived in the box, there was a possibility she had hillbilly Santas lurking who'd accept Winnie ears in lieu of frog legs.

"I just moved in last month," Cassie replied and I stared at her.

"You... did all of this," I gestured to her house. "After Christmas was already over?"

She nodded and I decided there must not be an HOA. They definitely would not have let her do this. A door creaked in the hall and I saw Winnie's tail disappear into a room. I followed without taking my eyes off Cassie.

"So..." a howl carried from the room, and I ran.

"Winnie!" I called and she let out another whimper. There was an open bedroom door to the left and I walked in to see my partner, cowering in a corner. Her ears were flat against her head, her body hunched and her eyes bugging out of her head.

In front of her... was the biggest spider I had ever seen.

"Crush it!"

The dog cowered and got smaller.

"Winnie, come!" I said, paralyzed in fear. The dog did not move.

"Cassie, I need a shoe or a..."

The woman appeared behind me and let out a delighted squeal.

"Arnie!" Then she went and picked up the tarantula, producing a small Santa hat, affixing it to the spider's head, and carrying him out of the room. Winnie whimpered, I felt my limbs go weak, and we shared a look of confused horror.

Cautiously, we ventured back out of the room, down the hall, and into the living room. Cassie was now adding small mittens to each of the spider's eight legs.

"Are you... serious?" I asked, voice trembling and she beamed at me.

"He's the best. Do you want to hold him?" She asked, moving toward me with the spider in her hands. Winnie howled, and in complete agreement, we turned tail and ran.

"Why are you red and out of breath?" Larry was leaning against my sunshine yellow Jeep, scowling.

"Spider. Really big spider. Crazy lady," I panted and he gave me an eyebrow raise.

"Seriously? That's the best you can come up with?"

"She put a freaking Santa hat on it, Larry!" I shouted and Winnie tucked in her tail. Larry's eyes went from suspicious to amused horror.

"Oh, you met Cassie... or Noelle..." he nodded and pushed away from the Jeep. "She's... out there."

"Spider, Larry! Spider!"

He wrapped me in a hug and I started shaking and trying to swallow all of the air around me.

"It's OK, Cyn. The spider is not here." He rubbed his hand along my back, and Winnie leaned against our legs, also needing comfort. "It's OK, girl. I know Florida was traumatizing, but that woman's spider is harmless."

I pushed away from his hug and we both stared at him.

"Big spider, Larry. Really freaking big spider! Not harmless!"

"Seriously, you two were in the Army."

Winnie and I exchanged a look. I crossed my arms.

"You lived in Florida for two years, you've seen worse things than a tarantula. Though... the Santa hat is a little..." he struggled to find an in-offensive phrase.

"What about the mittens?" I demanded, eyes wide. "There were boots and mittens, Larry. Eight of them because it's a freaking spider!"

He decided I needed more hugging and pulled me back against him.

"I've missed you these past few nights," he said against my hair and I felt a shiver of excitement.

"I'm still waiting for my cookie."

"Just the cookie?" he asked and I felt my lady parts stand at attention.

"Well, I wanted the orgasm until you mocked my fear of spiders. Now it's going to take a lot of cookies for us to forgive you," I teased and he tickled me until I squeaked.

"You're going to eat those words, Cyn."

"What did you think I wanted to do with the cookies, Larry," I stuck my tongue out at him, and he slid his fingers into my hair, pulling our faces together. Our lips had barely touched when I discovered we had an audience.

"I see you're working really hard." I pulled away to see Daniel scowling at us.

"I mean, you'd have to ask Larry about the *hard* part but..." Larry moved behind me and covered my mouth.

"Any leads on the vandalism?" His brother scowled at both of us, but he decided to answer Larry's question.

"No. Aside from being childish, he accomplished the feat in one of the town's many, many blind spots. I'd take a report, but someone hasn't proven me innocent yet so I can keep my job." The older Kirby was now scowling at me and I flipped him off.

"You're not innocent, you're just not a murderer," I muttered against Larry's hand. With his fingers half in my mouth, I sounded like an adult in a Peanuts' comic and neither seemed especially interested in knowing what I said.

"We were just going back to her place to work on it," Larry said and my good spots tingled.

"No, you aren't. She's going back to her place. You are going with me to help mom dig ditches for the new sprinkler system," Daniel said and my eyes widened.

"You dig ditches? For the snitches?" Larry had let his hand fall, and both men rolled their eyes at me. "Fine, whatever. Have fun digging, Governor Ratcliffe."

Larry still had a grip on my waist and I glanced at him.

"Problem?"

My back was pressed to his front, and I could feel more than see his affliction.

"I don't want to spend the day with my brother or my mom," he said against my neck, brushing a soft kiss just below my ear.

"Yeah, it's unfortunate. But you never made good on your cookie promise for enduring 'the talk' so I'm not going to save you." I wiggled out of his arms and he took hold of my wrist. "You also picked another woman over me. In my own home! So... talking clearly didn't do anything, and I don't have a cookie."

"We never had the actual talk, Cyn," his voice held a warning. "I want you to be my girlfriend. Only mine."

My stomach fluttered, and I saw Daniel shuffle his feet.

"Kind of late after the other night, don't you think?" I asked, my pulse kicking up a notch. I'd never been anyone's girlfriend. I'd been their friend, their *friend* and their anonymous hook-up, but this... this was new and terrifying. New, but also... it was Larry. I'd known him forever... I hadn't been overly fond of him for parts of it, but he wasn't unexpected.

"I just wanted your help; I didn't pick her. I don't want to just be your plaything and personal space heater, Cyn. I have no interest in Carla or doing anything with her besides proving she didn't murder people. I'm interested in you. So... I guess... if you can't commit to just me, I can't keep seeing you," he said quietly and the pulse in my chest went to my head. Little bursts of light filled my vision. "I don't need an answer now, but I do need an answer before you get any cookies... or orgasms."

Daniel started choking behind us, and Larry gave a small smile.

"Think about it?" he asked and my tongue was stuck to the roof of my mouth. Instead of answering, I nodded and opened the Jeep door for Winnie. She hopped in and I waved, climbing behind the wheel.

I sat that for a moment, not daring to start the engine and risk driving.

"What do you think, girl?" I asked Winnie. She let out a wide yawn in my rearview mirror, and I dropped my forehead to the steering wheel. "You could be more helpful."

Winnie let out a fart that forced me to turn over the engine to roll down the windows.

"Seriously, dog, what am I feeding you?" I grumbled and watched Larry walking down the street beside Daniel. The Kirby brothers could not have grown up more different from each other, but there was a bond there. A bond and a similarity I'd missed before. Neither had left or gone very far from home. They liked stability, consistency, and permanence.

I'd joined the Army to avoid becoming another townie who never left.

Being with Larry, really being with him, probably meant I never would again. My heart skipped a beat and I wasn't sure if it was the fear of staying or the excitement at being with him. I put the Jeep in gear and tried to distract myself with murder and giant spiders.

It was barely a block to where we parked beside my building, but I drove past it twice in my daze. We'd circled the town, driving past Mo's bakery and Amber's shoe store. The next pass we ended up out in the farm area where I had to take a moment parked in front of the dairy to reorient myself.

Joseph poked his head out of the ice cream shop and shooed me away.

With both hands, he actually gestured for me to scoot and then turned the business sign to closed.

"That was rude," I muttered and backed out of the dirt parking area. We drove back into town and I carefully avoided the street where Mrs. Kirby lived. We made it to Main Street, a confused bunch of muscle heads looking baffled at the lack of sunshine yellow Jeep in front of Marvin's shop. We passed Mo's, Casey's Bar and...

As I nearly passed it the third time, my brain had a sudden burst of brilliance.

"He was too dazed to go very far," I said to Winnie in the rearview mirror and pulled up the map on my phone. Carla's address already had a pin drop, and I'd drawn a circle radius based on fuel mileage, but it wasn't necessary. The gas station was barely two blocks from Jessop Rockwaller's house. I consulted the great Google and after a few, possibly illegal, back door searches I found the address of Senator Tim Thomas. Wouldn't you know it, the men lived a mile away from each other and even in a dazed stupor, I bet Mr. Rockwaller could find his way.

Chapter Eleven:
Malicious Mail

When we arrived in the senator's neighborhood, Winnie and I had to double check that a twister hadn't carried us to Oz.

Every house was brick front with a grand staircase up the center. Each had a wrought iron gate set in stone obscuring all but a few peeks of the houses that lay behind. We paused in front of the senator's house, trying to see through the trees peppering the interior fence line. A fountain graced the circular drive and a courtyard at the manor vibe graced all the spots Winnie and I could see.

"I don't think we're in Ohio, anymore," I whispered and she let out a low woof of agreement. I pulled parallel to the gate and checked the roof of the house for turrets or cannons.

"I think it's just a house," I said to Winnie and opened the door. She followed me out and we didn't bother to lock the yellow monstrosity. Partly because I wanted it to get stolen, and partly because even if it did, the joy ride would be short-lived.

Winnie promptly got to work, sniffing the gate and marking spots she found interesting by peeing on them. While her nose worked, I tried to get a visual idea of the house's layout. There was no garage on the front, no cars parked in the circular drive. A bay window overlooked the rose bushes on the right-hand side of the staircase, but the curtains were drawn. Same with the windows above and beside it, making the windows of no help to prying eyes.

"Excuse me, can I help you?"

I nearly leapt out of my skin as the disembodied voice crackled from the speaker box.

"Uh..." I said, looking around for a camera and finding one mounted every ten or so feet along the boundary. "I'm looking for someone."

"Who are you looking for?" The voice wasn't familiar, but it was definitely human and male.

"I'm looking for Mr. Rockwaller and Senator Thomas," I said. A long silence followed, and I gripped Winnie's collar to pull her to the ground in case machine guns rose from the columns and open-fired on us.

"You have the wrong place," Speaker Man said and I shook my head.

"I don't. We both know I don't. My name is Cynthia Sharp, and I'm just trying to find a killer."

"There are no killers here, Ms. Sharp." The voice was clipped and I nodded.

"If you'll allow me to ask you some questions, I'll go away," I offered and despite the speaker being inactive, I could feel him thinking on the other side. At the last second, I decided to show my hand. "I've seen the video from Derby's and the photos in Yvette's office. I don't care about gossip, I just want to find the murderer so people will stop confessing how they planned on murdering her to me and get my hands back into the uteruses of pregnant cows."

The gate swung open and Winnie and I walked in.

The paving stones were grey, as were the stones making up the front of the house. Trees lining the fence and along the driveway made the area cooler than the space a mere foot outside the gate. Winnie's claws echoed on the flagstones and it was eerily quiet, even for the country. A breeze sent the smell of pine and the whisper of needles into the air, and I stopped to absorb the calm.

"Are you going to come in or just stand there?"

My eyes opened and I stared at a man that was neither the senator nor the heir to a rock fortune.

"I don't know yet. Is there a permit I could file to live in this driveway for a week?"

He stuck his nose in the air and sniffed in disdain.

"Yeah, fine," I said, and Winnie and I moved to the staircase, ascending it slowly.

"What is that?" he sniffed at Winnie and she extended a paw.

"A wizard in animal form."

Without waiting for him to process that, we entered into a foyer that was neat and impersonal. A wooden table sat beneath a shiny mirror. There was a coat rack beside the door, but no coats were on it. Across from the rack was a closet and without regard for decorum, I opened the door and looked inside.

It was full of coats.

"What are you doing, Ms. Sharp?" I turned to see the senator standing in a doorway.

"Trying to understand why rich people need a coat closet and a coat rack within five feet of each other. Who does that?"

I watched the man carefully as his eyes examined the closet and the rack. Beside me, the man who had opened the door spoke up.

"The coat rack is for guests and items damp from the elements, miss. The coats of the house go in the closet," he sniffed again and I shrugged.

"What happens if the coat dries and it just stays there? Does Martha Stewart come and yell at you?" I asked him, shrugging out of my coat and considering the ramifications of throwing it on the floor just to annoy him. As though detecting my intentions, he plucked it from my fingers and hung it on the stand.

"Sir," he said to the senator and Tim Thomas raised his hand in release. Another sniff and the man walked away.

"Who's he?" I asked and Tim looked mildly relieved to see him go.

"My mom insisted I needed an Alfred Pennyworth to keep my ego in check. I personally think she just wanted someone to stand around and judge me into behaving properly in all social and private settings. Every time I try to fire him, my mom gives him a raise. He might have more money than I have at this point," he said with a shrug and gave me the once over. "You don't look like I expected."

"You expected me?" I said, not sure I was impressed with the senator himself. He seemed young and soft. Not someone who had ever worked or needed to prove himself. Mr. Thomas had been handed from one stage of life to the next without any real awareness of the hows or whys of it.

As he was in government, that was probably for the best.

No one ever wanted a politician who thought for themselves. At least not when it came to important things like public appearances, opinions, and beliefs about life, liberty, and the pursuit of money.

"Not exactly. I expected at some point I would meet you due to your notoriety in the community. Either at your sentencing or to give you a medal for services to the community, but never in my home," he said thoughtfully, leading me through the doorway into what could only be called a parlor and only be in the house of rich people. There were two floral davenports, a fireplace, and potted plants that couldn't be real or they'd have died in the lack of sunlight. Sitting on one of the stiff, wood and fabric seats, was Mr. Jessop Rockwaller.

"It's a very fine line between criminal and hero," I said, looking at the pristine room. It looked as sterile and uncomfortable as the entryway. "Do you live here often?"

The two men exchanged a look that told me more than anything they said would have. This was for show, no one really lived here and it was as uncomfortable for them as it was for me.

OK, maybe not as uncomfortable as it was for me, since they weren't wearing shoes and the mogul's fly was down.

"Never mind. How long have you two been dating?" I asked, crossing my legs and sitting on the floor. The floor looked more comfortable than the stiff, formal sitting surfaces. Winnie circled the whole room twice, stuck her nose in both men's crotches, and then lay down with her head in my lap.

"You're quite direct, Ms. Sharp," Mr. Rockwaller commented and I blinked at his surprise. "Apologies, you are the second person to arrive today with questions, but the first to do so in honesty."

"Who was the other person?" I asked, wondering if Cruz would come here without me.

"It's not important. He's an old family friend," Senator Thomas dismissed and Rockwaller fell silent. I filed that away for later investigation and instead stroked Winnie's head, waiting them out. A grandfather clock chimed the quarter hour, and a quiet sniff indicated the butler was lurking nearby.

Tim tapped his hands on the back of the couch, walked around, and sat facing Jessop. He picked up a glass tumbler with an amber liquid, swished it around, and then set it back down without drinking.

"Aren't you going to ask questions?" he demanded and I tilted my head.

"I did ask a question. Two actually. How long have you two been dating and who else was here asking questions?"

A long-suffering sigh escaped his lips, and Jessop stretched a hand out to rest on his knee. Gripping the other man's hand, they shared a look filled with affection. At least one thing in this room was real.

"We've been dating for a few years now," Tim said and Jessop nodded. "The friend is a town council member, Burt Kielder. He's making a play for governor, and I was backing him. Unfortunately, or fortunately depending on your perspective, my support won't mean much as a gay Republican."

I snorted and tried to mask it as a cough.

"Problem, Miss Sharp?" Jessop spat and I shook my head.

"Nope. Just... you are probably not the first gay Republican. Fairly certain there are and were a lot. You could be notorious as the first one to be so honestly. I mean... Ronald Reagan was a movie star, but straight men don't have hair like that. So is that why you married Carla?" I asked Jessop and he furrowed his eyebrows together.

"No. That was... family pressure. They said that I needed a woman to run my house and balance my stiff and impersonal nature." He swirled his drink and took a small sip. "Carla was perfect in her own way. She had wanted stability and freedom, and I gave her both. My only request was that she be cautious and discreet. The woman, for better or worse, was neither. There was another aspect to our marriage but I don't fully understand it. She had another job besides the newspaper."

"What other job?" I asked.

"Something with the government. It was probably the only thing she was able to keep her own counsel on."

I nodded, considering the next question and studying the men. Both had trim, but not athletic frames. Soft hands, adorned with rings and the shine of lotions didn't look capable of swinging a wooden bat, let alone crushing a woman's skull with one.

"What did Yvette blackmail you for?" I asked instead and they both looked at me in surprise.

"Yvette?" Tim asked and he shook his head. "She's the one who told us someone was trying to ruin us. The pictures were given to her in error, I think. That's what she said. Her only suggestion was that we be more careful and discreet. Jessop left his house when he got a threatening note."

The other man nodded and set down his glass. He rose, pulled his wallet from his back pocket, and removed a neatly folded sheet of printer paper.

"You... keep it in your wallet?" I asked and then looked at the size of his wallet. "You've been sitting on that? Dude, you're going to need a hip replacement."

"Ms. Sharp," he scoffed and I shrugged, accepting the paper.

As expected, it was printed in generic looking ink in a generic looking font.

Tell her you are leaving. Get out while you can, there is no reason to go down with the ship.

"This... is threatening?" I asked and he sighed, taking the paper from my hand and flipping it over. On the back was a collage of images. Jessop and Tim, Carla and Larry, Carla and Mr. Carter, Carla and Seth, Carla and...

"Who's the man in the lab coat?" I asked, trying to figure out if he'd been in the boxes behind Yvette's desk.

"Him?" Jessop asked, coming closer and squinting.

"I think that's the head of neurosurgery at the hospital. He was the most surprising to see with Carla to be honest." He rubbed the space between his eyes with his thumb and index finger.

"Why?" I was looking at the other men in the image, trying to see if there were any consistent background lurkers. "Does she not usually go for the medical type?"

My eyes landed on another image and went wide before looking back at Mr. Rockwaller.

"Yes," he sighed and I tried to make the stationary image zoom in. Mr. Rockwaller and the neurosurgeon were lip locked with their hands exploring each other... shirtless. The image ended at the abs, and I chose to believe there were pants in the part of the image I couldn't see. "I'd thought he was... but I think he's just curious to see what's out there. Carla spent more time with him than I did, but he's an honest man. Thankfully for him, he's brilliant and the hospital firmly believes your genitals are your business. Unlike politics and business, where there are no sanctions on publicly traded information."

I nodded, still scanning when I saw a familiar face in the background of two, then three and a fourth photo.

"It's probably a long shot, but do you know who this is?"

I handed over the paper and the two men squinted at it together.

"Can't be certain," one muttered and the other nodded in agreement.

"Does look a bit like him though," another look exchanged and Jessop tucked the paper back into his wallet.

"No idea," he said and the Senator agreed.

"You just said it looks like someone, who does it look like?"

"I believe this conversation is concluded, unless you believe either of us to be a murderer," Tim Thomas gestured with his hand toward the door, but I remained seated.

"I believe you are withholding information that could help me find a murderer," I crossed my arms and he mirrored the gesture.

"I have no legal obligation to answer you, Ms. Sharp."

"I can have the new deputy come ask my questions," I snapped and he shook his head.

"You can't. I have the whole community caught up in a ridiculous gag order. It won't hold up, but it gives us time to come up with a plan. A strategy for proceeding." Tim nodded his agreement with himself.

"A plan for what?" I asked, surprised when the butler appeared and grasped my arm. He tugged me to a standing position, and I was too shocked to fight him on it.

"How we will address this with the public." I was being guided toward the door, Winnie in tow. "Don't forget your coat."

My down jacket was thrust against my chest, Winnie and I were each given a brown bag, and the door snapped shut on our noses.

"What just happened?" I asked, looking in my bag and seeing a bottle of wine. Winnie set hers down and stuck her nose into it. She came out crunching a dog biscuit and I wondered. Had there been dogs in that house or did they just have guest gifts on hand for all manner of guests? Was there catnip and bird seed to?

At a loss, we walked down the driveway to the fence, it swung silently open as we approached, and I walked through half in a daze.

"Thank you," I said to the empty space, assuming they were watching and listening in security.

"Good day, Miss Sharp," Alfred Pennyworth's unfriendly uncle sniffed and I rolled my eyes. We walked back to the Jeep only to stop part of the way there.

"Oh no," I muttered, seeing the ringed tails of raccoons peeking through the open windows. "No, no, no."

I'd forgotten to roll up the windows, and my Jeep was full of raccoons.

"Winnie," I said and she started cowering.

"If you chase them out of the car you can have any snacks they didn't eat."

She charged the Jeep barking until they scurried out and up the trees. She leapt into the open window and I heard a sound of despair.

Cautiously I approached the driver's side and squeezed my eyes tight.

"Please don't let them have pooped in it. Please..." I begged the universe and slit one eye open. The raccoons had ripped the pink fluff off of the seats, attacked the lacquered steering wheel, and... scratched nearly every inch of the paint on the Jeep doors and the runners. The only thing completely untouched was the death threat smiley.

The death threat smiley was either made of raccoon repellant or the substance they use to make the black boxes for airplanes.

"Just great," I muttered, opening the door to get in and seeing the biggest horror of all.

"My coffee!" I cried and watched the liquid pooling on the floorboard while Winnie curled up in despair.

Now there was no coffee, no snacks and no answers.

Chapter Twelve: Elf on the Shelf

"Slow day, chica?" Cruz asked, and I shot a spitball at his forehead. He caught it and tossed it easily into the can beside my desk.

"Go away," I muttered. Ripping off another small piece of paper, sticking it in my mouth and firing it out of the straw at my hand drawn target. It was three rings on a picture of Amber's face I'd ripped from the newspaper.

"You're losing your touch, hardly any are in the ten ring," he said, snaking a spare straw from my coffee cart, grabbing some paper, and landing one dead center between her eyes.

"Whatever," I muttered, impressed despite myself. Setting down my straw, I looked at him again and saw he was in jeans and a t-shirt. "Day off?"

"Something like that. What happened to your Jeep?"

"Raccoons," I sighed and grabbed my coffee mug from my desk. It had a dog dressed as a ghost on it, declaring "Licks or Treats". My mouth found the brim, I tilted the cup... nothing. "Oh, right."

Winnie had four paws in the air on her dog bed behind me.

The whole spitball game had started when I emptied my coffee and Jessica Saller had come in trying to demand I find her keys. She went on for forty-five minutes and I'd remained hiding behind my desk. Jessica, for better or worse, had an aversion to deodorant. In school she'd claimed it was some sort of allergy, but I think truthfully she just forgot more days than she remembered. Normally, I'm a live and let live kind of woman, but she did not respect personal boundaries. Without an end to her rant or reek, I'd started ripping up paper, and then I saw straws on my coffee cart.

I'd had to move even closer to her to get the straw and my nostrils would never be the same.

She only shut up when my first spitball went straight into her mouth and I could tell her the keys were in her back pocket. I then demanded reparations for having to look at her rhinestone clad ass. She'd huffed, left, and thus the game began, but I'd never made more coffee. Sensing his life may be in jeopardy, Cruz took my mug to the cart and popped a pumpkin pod into the single serve maker.

"I need your help," he said and I considered shooting a spitball at the back of his neck.

"I'm already helping you. Helping you means that yesterday I questioned a senator, a mogul, had my Jeep destroyed by raccoons, and slept alone with Winnie and an extra-large two-topping pizza. Now I'm shooting spitballs at anyone who wants my help."

Cruz handed me the coffee and crossed his arms, the picture of patience and understanding. The muscles in his biceps flexed and my brain went a little fuzzy. The man was hot, muscular, smooth, and flawless with his mocha skin and caramel eyes.

I got hungry just looking at him when he wasn't making me coffee.

"Are you going to drink that so you resemble a human?" he asked with a smirk, and I glared at him.

"Did you poison it?" I sniffed hesitantly and he looked behind him.

"Your coffee cart. Do you keep poison over here?" His body shifted and I appreciated the view. "Stop looking at my ass, chica."

"I wasn't!" I lied, gulping coffee and looking out the front window.

"Liar," he said, lips brushing my neck and I choked, sputtering coffee down the front of my shirt.

"You made me spill coffee!" I hissed, even as my throat burned and my eyes watered, I couldn't help but notice his hand on my waist.

"I can make you do other things," he whispered and I think my underwear disintegrated. "But you'll have to wait."

"Why?" I whined and then clapped my hands over my mouth. "Damn-it, stop that!"

"Making you want me?" His eyes lit up and I smashed my elbow into the desk.

"Son of a..." Winnie let out a bark and went over to love up on our former training sergeant.

"Hi, girl," he said and she melted into a puddle of goo at his feet.

"Hussy!" I yelled as she showed him her belly but I had to admire her lack of shame. If I were that willing I'd... my head fell to my desk and I banged it twice until a warm hand placed itself between my face and the wood.

"I need your brain, Cyn. Don't damage it," he said quietly and concern replaced the arrogant self-assurance in his voice. "What's wrong?"

"I'm having a life identity crisis," I said into his palm, and he lifted my head. "What?"

"This isn't new, chica. Why is it knocking you on your ass now?"

"What's that supposed to mean?" I scowled but my heart wasn't in it so I pulled my face away from him and drank the rest of my coffee. When life gives you indecision and crisis, drink coffee. New life philosophy.

"It means when you showed up to military police canine school, all you wanted was a dog. You were willing to build the bond and do the work, but you had no real interest in fighting crime, stopping terrorists, or fighting for this country. You just wanted to see the world with a dog and shoot stuff." He wasn't judging, his hand rubbing up and down my back to take the sting out of his words.

"You're a restless spirit. You're never going to be satisfied, even driving a truck through a wall. As soon as it's over, you feel empty again. You're just waiting for the next drop, the next loop on the roller coaster so you can feel alive for a moment."

"How do you know that?" I asked, looking at him, really looking at him, for the first time.

"Because I'm the same, chica," he said quietly, and I tried not to wonder too hard how he knew all that... about both of us. When I was younger, I used to ride the wheel that spun so fast you stuck to the wall over and over just for those few seconds of terror that I could fall off at any second while defying gravity when the wheel tilted. The only thing between death and me was a single metal chain that would cut me in half if gravity failed.

I was always secretly disappointed that gravity never once failed.

"So... why are you in Ohio?" I asked, deciding that answer seemed relevant now. Once a man admits to knowing you have no overarching motivation in life, you might as well learn *his* motivation for reappearing.

"Mostly?" He asked, looking me in the eyes without blinking. "I'm here for you."

"Why?" I asked, stomach doing small flips while my palms started sweating. Was this a death threat? Was this an invitation to be kidnapped?

Was this a booty call?

"We'll have to talk about that another time," he said softly, kissing my temple as the door opened. Ian moved away from my desk and I saw Mo standing there, holding a pink box.

"Where the hell have you been?" she squealed and I took in her flour dusted apron, red hair, and green glasses. Beneath the apron she was wearing red and green, and I nearly laughed.

"You look like a damn elf," I laughed.

"Your personal Elf on the Shelf and you are being naughty!"

"How am I being naughty?" I asked, shaking my head as some flour fell from her hair to her nose.

"I have eyes, Cyn! You were all up in his space. What would Santa say?" She fisted her hands on her hips.

"He'd tell you to stop being a creeper who watches people..." I looked behind me at Cruz as something clicked.

"What are you thinking?" He was wearing his blank face, his thoughts a mystery while he stroked Winnie's fur. I used to think it meant he was giving me room to reach my own conclusions, now I was pretty sure that he was intentionally keeping things from me and didn't want to look surprised when I figured them out for myself.

"Elf on the Shelf, they are used to manipulate/bribe kids to be good with the idea they're always watching and reporting back to Santa," I looked between him and Mo and saw that she wasn't quite meeting his gaze. "Mo?"

"Why him?" She shouted and I clapped my hands over my ears at the volume.

"Inside voice, please," I cautiously took my hands off my ears and she swallowed twice.

"Why are you here with him? I know I gave him the coffee and doughnuts, but they were supposed to be a parting gesture! Like he'd give them to you and you'd throw them at him and then send him packing. Then you'd eat the doughnuts Larry brought you and you'd make up and I'd be your Maid of Honor. Now I walk in and this man..."

I again looked between the two and was completely baffled.

"Is this about your cookware? I know he threw you off when you met for the first time..."

"No! It's about Larry," she snarled and again I felt I was missing something. "It's about Larry and the fact that he's here and loves you. This guy just pops into your life, spikes your hormones, and leaves you wanting. He isn't healthy, not for you! Which isn't healthy for me because then we drink too much and eat too much ice cream and I hate going pants shopping."

"Mo, I'm helping him with a case... one Larry, Daniel, and Joseph all insist I solve. I promise not to make you drink or eat ice cream if that's a problem. We could go to the shooting range right after you get that felony conviction thing cleared up."

Ian choked on a laugh, and her eyes filled with hostile fire.

"He's not even a deputy," she crossed her arms and I looked back to Ian's carefully blank face. "Chris told me, he knows some guys in Yellow Springs. He's working there undercover to get access to information about something larger. They don't even know who he's working for!"

My eyes went back to him and he was leaning against the wall, staring at his shoes.

"So... not for me?" I asked, not feeling as disappointed as I thought I would. Work made more sense and it was almost a relief. He was the gravitational pull of the spinning ride, that smothering sensation that made you feel safe as you faced the ground with nothing in front of you but a thin metal chain.

He was a rush, but one that had a habit of ending just before it killed you.

"It's complicated," he responded, eyes sparkling dangerously. Be it at me or Mo, he was angry enough to burn from the inside out. "Why don't we get back to the Elf on the Shelf?"

"Yeah, distract her so you don't have to answer for your crap. Same as always," Mo seethed, and I held up a hand to her.

"Mo, I love you," I said and her eyes softened. "But this, right here, really is work. Larry... picked Carla. Whatever the reason, he picked Carla and then asked me to be his. Exclusively just his and it would have freaked me out whether Ian was here or not, but now it's just part of a long list of mixed signals."

"But why?" Her eyes were misting, and I dropped my gaze to my hands. It was a valid question, one that had kept me up all night watching Gilmore Girls and binge drinking pot after pot of coffee... with Bailey's.

"Mo, why did you join Teach for America?" I asked her instead and she cocked her head to the side.

"To see the world and help people. Then I discovered that teaching is hard, people are mean, and I like baking things better," she shrugged and I felt Cruz laugh behind me. "What?"

"Nothing. I just realized I never asked and I was thinking about carnival rides."

"Carnival rides?"

"Yeah, the kind that would probably kill you if they didn't make the operator stop them. It made me wonder what everyone's gravitational moment was." I tried to shrug it off, but Ian's eyes were boring a hole into my head.

"I was also thinking about how Yvette had all those pictures and wondering how she got them. Some are clearly shots from the bushes outside meeting spaces, but some make it look like she was right there in the room." I was getting this conversation back on track if it killed me. I wasn't ready to examine my fears of commitment when it came to Larry.

Or the more prominent fears of rejection.

"You think she was an Elf on the Shelf? She's not that short, Cyn," Mo said, fisting her hands on her hips, but Cruz was following my thoughts.

"The device in Carla's key chain was a tracker and audio recorder, Cyn."

"Exactly! But maybe she also had nanny cams, or the adult equivalent of an Elf on the Shelf," I looked between Cruz and Mo and she was looking around nervously, checking the corners of the room. "What are you thinking about right now?"

"The crucifix," she said softly and I nearly smiled.

"That is your adult equivalent of an Elf on the Shelf?"

"God is always watching, Cyn!" she hissed, and this time I did smile. One could always count on catholic guilt to continue long after one stopped practicing Catholicism.

"I wonder if he watches you and Chris when he's feeling... frisky." I waggled my eyebrows at her and she opened up her bakery box to throw a doughnut at me. I caught it and took a bite while she turned red and gave a wide-eyed look of horror at Cruz.

"Do not talk about what I do with Chris in the same sentence as God and in front of strangers!" She pulled out another doughnut and threw it at me. She missed and toppled the bottle of wine Senator Thomas had given me. In the bottom of the bottle was a hollow. Curious, I picked it up and placed my finger inside while Cruz moved over to take custody of the doughnut. Smaller than a keychain...

"Do people normally bring home gift wine and drink it?" I asked, trying to picture Yvette's office and the photos on the shelf.

"Not usually," Mo said, deciding to eat the third doughnut she pulled out of her box rather than throw it at me. Box... the books were boxes where she hid the pictures. But what if...

"I have an idea," I said to no one in particular and Cruz raised a brow. "But I need to see the pictures and the book boxes from Yvette's office."

"What does that have to do with wine, chica?" he asked, fingering the label on my wine bottle. Temporarily mesmerized I lost all rational thought watching him trace the letters of the winery with his finger, slowly and gently.

Mo beaned me in the head with a doughnut and I shook it off, giving her a thumb up.

"It doesn't exactly. But when people give you wine, you don't immediately crack it open. Same with books, especially if they're older vintage editions. What if the books she kept the photos in were the rejects from her book nanny cams?"

"You think she bought a bunch of old books, made them into cameras, and then gave them as gifts hoping no one would notice?" Cruz considered it but his eyes were skeptical.

"Or..." Mo chewed on her lip and again scanned the ceiling and checked the doors. "If you gave someone a really nice bible, they'd probably keep it but never open it. No one throws away bibles, but hardly anyone reads them."

I scrunched my face, nodding at her when a visual popped back into my head from my visit to the senator's house.

"Crap! Do you think maybe Yvette really didn't take those picture's?" I asked, grabbing my bag from the corner and checking that the rear doors were locked.

"Slow down," Mo said, trying to grip my shoulders but only managing to reach my elbows. "What the hell?"

"Sorry, it's... the senator said Yvette tried to warn him and Rockwaller that someone was watching him. I thought it was a ploy to gain their confidence, but what if she was telling the truth? What if she found the photos that were nanny cam style? What if someone else was doing the indoor spying?"

"With... bibles?" Mo whispered and I nodded.

"There was a super fancy white and gold bible on the entryway table at the senator's house. I need to look at it, and the other pictures... and..."

I was bustling around, mind working but I couldn't seem to connect anything concrete. Shoes, I was going to need shoes. My clean shoes sat beside the sad concrete encased one a con man had left with a warning note. The concrete was my fault, that the shoe was still here was really more a commentary on my housekeeping skills.

Concrete... rock quarries... visiting men who want to be governors...

"I need to go back to the senator's house. Can I meet you... at the picture evidence storage place?"

"Property room?" he asked and I shrugged.

"Is that where they keep the pictures?"

"Yes, chica."

"Then yes... where is the property room?" I asked, grabbing a leash for Winnie.

"At the Sheriff's Station. I'll see if I can check them out."

I clipped on her leash and glanced around the room. My shoes were still next to the one covered in cement. I looked down at my feet- rainbow heart socks.

Back to the shoes and this time I definitely got them on my feet. I checked twice.

"Check them out? Like a library book? I thought you just walked around and picked up boxes like on Cold Case..."

"No. Stop watching TV." He grabbed my hand, pulled me in for a hug, and kissed my cheek. "See you in an hour?"

"I think so... If I need to bring something to become evidence..."

"Don't touch it and call me," he warned and I nodded, but we both knew I would touch the crap out of anything I found and completely destroy its evidentiary value. "At least wear gloves."

He threw two balled up pairs of latex gloves at me, and I nodded before wiggling my eyebrows.

"But if you give me your rubbers, what will you wear?"

Mo threw a doughnut at my head.

Chapter Thirteen: I-Spy

"No," the butler sniffed into the speaker and Winnie growled.

"You can't just..." the gate opened and I stared in confusion between the box and the open gate wondering if it were some kind of trap. If I went in, would he call the police?

A new voice came over the speaker.

"Come in, Miss Sharp," and I drove up in my raccoon tarnished car that smelled strangely pine-y with a hint of fish.

"That you?" I asked Winnie and she tilted her head, scenting the air. Her tail wagged and she put her head down.

We stopped in front of the house, and I again marveled at the Scottish mansion style architecture in the middle of Ohio. The solid wood doors opened before I'd even secured my car, and both men stood shifting in the doorway, no longer concerned with discretion, the curtains flung open on every window.

"Is everything OK?" I asked, noticing the fish scent was somehow stronger outside of my car. "Why does it smell like fish?"

"No, our privacy has been invaded, and you are the only person who's been here! You and your stupid raccoon Army who tossed the trash!"

The senator looked red, and I wondered if he was drunk or if he was really angry.

"More than it already had been? Also, I don't have any raccoons..."

"You know perfectly well..." he trailed off as Jessop squeezed his hand. "What? Look at her Jeep! She brought those raccoons who pulled out all the fish scales and papers!"

"I don't think she does. Also, you don't really believe she controls raccoons do you?" he said and both men studied me. I tried to look competently innocent, but their expressions indicated I managed nothing more than deer in the headlights. Winnie pranced up the stairs, nosed both men in the crotch, and let herself into the house.

"Your dog has very poor manners," Tim said and I shrugged. "Those were not your raccoons?"

"She's an Army brat. Lived all over the world and is still adjusting to being back in America," I inclined my head for permission to ascend and follow her, feeling my comments on the raccoons were unnecessary. Jessop granted me permission while Tim cocked his head to the side.

"Weren't you last stationed in Florida?"

"Yes, but that's not America. That's hell above ground. You know Disney World was built there because they rightly believed no one could tolerate living there long term." He still didn't look convinced.

"But people *do* live there."

"And they are miserable unless they are at Disney World. Just trust me, the only happy people in Florida are old and or heavily medicated." The two men exchanged a look as I reached the top of the stairs, and I waited for whatever they were thinking to be decided.

"Your brother was here," Tim said simply, and I felt the air leave my lungs.

"Seth? Is he OK?" I pushed past them and ran into the parlor where Winnie was whimpering in front of an empty couch. I looked behind the curtains and in the closet, I dashed down a narrow hallway but got lost and promptly turned back. Winnie's sad eyebrows said it all.

"He's gone now," one of the men confirmed, and I felt my eyes burn.

"A video surfaced of him in the house with Carla and us," the same man said and I looked back at them trying to hide my tears. "She followed you and discovered I wasn't dead. She wanted to talk... about getting a divorce. She really does love your brother."

Again, the tears, so I tried to focus on something besides my brother and his kids. Something that wouldn't make me sad... Then, I tried not to choke on the nausea that my brother and my Larry had banged the same chick... or on the ball of emotion that welled up in my chest at the idea of *my* Larry.

What the hell was wrong with me?

"They... haven't done anything," he said, looking concerned for my health, so I did a few deep breathing exercises... there were still bells clanging in my head but the floor and the ceiling had righted themselves.

"They're adults. I just... wanted to see my brother. Also to not think about your wife doing my boyfriend and my brother... maybe at the same time. It's only gross because its once separated incest, and also I might I-"

I closed my mouth and the room started spinning. At a loss, I sat down on the floor, and the men shared another knowing look. It would have been easier to be offended if my face wasn't pressed into their carpet while my body threatened to hyperventilate.

"I am serious. Your brother said that he wasn't going to bring her into his bed while she was committed to another. He'd been 'that guy' before, and he said that the only way he could be with her was if it was only them. It was sweet..." the two men squeezed hands, and I nodded, giving my cheek rug burn.

"Right, so if you haven't seen the video, why did you need to speak with us?"

A glass of ice water on a silver tray was set beside my face, and I looked up at the butler.

"Miss," he sniffed and stalked off.

"Poison?" I asked the other two men and neither looked certain.

"Is that a common thing? People trying to poison you?" the senator looked concerned and I shrugged, shifting into a seated cross-legged position. I picked up the glass and gave it a cursory sniff.

"Not recently," I took a small sip and it tasted like water. Possibly tap water, which I found reassuring. If I wasn't good enough for the bottled stuff, I probably wasn't worth wasting poison on. A longer drink of the water and my tongue unstuck from my throat, allowing in the air I needed to keep breathing.

"Sorry, I'm here because I need a bible."

"You... excuse me?"

"Well, I need to see your bible. The white one that was on the entryway table yesterday to be specific, and I was told I should wear gloves, but don't take it personal. It's just we think it's a spy cam."

"You... what?" It was Jessop's turn to look ill, though he had the grace to collapse on the couch and not the floor.

"I guess... I'm... OK..." I stammered, trying to figure out where to start and knowing pretty clearly these men would be skeptical regardless. "Do you have that note?"

Jessop nodded and looked at Tim.

"I just want to show you something," I said, pulling up Yvette's blog on my phone. The man pulled out his note, and I flipped it over to sit side-by-side with my phone.

"Yvette's photos, the ones that were definitely hers, were taken from bushes and through windows. The pictures on your paper, and some of the photos found in her office, were taken indoors. More clear and like a person stood in a room taking them. But obviously you wouldn't have done..." I gestured to the paper and the men blushed. "No judgment, but you wouldn't have done it with some rando in the room. Which, in a nutshell, leads me to believe the recording device would have to be in something that one would receive as a gift, but not promptly do anything with. Special edition books, fancy wine and..."

"Bibles," Jessop nodded and it was Tim's turn to sit down hard on the couch.

"That bible on the entry table was there for a month. We left it on the entryway table because I thought one of my guests must have left it and they would see it and take it back home. We just moved it yesterday," he was breathy. Jessop rubbed the other man's back, and he dropped his head to his shoulder. It was a sweet gesture, one that spoke to a love and familiarity that poked at the mushy spot in my chest.

"Where did you move it to?" I asked and he held his breath.

"It's right over there."

He inclined his head to a sturdy, built-in bookcase. The volumes were all the same size, free of dust and anything remotely acceptable on BookTok. I went over, inspecting the volumes to find Jane Austen, A. A. Milne in a gold leaf edition of Winnie the Pooh, and Tom Sawyer. I traced my finger along the spines, marveling at the untarnished covers while Winnie sniffed, nudged a book, and sat beside me.

"Do you read these?" I asked, glancing over my shoulder. Winnie whimpered beside me and stood, turning in a circle.

"No, Ms. Sharp. The actual reading books are in the library. Those were purchased purely to be decoration," Senator Thomas said, and I paused to study his face.

"I can't tell if you're joking or not, but if this place has a library, I'd love to see it," I turned back and spotted the small white Holy Bible on the shelf, spine aligned perfectly with the neighboring pieces. I pulled on one of the pairs of gloves in my pocket and carefully, I slid it out. When I opened the volume to hear the spine crack like an encyclopedia tomb I had a moment of discomfort at the idea that I had been the first to open this book.

It had been a long time since I'd been any book's first, and that bothered me for some reason.

Winnie sniffed the spine and sat, again, looking between the book and me.

"I know girl, but we have to look inside."

I flipped through the first few pages, looking for something amiss. It was a standard bible, beginning with Gensis and carrying on from there. I switched to the back and heard the spine creek open again.

"Please, Ms. Sharp, could you be more gentle?" I turned and tilted my head at him. Senator Tim shook his head and gestured for me to proceed. "I'm sorry. I really don't like when people touch my things. Even when they aren't mine and possibly being used nefariously."

My eyes took in the room again before turning back to the book. A few pages in from the rear cover, small squares appeared in the center of the binding, gradually getting wider. It was a square telescoping opening and at the widest part was a small black wire taped to a flat battery. The wire disappeared into the spine and I turned the book to the outside, seeing the lens of the camera looked out from the *O* in Holy Bible.

"That's impressive," Tim said from right beside me, and I jumped, dropping the book just as a small hum started.

"Maybe we should move," I said as Winnie alerted on the book a third time, and this time I understood why she sat. I grabbed the man's arm and dragged him back to the couch as sparks shot from the bible and it smoldered from the spine outward. The ice water I'd been drinking sat on the table and without thinking, I tossed it on the fire just as I remembered the battery.

"Crap!" I said, using Winnie's shepherd skills to push the men back. "Crap, crap, crap."

Sparks arced from the battery to a nearby lamp and the whole house went dark, backlit from the open curtains so everything was half illuminated.

"I'm guessing that might be my fault," I said into the semi-darkness, and Winnie let out a long fart as another voice joined the darkness.

"Actual professionals are here," sniff.

"Chica, why do things near you always end up on fire?" His hand wrapped around my wrist and in the semi-dark, he stole a kiss. When our tongues touched, I felt my toes curl as I fisted my hands into his shirt and tried desperately to swallow his life force. The lights flickered back on and I jumped away from him like he had electrocuted me. Something like triumph flitted across his face, and I fought between wanting to panic and wanting to punch him.

Both with a heaping desire to rip off his clothes.

So basically, I was exactly the same person when I was in Afghanistan, and it would be great if my body could grow the hell up... maybe taking my brain with it.

"I thought you were going to check out the pictures?" I asked, trying discreetly to check my mouth for drool.

"I have checked out the pictures, and there's something I thought you and these gentlemen should see."

"Perhaps this show and tell could move to a room with... fewer flammable collectibles? The sun deck, perhaps?" the butler sniffed, and I stuck my tongue out at him.

"I didn't booby trap the book."

"Based on your history, it wouldn't seem you'd have needed to. You tend to cause fires completely without intention."

Cruz chuckled beside me but disguised it as a cough when I elbowed him in the gut.

"You're going to pay for that," he promised against my cheek and I flushed red.

Donning a new pair of gloves, Cruz picked up the bible and examined it for an ignition source. Winnie nosed at the spine and he passed it to me to inspect.

"Explosives are more your thing," he said and I studied the book. Between the glue binding and the leather of the cover was a metallic coated piece of plastic.

"Do you have your knife?" I asked and he flipped it open. Carefully, I inserted it into the leather and made a single slice, peeling back the two sides. I passed it back and he came to stand flush against me, sending my brain on a temporary vacation.

"Cyn," he said against my ear and I shuddered.

"Yeah?"

"Is it going to go boom again?"

"No. It burned through the accelerant... and destroyed any stored images," he nodded and snaked his arm around me to take the book and place it in a bag.

"Then, for now, we will move on," he said and everyone turned to the man of the house who looked mildly panicked until the butler took charge.

"Follow me." The man placed his nose firmly in the air and led the way past the foyer, through the kitchen, and into a well-lit enclosed back patio. It was well furnished in squishy cushions on wicker furniture, painted a sea-foam green that somehow complimented the AstroTurf beneath our feet. "I'll get drinks."

Cruz, comfortable in all situations except being reprimanded by old ladies, gestured for Tim and Jessop to take the first seats. They chose a love seat and he pulled a coffee table into the center and another love seat opposite. The room lost some of its visual appeal, but home decorating probably wasn't on Ian's résumé as a skill.

"I didn't bring all the pictures in, just the ones I thought may be of interest to you specifically," he pulled a small stack of prints from his cargo pocket. They were carefully wrapped in an envelope and he slid them out across the table. With gloved hands, he arranged the images and they all featured the men across from us, but also another man. It was the same man I'd seen in the background of the threatening collage.

"I asked you about that man," I said and the men leaned in closer, shifting uncomfortably. "You did know him!"

"Yes, Ms. Sharp," Jessop let out a dramatic exhale and leaned back to cross his arms. "That is the town council member, Burt Kielder, we informed you was at our house yesterday."

"Why didn't you tell me yesterday?" I asked, and Cruz pulled out another print and placed it beside the others, this one an outdoor shot through a window.

"Because he had been photographed having sex with my wife and Yvette blackmailed him."

Chapter Fourteen: Sudden Drops

W e were on our sixth pot of coffee, night had fallen, and I still had no new ideas.

The Sheriff's Office had granted us access to a conference room with a massive wooden table, and we had sorted the pictures into indoor nanny cam shots and outdoor snooping images. There were thirty different people in the outdoor shots, most of them living in Sweet Pea and most of them had sworn they were innocent.

Which, of murder, was probably true but holy crap the debauchery.

My dentist liked to touch himself watching livestock breed. Joseph was growing marijuana in a secret patch at the dairy that he shared with the owners for their "glaucoma", and Mrs. Charles and her husband liked to have sex in public spaces.

The last wouldn't have been so disturbing, but my parents were part of the group in the background sketching it. Apparently, they'd had a permit to host an art class. Daniel was far too squeamish to argue over the definition of art.

At least according to Yvette's articles. Though frankly, given what a hoochie Daniel used to be, I was more inclined to believe they kicked him out when he asked if he could watch. The man was nasty and shameless.

Also his wife used to smash pudding on girls clothes so it would look like diarrhea, and I heard rumors she lets her children do things that are just as bad. Not really a family I wanted to join, but arguably my family were outcasts and freaks in their own right.

Though at least we weren't mean... just disturbingly interested in sex.

"Where do you want to start, chica?"

I tore my eyes away, eyes imagining the scene extending before and after the picture. When I realized my parents had watched, I just stared at him in horror. No one wants to see their neighbor boinking her husband while their parents watched.

"With a fifth of tequila and a rusty spoon to dig out my eyeballs."

He laughed and shook his head. Either he didn't have tequila and rusty spoons, or he was declining to share. The rat fink was pretty selfish so I was leaning toward him being against sharing.

"What do all these pictures mean to you besides you live on Shutter Island and our industrious reporter was a creepy little voyeur? I mean none of this is especially damning... unless photographed and disseminated with a story."

"Ugh, were all of these disseminated?" I asked, noting that some of the pictures had post-it note explanations attached to the back, and some simply existed. While the images of Larry and Carla weren't unfamiliar, the one of my mom hosting a sex toy party and shaking a dildo at the window was. It didn't have a post-it, nor did it appear on her website. I started a new grouping of the images: online, undocumented, and detailed notes.

I pushed aside the pile of the online images. There was no leverage if you'd already told the world. Which left the pile with notes and the pile without, none of which had been made public. I tried to arrange them by content: explicit or suspicious behavior. I tried to arrange them by the occupant's known occupations.

I tried arranging them by whether or not my mom would sell them a sex toy.

"Ugh," I grumbled again and pulled out my phone.

"Ma, did anyone try to blackmail you or dad?" I asked when she answered.

"Cynthia, I did not raise you to be impolite," she chastised me and I thunked my forehead on the table. It wasn't as though I hadn't *just* seen her yesterday. It wasn't as though we hadn't been texting throughout the day.

It wasn't as though someone had been murdered... oh wait.

I let out an exasperated sigh.

"Hi Ma, how are you? Done any sketching of fellow seniors having sex in a public place? Sold any dildos? Have you been blackmailed?"

Ian threatened to laugh beside me and I dug my fingernails into his arm. It was probably less painful than this phone call, and I considered other more sensitive places I could dig my nails that would be more satisfying. My mom, true to herself, ignored the sarcasm and started telling me about a new cheese infused bread recipe she came up with while Ian walked around the table toward the other end. I was appreciating the view when the corner of a picture poked out of his back pocket. Quietly as I could, I moved up behind him and pulled it out, studying the post-it note affixed to the back first before flipping it over.

A man in full Army dress greens was shaking hands with Burt, but in the background, Carla was standing in uniform guarding the door. It wasn't an Army uniform, but it was either military or Law Enforcement. Her hair was pulled back in a tight bun and one of the men shaking hands was looking... to her. It was a still image, but they were communicating... something.

"Ma, I gotta go," I said and watched Cruz's carefully blank face when he saw me holding the picture.

"Who is she really?" I demanded, anger flaring.

"Same thing I am. An informant and a patsy, the government sticks us places to get information with different letters on our paycheck. Carla isn't military, she's... some alphabet agency, but the Army had benefited from her information. She is particularly gifted at honey traps, but she wanted out. For the same reason she wanted out of her marriage, she wanted to be done with the life and the service," he took the picture from my hand and put it back in his pocket. "Most of the indoor shots, the spy cam style, they are hers."

"So she placed the nanny cams and killed Yvette?" I asked, and he shook his head.

"No, these..." he shifted a pile toward me. "These spy cam style, are hers."

The images were indoor events with suits and ties, lots of jewels, and pomp. A few times there was a glimpse of a mirror and there was Carla, on the arm of her husband. Mr. Carter appeared in some, as did the councilman and the senator. A man I recognized from an Army hearing, and leadership from the entire county were in attendance at several photographed gatherings. All of the events were recorded by Carla.

"To what end?" I asked and he studied his shoes. Whatever he said next would be a lie, and I shoved the pictures back at his chest. "Forget it, I don't want your lie. You're here for those pictures, then? Why didn't you just arrange them by the ones she'd taken and the ones that weren't hers or Yvette's in the first damn place and save me a crap ton of hours in your company?"

"Maybe I wanted to be in your company. Cyn..." I interrupted him by holding up a finger.

"Save it. I don't care what you are. Not anymore," I shook my head and decided to study the indoor images that weren't hers. Whereas the first set took place in public settings, the second set crossed a line. Cameras had been placed in bathrooms, bedrooms, and people's private areas that even I couldn't identify, but were quite red, or pink, or furry. Most were sexual, some just awkward, out of context, and potentially damning.

Carla was a spy. Cruz was a spy... or cleanup crew, or both. Carla was getting information on wealthy people in the area by posing as the wife of a wealthy man. I opened my mouth to ask Cruz what was in the area of interest to the feds but closed my mouth. He wouldn't tell me and I was tired of lies. An image from Carla's pile was sitting beside an image from Yvette's and above them was a nanny cam image.

The quality was similar between all of the images, but the lighting wasn't. Yvette's had been reliant on ambient light, Carla's designed for soft lighting in large spaces, and the nanny cams... I saw the bag with the bible and pulled it out, Winnie getting to her feet from beneath the table, prepared to save all of us.

"Are you concerned about explosives or organized religion?" I asked her and she flattened her ears. "Yeah, both scare me too."

I checked my gloves for holes and when they looked to be intact, I dumped the book on the table and pulled a pen light from my cargo pocket. There was also a Chips Ahoy so I decided to eat that and toss Winnie a biscuit from my other pocket.

"I can get you real food, Cyn," Cruz said, but I elected to ignore him. His idea of real food would probably be a salad, and I wasn't in the mood for a salad. I wanted answers, candy corn, and a nap. Maybe also... my eyes tracked to Ian's pants and I mentally slapped myself in the head as he let out a very male laugh.

The man missed absolutely nothing.

"I can be your food, too," he moved closer and heat flooded everywhere.

"Damn it, you lie and keep secrets and disappear. Why do you do anything besides piss me off?"

"Because, I'm cute," he rubbed a hand on the small of my back and awareness hummed outward from his touch. "And I'm fun."

"I've never seen this fun before," I grumbled.

His lips brushed just beneath my ear and my knees gave out, but he caught me. This fun I had felt before and despite all the promise in his touch and his gaze, he'd never come through once.

"We're also surrounded by some very... inspirational images," he pulled one toward us with a woman bent over a kitchen counter. "This table is high enough, we could practice angles."

My breathing shuddered, and I zeroed in on the image.

"Wait," I brought it closer to my face and studied the man behind her.

"What am I waiting for?" He dragged his hands over my hips but I shoved him off to study the picture. I grabbed another and then another, all of them the same. In each one, an occupant of the photo was looking at the camera, making eye contact, winking or smiling wide. They'd arranged to capture the moment. All, except for two: The senator with Mr. Rockwaller, and a man I didn't recognize with a woman I did.

It was Yvette, in a wig and the man... he looked well off. They weren't having sex though. Her eyes were moving around too much. It was dark but not outdoors, at least not entirely. A faint reflection was in the right corner. Car, maybe? Were they in a parking structure? Where the heck was there a parking structure?

My eyes went back to the man. Who was the man?

Cruz moved closer, studying the image beside me.

"Do you know him?" I asked and Ian slipped back into his role as professional crime fighter as though he'd flipped a switch and shut down his humanity. It was an impressive skill, one that left my head reeling, and now I had to wonder if he was a honey trap. I stared at him, watching his eyes study the photo. Cool, calculating... robotic.

How had he looked kissing me? The same?

"No, but I think I know someone who might be able to help," he said and excused himself to make a call. I shook off the eerie feeling that the man was still keeping secrets. Secrets about himself, secrets about me... secrets like why he kept showing up where I was and trying to get into my pants.

The room dropped five degrees without him and I picked up the bible without much enthusiasm. The cover was singed but intact. Inside all the pages had yellowed, but only the back pages had burned. The pattern started at the hole cut for the device and radiated out. It was low heat, low fire... so how did it make that noise?

I traced the cut I had made into the binding and peeled it back farther. A paper wrapping that twisted at the top sat in the binding and I lifted it out. The piece was smaller than the tip of my pink fingernail and I'd seen it before. Absently, I held it out to Winnie who sat.

This was the source of the explosives.

I sniffed at the binding, but there was no scent. Just a filmy residue like the opening of a lighter after it's refilled.

"What are we looking at?" Cruz asked from behind me and I showed him the paper.

"Explosives were in here, and I feel like I know what it is, but I can't place it."

"It's a Party Snap," he said, taking the paper. "Those things kids throw on the ground to make a sound."

"Doesn't the sand in those moderate the explosion?" I asked, trying to remember the chemistry of the reaction. "One of the reasons it's stable is because of the sand, that's why it is safer than a cherry bomb."

"I don't think this is stock," he said, twisting it in his hand. "The tail part is too long. I think someone made a home version and left out the sand."

"OK, so I drop the book and it pops. The pop triggers the little capsule of butane, the images are burned, and then what?"

"Whoever had the Bible in their house thinks it's a sign from God that they are the devil and put an end to their evil ways?" He offered, putting the paper back in the binding. I set both down and stroked Winnie's ears.

"Why something that needs to be dropped though?" I was looking at Winnie, watching her nostrils flare and eyebrows wiggle. Cruz moved around the table, shuffling the images. A stealth observation device with accelerant and an impact activated explosive, in the house of a senator who was dating a man who sold rocks. The Bible had been there for over a month, it was just moved to the shelf without incident...

I rubbed my temples and stared at my shoes.

Cruz wrapped an arm around my waist, pressing his entire body against the back of mine. I jumped, dropping the pen in my hand.

"Did you forget about me?" he said softly, and my lady parts warmed. My brain sent out sirens and warning bells. The man was basically a gifted actor in espionage.

My eyes went to the pen I dropped... dropped.

"No, but... what if this wasn't a storage photo taking Bible. What if this was a live feed? If whoever held it started getting too close, make a sound, startle the holder, they drop it and fry the transmitter."

I picked the book up again and this time searched for a wire and mesh imprint.

"There," I said, showing the indents to Cruz.

"There was a speaker in there."

I stared at the impression, the residual explosive, and the singed casing. Who would need live access to information? My eyes tracked to Cruz, the informant. Carla wouldn't need a live feed though... would she?

"So... who's the man having secret meetings with Yvette wearing a wig?"

Cruz hesitated, turning me in his arms to study my face. He tried to press himself closer and I pushed him back.

"No. No more freaking honey traps. Answer or leave, Cruz."

"Andrew Scott, he's a foreign correspondent, worked with Special Ops overseas before coming back and writing a tell all. His trademark was stealth observation. Hiding surveillance in ordinary objects. He was ultimately fired." Cruz tried to pull me back in and I growled at him.

"For writing a book?"

"For selling people inappropriate images and the option to blackmail."

"What do you mean?" I asked, looking back at the pictures. "He took all of those?"

"No. The photos *he* took are evidence. His post-retirement enterprise was selling the option for others to follow suit. He fell off the radar for a while, but they're going to try and track him down."

"Do you think Yvette bought his services? She had her own camera," I said, gesturing to her stack of photos.

"I think she stumbled onto something and thought he could help her get leverage or evidence," Cruz speculated and I sighed.

"So what? She's meeting with a man to get him to help her with something? How did she get the picture of them meeting? How did she get these spy cam images if he sold them to someone else?"

"You can ask him all those questions when we find him," Cruz said, pulling me against him. "For now, would you want to..."

His phone rang and he answered with a simple "Cruz".

He listened, made some noises, and shook his head.

"I have to go," he said, pressing his forehead to mine. "I'm sorry."

"At this point, I'd be more surprised if you stuck around," I pushed him, taking a step back and clipping on Winnie's leash. "Let me know when you find him."

"Cyn-" His phone pinged a message and he grimaced.

"Later, Sgt. Honey Trap," I waved at him over my shoulder exiting the room. "Watch out for yellow bears in red shirts."

Chapter Fifteen:
Fly Fishing

I was in bed and staring at my ceiling.

It had been two hours. I had tried counting sheep. I had tried counting the furs on one of Winnie's ears.

I'd tried drinking decaf.

My ears pricked as Winnie lifted one of her own at the metallic click of the exterior door opening. Winnie lifted her head, nose working while I reached under the bed and entered the code to release my handgun. Footsteps started moving up the stairs and Winnie's nose worked faster until she paused, flopped over and let out a fart.

"Dog! Guard!" I hissed at her, and she rolled on her back for me to rub her belly as the light blinked on. I leveled the handgun at... "Larry?"

"It's barely nine, why are you in bed?" he asked, indifferent to the semi-automatic pointed at him.

"Why are you in my house?" I asked, lowering the gun but not willing to lock it up yet. "I could have killed you!"

"Yeah, but you didn't, and Winnie would have gotten me before you shot me if I was a baddie. Calculated risk," he shrugged and started moving through my kitchen, pulling out snacks and heating water in the kettle for the hot cocoa packets he pulled from a bag he'd brought with him. Just earlier I'd been willing to live and let live, forgive and forget, but now...

"I repeat, why are you in my house?"

"Because," he shrugged and I crossed my arms under my chest. His eyes went wide and I looked down. Tank top, no bra... mild slippage that I carefully tucked back into the shirt and I looked back at him. He was still staring where my boob had been and stood there, licking his lips and looking like maybe his pants were a little tighter than they had been.

"You aren't allowed to come back here," I said, petting Winnie. "That was the rule. I help Carla and you leave and never come back. I spent all day helping Carla and now you are in my kitchen. Touching things!"

Larry still hadn't managed to look up from my chest.

"God damn it, Larry. You made your choice and while we aren't necessarily on bad terms, I'm tired and cranky and just now I want to hit something. Get out!"

"I thought... after we talked and she was with your brother maybe... we could talk some more... but maybe with fewer clothes," he followed my body down to where the blankets pooled at my hips. "I really miss you without clothes."

I wasn't wearing any pants.

Freaking great.

"You thought wrong, Larry. You chose her and even though I get it, I'm still hurt. You chose her, like you chose your image over me for years before, and then claimed you wanted to be my one and only, but what about your one and only? You never mentioned giving up your image for me!"

"I didn't choose her!"

"You did! I said you could ask me to help her and leave without ever coming back and you agreed. So what? Did you think just because I can prove she probably isn't a murderer it's OK for you to just show up here? Show up here, look at my boob, and then I'd just open my legs and arms for you?"

The metallic door clicked downstairs and again Winnie scented the air.

"You going to do something about this one?" I asked her and she flopped back against the bed. My gun was still in my hand, but I was pretty sure I wasn't going to need it.

Mo poked her head around the corner and Cruz came in behind her.

"Great. Just great. I go to bed and you decide to throw a party in my house. I drank decaf, people. DECAF so that I could sleep. If none of you is dying, get the hell out."

"Cyn," Mo was staring at the gun in my hand and I sighed, locking it back into its under-bed holster. There were very few people I would put my weapon away for, and unfortunately one of them was Mo. "Thanks. I need your help."

"With what?" I flopped back against my pillow and pulled the blankets up to my chin.

"Ummm…" she looked at Larry and Ian, turning red, and then looked back at me. "Man help."

She whispered the last and the two men in the room choked; Larry with discomfort and Ian… was laughing.

"You brought Cruz. Do you need help with him?"

She looked at him, eyes traveling up and down his jeans and T-Shirt. I looked at Larry in his and decided that neither of them looked appealing. A first for both of them and I suddenly wondered if I'd broken my lady town with unfulfilled want and frustration at their stupidity.

Damn them both.

"No," she said, looking away with a sigh. "Do you need me to help you with him?"

"Like… take one for the team?"

Mo turned burgundy, Cruz gave me a look, and Larry busted up laughing.

"No. I… seriously? You'd consider it a favor to *do* him?"

I shrugged and closed my eyes.

"I don't want him." I lied and Ian made a sound. Larry dropped something in the kitchen.

"I don't want him either. Take them both, have a nice little reverse harem. Keep your blinds closed though. Apparently the town is full of snoops and spies."

"Cyn," Larry warned, and I turned to him. "Mo isn't my type. She's far too nice. I prefer women who threaten bodily harm against me... and put their body against me."

"I can do that and she can do the rest. She and Chris..."

"Cyn, that's why I'm here, Chris... is in some of those images. He... was trying to provide CPR to Amber when she nearly drowned and it was photographed to look like he was making out with her," I opened my eyes to watch Mo knot her fingers and shift awkwardly.

"Do you believe him about the content of the pictures?" I studied her face. She wasn't upset or hurt, so the problem wasn't that she thought he wanted Amber.

"No. Amber sent him the pictures as blackmail to get some information or stop him sharing information. The message was vague and weird. I don't know if... well, she might not have noticed, but I'm in them. I'm in them and Chris and I are both..." Mo held up her hand so Ian and Larry couldn't see her mouth the word *naked*.

"Outside?" I asked, tilting my head as Larry brought me a hot mug of chocolate, and Mo nodded.

"By the creek? We... he wanted to go camping but I needed to make this really elaborate cake so I told him we could do a day trip. We were at the creek... practice camping on a blanket, and we heard the sound of someone flailing. He hopped up and ran to the water. It was Amber, and he saved her. But now a month later..."

I rubbed my temples and pulled up the photos app on my phone. I scrolled through the pictures I'd taken working with Ian at the station, studying all of the images for content and style. There were no photos outside in daylight or by a creek. These were all interior shots, staged and clean aside from those taken by Yvette and Carla.

"Aside from the fact you were naked outside in February, when it had been snowing and for some reason she was swimming, was there anything weird in them? Was she looking at the camera in the picture?"

"It was in the sixties that day, and her eyes were closed," Mo shrugged, and I got out of bed, taking the cocoa with me. Sixties was a reasonable temperature to be naked outside, but no way for swimming.

"Guess I won't be going to bed," I grumbled, and Winnie followed me to the closet where I sought out some sort of underwear covering. The mug Larry had picked for me had a Hershey's kiss on the mug and declared the reader could "Kiss my Sass".

"Where are you going, chica?" Cruz spoke from the door. A warm arm wrapped around me and I looked down at Larry's hand.

"Remove it," I growled and he held me tighter.

"Cyn, please," his voice was pleading and I turned to study the pain on his face. "Your underwear are showing."

"They are my underwear, Larry. If you try to cover me again, I'm going to remove your hands by force."

"I want to be the only one who sees your underwear."

"You chose, Larry."

"I chose you, Cyn. Every time, I chose you. I just couldn't let Carla get arrested for something she didn't do. You're the best and... and I love you," he whispered and my stomach did a flip.

"Aww..." Mo cooed from behind him and I glanced at her standing next to a carefully blank Ian Cruz. He was perfectly still, his thumbs hooked into the front pockets of his pants. He looked neither concerned nor disinterested. "Cyn!"

I shook my head at her and then looked back at Larry.

"I need time," I said, grabbing sweats and pulling them up. This was not a jeans or slacks mission. This was an *interrogate Amber, offend her with my appearance, and get away from Larry* mission.

"Need time to decide if you love me?" his eyes were haunting and I shrugged. It can't hurt more to not be informed the feeling was mutual than it did to watch the man you love agree to leave your life to help another woman. A woman you'd seen him naked with... kissing...

"Time to decide if it matters that I did."

"Did? You... don't anymore?"

I shrugged and pulled on my shoes.

"I don't currently have time to figure that out. Whoever leaves last, lock the door? Let's go Winnie."

Amber was possibly the only nearly thirty year-old who thought living with her parents was cool.

The house was a brick and iron mansion modeled after a Brooklyn brownstone with Midwest charm. Unfortunately,

Midwest charm and Brooklyn are not friends. The whole thing looked tacky and visually offensive.

Since that defined the people who lived inside of it, it was arguably truth in advertising at its finest.

The speaker box at the front was static-y, but the gates were propped open and dozens of cars were parked in the circular driveway. The bright yellow jeep with the death emoji on the hood stood out like Big Bird next to the cast of Finding Nemo. Every other car was sleek, shiny, black, and more expensive than my parent's house.

Normally, I tried to be more discreet, but since this was Amber's house, I parked dead center in front of a giant ice sculpture.

The Jeep door tapped it as it opened and I smiled.

"Winnie, take a break," I said, pointing at the base of the ice Carter Family. Winnie sniffed, lifted her back leg, and peed on Amber's frozen foot. It was childish, petty, and exactly what I needed so I tossed her a treat. Behind me a man sniffed and I turned into Senator Tim's butler.

Behind him, Tim Thomas was wearing a tuxedo on the arm of Mr. Rockwaller.

"Cynthia, you were invited?" the senator asked and I shrugged.

"I'm not usually invited but people are never surprised when I show up."

All three men nodded and I tried not to feel a little annoyed; not that they believed I just appeared in places, but that they looked fabulous, happy, and immaculate. A leaf fell from a tree and landed in my hair, but Mother Nature dared not mar *their* flawless perfection.

"I need to go find Amber," I sighed and started to move away when Mr. Rockwaller called me back.

"Cynthia?"

I turned and he handed me a piece of paper.

"This is from your brother."

It was a sheet of lined notebook paper, nothing odd or unusual about it. The men moved along and I just stared at it.

"Ew! Who let you in?" Amber said from behind me, and Winnie growled.

"Amber, look, they made a realistic statue of you. Ice cold and completely disposable." I smirked and then shook my head. "But I need to see the thing you used to take that image of Chris."

For the first time in her life, Amber looked uncomfortable.

"Who told you about that?" Her stage whisper carried the scent of alcohol, and I took a step back.

"Woah," I fanned my face. "What are you drinking and when did you start?"

"I started three days ago when that stupid picture showed up with those stupid instructions." Again I felt light-headed sharing her air space. "I don't get it, that picture was from a month ago. Why the hell did this *just* happen?"

"Run that by me again?"

"Ugh, you're so annoying. That day at the beach, I was trying to get Stephen to make out with me. So I was showing off and then I got too much water and that fire guy showed up, naked. I'm glad he was there or whatever, but when Stephen came to check on me, I was so over the idea of just making out and I took him to my car. Then his house. Then... well, you wouldn't get it. I completely forgot about that day. Found the bag I'd taken to the creek in my car and brought it inside a few days ago, then two days later I get those pictures and instructions to send them to the firefighter with a warning or like... a threat or whatever."

I rubbed my temples.

"What was the warning?" I asked, and she pointed at the x-eyed character on the car.

"It was basically that, but I didn't want to send mail because ew. So I texted it to him and there wasn't one of those emojis, so I just recreated the idea of it," she jutted out a hip and propped her hand on it, a half dozen bracelets clanking together on her arm.

"Did the pictures come to you in the mail?"

"I don't know, maybe? I don't check the mail," she plucked imaginary lint from her tiny camisole top and I considered letting Winnie pee on her. She was given pictures, a warning for Chris and...

"Can I see the bag you took to the creek? Did you unpack it?"

"What? Why? No," she crossed her arms and then uncrossed them before stomping her foot. "Whatever. But you have to go in the back door and *that* has to stay outside."

"If *that* is your attitude, I agree," I clipped Winnies leash on and marched to the front door, flinging it open. Amber struggled to catch up on toothpick heels and I marveled that the woman could stomp her foot in them but fast walking was a problem.

On the other side was a scene from an animated show where pompous people worked to look important. While it was clear all of them had money, it was equally clear that none of them had taste. A sharkskin three-piece suit stood beside a woman in a gown adorned with peacock feathers. A crystal glass was in everyone's hand yet not a single person was drinking.

"It's like an episode of WandaVision in here," I said to Winnie and she let out a small whimper of agreement. No one looked at me, Winnie, or Amber after she made it inside. "Are they alive?"

Amber rolled her eyes and then paused.

"I think so," she walked over to a suited man and said hello. He shook her hand, smiled with a wide-eyed madness, and then went back to staring at the wall... or the woman beside him... "That one might be a robot."

I choked on my laugh as I realized it was the first time Amber had ever made a joke.

"Lead the way," I gestured and she nodded. I anticipated going upstairs, but she walked past them to a small section of the house. It was quiet, peaceful. A single door with a peephole sat in an opposing wall, and she pulled out keys to let herself in.

Cautiously, Winnie and I followed her through the door.

We're probably going to be murdered now, I thought, and the feel of Winnie leaning against my leg said she agreed. Definitely do not go into a random locked room of a house with a stranger. We paused in the doorway; Winnie scented the air and then flattened her ears.

The room smelled like Bath and Body Works had a baby with a flower shop and took only their worst personality traits.

"Oh god, what's that smell?"

Amber turned to look at me and I saw we were in a small one-bedroom apartment. To my left was a small kitchen, to the right a love seat with a television and on the opposite wall another sturdy door. This one appeared to lead to the outside. To the right a bedroom door sat off of the living room.

I was not surprised the place was devoid of books.

I was not surprised that the place smelled.

I was surprised that it felt comfortable.

"The bag is in my room. Don't get comfortable," she sneered, and I decided Winnie should pee on her couch. She stalked off toward the door and she swung it open, revealing a four-poster princess bed, teenage girl colors and clothes strewn everywhere. She disappeared from view for a second and just as I was about to give Winnie the command to pee, the woman reappeared carrying a canvas beach tote with a contrasting bottom and a scarf tied around the handle.

"Everything is still in there," Amber shrugged, apparently it was not important to replace her belongings where they belonged. "You can just take it."

Ignoring her, I carefully set it on the table and opened the magnetic snap at the top. Inside was sunscreen, a towel, wedge shoes, four pairs of sunglasses, lipstick, three trashy magazines, and a bug.

"Ew!" she said, watching me pick up what looked like a shimmering beetle. The bug had been the only thing in the front pocket of Amber's tote and I set it aside to look at the bag. There was a small tear in the liner and another in the outer layer. "What is it?"

"Fly fishing lure," I answered without looking at her. The lure was small, but I was fairly certain I could see the tiny lens of a camera... that or my eyes were playing tricks on me.

"Why is it in my bag?"

"When did you get this bag?" I asked instead, and she bit her lower lip. The furrow between her eyes looked as though I had asked her to find the antiderivative of a cylinder. "Don't hurt yourself. An estimate is fine."

Amber huffed out a breath.

"Ugh! I don't remember buying it. I'm not even sure I did. It could have been a gift," she threw her hands in the air and I nodded.

"Who knew you planned on going to the creek that day?"

"No one. I didn't even know I was going until Callie called and said Stephen was there."

I rubbed my temples. How was this woman a year older than me and somehow still living like a high school senior who hadn't discovered what comes next? The chances were pretty decent the bag was sent to her for a specific reason and it captured something else instead.

But why the delay?

I studied the fly in my hand and looked at my Garmin watch. The data from the Garmin didn't sync unless I opened the app. Maybe the fly needed to be connected to something. An app or... Wi-Fi?

"Can I take this?" I asked for the bag and the bug and she waved her hands.

"I already said you could. Geez, listen much? I always knew you wanted my cast offs."

I rolled my eyes but caught the edge of a paper poking out on her counter. Shifting the unopened credit card statements and the lease documents for her store, I found an envelope with her name just written across the front. It had been torn open and was sitting on top of the pictures of Amber and Mo. Beneath that was the warning, typed and printed on generic paper in a generic font.

The symbol from the hood of my car was crudely drawn on the bottom and the message in between was vague at best, and childish.

FIREFIGHTERS MUST BE WARNED WHEN THEY PLAY IN THE WOODS,

TO BE MORE CAREFUL ABOUT WHO SEES THEIR WOOD.

STAND BACK IN THE TREES AND AVOID THE WOMAN, EVEN IF SHE SAYS PLEASE.

"What woman? Mo?" I asked no one in particular but when I looked around, Amber was gone. "Seriously? She just left?"

Winnie wiggled her brows at me and I shook my head. I put the pictures, envelope, and letter in the canvas bag and went toward the door, pulling my phone out of my pocket and accidentally sending Seth's letter to the floor.

With a sigh, I unfolded the paper. If there were any pictures in there, I was going to murder him. Between him and Carla, Heidi introducing my parents to bondage, and his mother-in-law having an interest in my sex life, I needed an adult emancipation. I scanned the paper and stopped at the X-eyed emoticon drawn at the bottom.

Be careful. We still don't know who's sending these messages.

Find the killer so I can go home.

Chapter Sixteen:
Primed to Parley

"What the hell, lady?" I shouted as a brunette ran up to my window.

"Please, help me!" She looked like an extra in a slasher movie, covered in mud and something that may have been blood. I was on a two-lane stretch of road between Yellow Springs and Sweet Pea, and aside from a few cows, there wasn't much out here.

"What's wrong?" I asked, scanning the area for hooks, hockey masks, and clowns.

"It's my son. He's stuck and I tried calling emergency but they said it's not an emergency and I'll have to wait. But it is an emergency! I mean not a fire emergency, but he's stuck!"

"What is he stuck in?" I asked, knowing that a well would be an emergency but stuck with a piercing behind a woman's tonsils would not be.

Also neither was something I would help with.

"His arm, it's stuck in the horse and he can't get it out," she pleaded and I shook my head at her.

"Why did he put his hand in a horse?"

"He said he was checking on the foal. We have a pregnant mare and..."

I let out a sigh.

"Lead the way," she climbed into the passenger side of the car and pointed to a T-intersection.

"We live right over there. My son, he's a bit impatient. We told him when the mare had the calf he could raise the horse to be his. He was trying to get the horse out now so they can start being friends."

As a child who'd grown up without many friends of my own, I could relate to the boy's plight. I followed a bumpy washed out road to a barn and turned left as instructed. The woman climbed out and took off to the barn. Winnie lifted her head, scented the air and tilted it with a low woof of questioning.

"This will hopefully only take a minute," I said, and climbed from the Jeep. Winnie hopped out beside me and we rounded the door to the barn. The brunette was cradling a man against her chest beside the horse and I paused.

"Please!" She called out and I moved closer, wondering if the little boy was just hidden from view. I got to the other side of the couple and... no. The man was the one who had his hand up a horse's backside.

It was also not a pregnant horse.

Or a mare.

"What in the actual fluff?" I asked and the woman wailed, clutching the man's head to her breasts. "Lady, that man is in his twenties, that horse isn't pregnant, and it's also not female!"

She looked at me and I noticed more fine lines than I had in the dark. The woman was realistically old enough to have birthed this man if she had him young. I studied the man with his hand up a horse's ass and tried not to gag on the visual. Sure, my hand had been up inside livestock, but based on what I was looking at, the man was either confused or sexually adventurous in an inappropriate way.

Not from the horse, though. He was now trying to motorboat his own mother and I gagged.

"I'm not trying to birth a calf from a male horse," he said, making eye contact with me over her shoulder.

"Because that's not how biology works?" I asked and he winced as she pulled him against her again.

"Yeah, but also we have a mare going into heat and we needed a specimen to inseminate her. This guy isn't quite in the best shape to make that work, so I was collecting a sample to fertilize the mare."

"Are you a veterinarian or trained in animal husbandry?" I asked, and he blanched.

"No, I work construction."

"So... you stuck your hand up a horse's ass and thought he'd ejaculate into your cookie jar?" I crossed my arms while Winnie got closer and sniffed the man, his mother, the stallion and the jar.

"Well, I watched a YouTube video," he shot back.

"And how's that working out for you?"

"Aren't you here to help me?" The brunette had moved away and was eyeing her son.

"Are you serious, Anthony?" Now her arms were crossed and I got a bad feeling I didn't want to hear the rest of this conversation.

"What? The internet is informative and I..."

"You know what? This is the goat and the donkey all over again!" She threw her hands in the air, and Anthony looked daggers at me.

"I don't know why you're mad at me. Donkey's don't even have the ability to produce offspring."

"Because my mom didn't know this wasn't a mare until you showed up!" He huffed and I looked under the horse at his exposed genitalia.

"That seems unlikely." The mom blushed and I nearly just walked away to leave him to wait for medical, but it seemed rude to the horse. Cautiously, I walked over and stroked the stallion's nose, his mane, and took the bridle. Slowly, I started walking him away from Anthony. "Relax your arm."

For his part, the man appeared to listen. The horse started to relax, releasing the pressure inside of him until he'd walked off of

Anthony's arm and was trotting away. Winnie sniffed the now exposed arm, gave me a look and...

"Don't you dare!" I warned her, just as she licked the man's arm.

"Don't breathe on me!" I warned Winnie as we drove back to our home. "How many times do we have to go over not putting your mouth in or on things associated with people's butts, sex organs, or mouths?"

The windows were down and she was getting the toothbrushing of a lifetime when she got home.

"Did you hear his mom? He does this a lot, Winnie! Do you know how unclean that arm probably was *before* it went into the horse?"

She wiggled her brows and brought her head back into the Jeep.

"Oh no, you keep that head outside!"

We pulled into a spot behind the building, and I clipped her leash on before she could jump out of the car and contaminate anything. I was halfway up the staircase when I realized the light was on and someone was inside my house. Silently, I unclipped Winnies leash and gestured for her to scent the air. The dog's ears were up, tail out straight behind her, paw lifted.

One sniff, two... I held my breath. A low growl came from her throat and a head popped around the corner, followed by raised hands.

"Calm the beast, it's just me," Daniel said and I reattached Winnie's leash. He wasn't welcome but he wasn't dangerous.

At the top of the stairs, I saw that Cruz and Larry had also elected to stay inside my house. It was a buffet for the eyes, but the rest of me wished they would leave. So naturally, they were all sitting on my sparse furniture and looked ready to torture me for the long haul.

Stupid eye candy.

I grabbed Winnie's care kit, some rubber gloves, and sat on the floor.

"What did she put in her mouth, chica?" Cruz asked and I rolled my eyes.

"A horse's ass."

Cruz laughed, Daniel went pale, and Larry looked concerned.

"Is the horse OK? Does it need medical attention?"

"Chill, Dr. Doolittle. The horse had a man's hand up his ass, Winnie licked said man's hand. He needs a new owner, but aside from that he's good."

I was pretty sure. Though of all the animals his mother had mentioned his hands inside of, I was personally most concerned about the goat.

Probably Larry shouldn't know there was a man out there DIY-ing his own sperm collection.

"Why the hell are all of you in my house?" I asked, brushing the complete length of Winnie's tongue while she thumped her tail on the floor.

"A buddy of mine called. The search warrant for Yvette's apartment came back and there are some alarming things in there," Daniel swallowed and I glanced at Cruz who rolled his eyes. It was apparently not that serious.

"She has letters, telling her to butt out and return what isn't hers. The X-eyes character is at the bottom of all of them. They aren't dated but there's a progression in intensity. The last one said for her to keep her head down or they would knock it off her neck."

Larry looked concerned but I shrugged.

"So you think that if I ignore the sad emoji I'll get bludgeoned to death?"

I was still wondering how a person gets bludgeoned to death and no blood ends up outside the building. Droplets down the hall, then nothing until the parking lot. Where there was...

"Did you ever find out about that animal blood?" I asked Cruz but Larry stepped between us.

"Damn-it! This is serious, why didn't you call Daniel like I told you to?" I held up Winnie's toothbrush in warning.

"Don't start with me, Larry. You said you wouldn't come back. I don't have to do anything you tell me to for as long as you don't do what I tell you to. Maybe even after because who the hell are you to tell me what to do?"

"Someone who loves you, you idiot!" he countered, and I was saved from a response by my phone ringing. No need to examine the flip in my stomach, the flash in Cruz's eyes, or the look of horror on Daniel's face.

Actually, Daniel's look of horror was absolutely epic, so I studied it until it faded.

"Hello?"

Cruz was back to stoic and blank. Larry looked to be in literal pain.

"Your paint is in, bring the Jeep tomorrow," Marvin gruffed into the phone and hung up.

"Great," I muttered, letting Winnie go after one last swipe of the inside of her mouth. I tossed my phone toward the empty couch and watched it bounce off the side to the floor.

"You should treat your belongings better, Cyn. My kids don't even throw things," Daniel scolded and my eyes flashed fury. "I'm just saying, you probably can't afford to buy a new phone if you break yours."

"Can your wife afford a new you if I break you?" I growled.

"Cyn, don't threaten my brother."

I turned my fury to Larry, who promptly raised his hands in surrender.

"I'm just saying, you shouldn't threaten him... in front of witnesses. Also, it annoys me when you threaten other men, I want to be special and think you only want to harm my body."

"Do any of you have anything *useful* to tell me that isn't 'You should have' or 'Why haven't you'?"

"The animal blood was cow and cooked," Daniel answered and I scowled at him. He wasn't supposed to be useful. He was supposed to be my next murder victim, but now he has the audacity to be helpful after years of being wall art. Not even good wall art, children's drawn pictures on your fridge wall art. A tangle of lines and colors that was the beginnings of a Rorschach inkblot test.

"Why are you looking at me like that?" His bewildered expression was more on par with his norm.

"How do you know that?"

"I'm a cop, Cyn."

"Barely," I grumbled and let go of the animal blood as a clue. It was a dead end if it was cooked. Lots of cuisine uses blood in food prep.

"I'm more of a cop than you are!"

"You wanna go, Kirby?"

Cruz took a step in between us.

"You look mildly terrifying right now, Cyn. Maybe you should take a breath, relax... I'll give you a massage," Cruz gave me a wicked grin and Larry went pale. At a loss, I looked between the two men and tried to work up enthusiasm for a cardio endorphin release. Sexy Cruz in his jeans and shirt, hot Larry in his jeans and glasses with a dimple in one cheek, my eyes scanned them both and I couldn't work up any sort of enthusiasm for sex, investigation, and conversation.

I just wanted cookies and a hug.

"Maybe another time," I said instead and got off the floor.

"What the hell?" Larry got to his feet and I rolled my eyes. It wasn't worth addressing that I was hoping to get my hug from him, as I now intended to punch him the next time he was within arm's reach. I put Winnie's care kit away and started opening cabinets in search of something with chocolate, empty calories, and no nutritional value. I opened the cabinet, closed it, and opened it again. I had coffee, I had cheese crackers, and I had food that needed cooking... no cookies.

"Where are my cookies?" I asked Winnie who had come to sit beside me. I heard movement from the men but elected to ignore them. I opened the lower cabinets, back to the upper cabinets, and then checked the fridge. "I know I have cookies. I always have cookies. They are on auto-ship!"

A warm hand wrapped over mine and I turned to see Larry as he covered my other hand at the same time.

"If you don't let go of my hands so I can get cookies, I'm kicking you in the nuts," I warned, and he rubbed his jaw against the curve of my neck. I let out an involuntary sigh.

"I owe you a cookie. Do you want a cookie or the other thing I promised?" He whispered and I leaned into him. "Remember the other thing I promised you if you were a good girl and talked to me? If you agreed to be only mine?"

His hands slid down my wrists and the skin tingled where he touched.

"Do you want me to remind you?" His lips brushed my ear and a loud crash came from just outside the door.

We both jumped and I elbowed him in the gut. Winnie let out a bark and then farted.

"What was that?" I asked, Larry doubled over with his arms around his diaphragm. Cruz and Daniel were gone.

Curious, I walked around and peered through the peephole.

No one was outside.

I pulled it open to check the staircase, but it was also empty. The metal fire door slammed shut at the bottom of the stairs and when I crept down, peering into the alley, no one was there. Winnie scented the air, tilting her head from side to side. A low growl came out and I wondered if we should follow.

"Cyn!"

Larry called from the top of the stairs and I started back up. There weren't many, but Winnie stopped to nose a small patch of rug. I probed it, but nothing came up.

Gunpowder residue?

Food crumbs?

I wasn't exactly neat and tidy, so it could be anything.

"Cyn!"

I shook off the thought and we finished going up. At the top, I stared at a hole in my wall, punctuated with a wooden spike.

I'M RAISING THE STAKES. BACK OFF.

Beneath it was the same X-eye emoji and a hand gesture that was either lascivious or threatening.

Chapter Seventeen: Photogenic Phonies

I woke up warm and relaxed. My eyes scanned the arm draped around my waist and the furry tail on my face. Larry had been pretty freaked out, I was annoyed that I had to fix a damn wall, but I'd let him stay when he offered as long as he didn't expect an answer about the dating/exclusivity/love thing. While the threat hadn't been especially bothersome, I was starting to feel like I was chasing my tail.

Winnie would be pissed.

She thought people or dogs chasing their tails were an insult to her people. So I tried, again, to piece together what I knew. First, a woman was definitely dead. Second, there was a crap ton of compromising images in her office that the killer either didn't know about, didn't find, or hadn't bothered to look for. If the threats meant anything, maybe the killer was trying to get them back, but how did they miss something on the killing floor? Third, the dead woman was being threatened and was also blackmailing people. Fourth, her boss was some sort of undercover government person that was gathering intel to leave and... I shuddered. She wanted to be with my brother. Her husband was dating a senator, the senator's house had a spy Bible in it, and I still hadn't been able to get in touch with the town council member who'd been in the house before me.

A glance at my phone said it was Saturday. Government buildings would not be open on a Saturday, so there was no hope of finding him today. The man had hooked up with Carla, and possibly also her husband. Someone else had mentioned him... he was related to someone else in this situation, but try as I might I couldn't conjure a source.

"Hey," Larry said, pulling me against him and I let out a sigh as we nested together.

"You know I have a rule about keeping food in the kitchen," I joked as his morning excitement poked me in the back. "You're not permitted to bring sausage into my bed."

"Haha," he said, adjusting so we could lay closer together. "How are you feeling?"

"Fine. Annoyed. Do you know how to patch a wall?"

I felt him shake his head behind me.

"I wish you were more concerned," he whispered and a shiver of tension coursed through me. "Every time you leave my sight I worry that you aren't going to do the bare minimum to keep you and Winnie safe."

"I'm a walking disaster. You should be more concerned about the people near me. Also, I always keep Winnie safe."

"Someone's threatening you and you're joking," his voice held fear that transferred to my heart. Larry was worried about me... Why wasn't I more worried about me?

Short answer, fear wasn't as effective an investigative tool as compartmentalizing.

Also inappropriate humor was as essential as coffee in my life. If you can't joke about your inevitable death, what can you joke about?

My brain kept processing the crime, the pictures, and the stakes. Bludgeoned to death was not the way to go. They found a tranquilizer in her system. Yvette had been drugged so she couldn't fight back. They suggested it was Trazodone, further implicating Larry, but when the animal blood turned out to be cooked, other leads had been pursued.

"I wish I knew why the killer left all of the pictures," I sighed and he tightened his grip on me. Shaking him off, I stood and stretched while Winnie did the same. She followed that with her potty dance; feed me face, and a low bark. "I need to take the Jeep to Marvin for a recoloring. What are you up to today?"

"Learning how to patch a wall from YouTube videos," he sighed and I gave him a smile.

"You'd do that for me?"

"I'd do anything for you. Except maybe go to one of your mom's key parties," he shuddered and I joined him in the sentiment.

"Definitely something to avoid. Those senior swingers are no joke."

"How long do you think it will take?" I asked Marvin as he took my keys and I signed the paper.

"However long it takes," the man was growing more unfriendly by the day. I checked the ground for lava, the backside of his pants for a bear trap, and his foot area for the same.

He appeared un-injured and not actively in pain.

"What crawled up your butt?" I asked and he bared his teeth in my direction.

"This damn murder business."

"Why? You aren't in any of the pictures," I said and he shook his head in frustration.

"No, but her damn car is here. I won't get payment for the repairs, no one will claim it, and it's embarrassing to have in my lot," he spit gum into the trash, unwrapped a new piece and stuffed it into his mouth. "Who drives a damn pea green Mini Cooper with red racing stripes. The thing is an abomination. Between that and your Hello Kitty Jeep, I'm going to demand feminism stay out of the automotive industry!"

"Can I see it?"

"You can do whatever you want as long as you get out of my face."

Behind me was a line of customers. None of them looked especially impatient or dangerous. My eyes tracked back to the man. He was spitting out another gum and replacing it. I noticed the yellow stains on the counter and the staining on his fingers.

"You quit smoking and it's making you cranky?" I asked and he narrowed his eyes. "What? If you're going to be rude and bristly, maybe you should rethink whether or not there's value in living longer without nicotine."

"Every second you stand here is another week I will keep your car, Cynthia."

I raised my hands in surrender and walked away. Winnie and I rounded to the vehicle storage area and my eyes immediately locked on to the abomination in question. It had been there when the Jeep went from pink to yellow, but I'd thought it was there for the same reason mine was: someone had wanted a cheap car and needed it repainted to something not hideous. The car gleamed in the light, a subtle glitter coat underneath that made the car two-tone. I gripped the silver handle and the car opened.

Probably not a good sign that the car was unlocked, and I made a mental note to take the cookies out of my car before I gave the keys to Marvin. The man was not getting my snacks stolen with his crappy car-locking habits.

The Mini's interior was a light grey. Calming and clean, there were no food wrappers and the whole thing smelled like jasmine. I glanced into the backseat, there were no food remnants, melted crayons, or nose art on the windows. Her center console held a cell phone mount, the cup holders devoid of coffee rings, fur, or anything...

"Did she even drive this?" I asked, studying the driver's side floor mat for signs of wear.

"Did who what, chica?" Cruz said and I looked over my shoulder to see him standing right behind my backside. Interesting image...

"This is Yvette's car," I sighed, climbing out and popping the hatchback. The back of her car was as empty and spotless as the rest of it. I lifted the little tab to the storage compartment and found the spare. "It looks sterile and blank. Makes me wish she were alive to see if her personality reflects her car or her writings."

I walked to the passenger side and popped open the glove box. Owner's manuals, tire pressure gauge, registration, and insurance. Her gearshift didn't have ponytail holders wrapped around it; the space between the seats and plastic didn't have a single crumb.

"The woman hid in bushes to take compromising photos of people. She had to have staked the places out. There is no evidence of snacks, dirt from hiding in planters, beverages to keep her awake. What kind of person has a car like this?" I flipped down her visor and a piece of paper fell out. I flipped it over and saw a job offer from another newspaper in Chicago. It was a gossip rag, her speed; the letter was flimsy from being read and re-read, but there were no notes or indications of her intentions with the paper or the offer.

My hand was halfway to putting it back in the visor when I changed my mind and stuffed it in my pocket.

"What are you doing here?" I asked Cruz when nothing was under the driver's side visor and I climbed out, locking the door before shutting it.

Even dead people deserved to have their belongings secured.

"I was wondering if you wanted to meet Andrew Scott," he said, face showing curiosity mixed with concern. "Why did you lock the car, there's nothing in there?"

"You found him?" I ignored the second part. If he had human decency he wouldn't have to ask.

"Yeah, he's in a five-star hotel outside Dayton. There are eyes on him," he continued to study my face. "He's been running up a tab for over a week under the assumed name of Seth Sharp."

"Peachy," I said, and then paused. "How do you know it's not actually my brother?"

Cruz pulled his phone out of his pocket and showed me an image of a white male, receiving oral pleasure in an elevator from a woman who appeared to be a pro.

"Not my brother," I said and was relieved. He didn't have the money for a five-star hotel, a pro, or any interest in either.

Also if I had just been shown a picture of my brother receiving oral in an elevator I would have been forced to murder Ian Cruz and throw his phone into a fire pit. Sensing my urge to wreak havoc he smiled wide, wrapped his arms around me and pulled me against him for a kiss.

"I agree with what Larry said last night. There's something about a woman who wants to kick you in the nuts that's pretty damn hot," he said into my hair and I rolled my eyes, stepping back to look him over.

His eyes were bright and alert, his clothes spotless, and his hair in the perfect military cut and style.

"Do you ever look like a human? Like... tired, unkempt and messy? Or are you just some sort of Stepford Soldier?"

He shrugged and gestured toward his car. I bit my lower lip, I wanted answers from Andrew, but I also wanted to get back in bed with Winnie and Larry.

With that thought...

"Let's go get Winnie," I said, leading the way to his black Ford sedan.

The ride to Dayton was quiet. Cruz drove in a zone that nothing else permeated. He didn't believe in the radio, rolling down the windows or small talk. When we arrived at the hotel, it was with relief that I discovered they were playing Christmas music... in March. I sang along happily to the sounds of busy sidewalks.

Anything was better than silence.

I started toward the front desk, but Ian grabbed my hand and tugged me toward a bank of elevators. The hotel's name wasn't on the front, but the rich floral patterned furniture mixed with leather was clearly geared toward old and stuffy. A fireplace simmered, filling the room with the woodsy smell of fire mingling with cinnamon and potpourri. Every wall was graced with a single, wooden-framed image of either a nautical scene or a stuffy looking white guy.

Two sets of elevators sat opposite each other and the middle on the left was the first to arrive. We got in. Cruz checked his phone and selected the fifth floor. As the metallic doors slid closed, he looked at me and I raised a brow.

"Problem, Sgt. Soldier Statue?"

"Just remembering what was happening in this elevator in that picture," he gave a wicked grin and I returned it with one of my own.

"You are more than welcome to get on your knees for me. The reverse is never gonna happen," I said and Winnie grumbled her agreement. His smile widened and he looped a hand around my waist to pull me against him.

"I'll need more than an elevator ride. Maybe on the way back down we'll take the stairs," he whispered as the door dinged our arrival at the fifth floor. My face was heated and a glance at my reflection showed more than a bit of alarm... and lust. "You want me."

I started to nod and then changed my mind.

"I want chocolate, cheese, a puppy, and at least a dozen other things before you," I declared and stepped out of the elevator before he caught me again in the hall and grazed his lips against my neck. "But yeah, sure, I guess you're on the list *somewhere*."

"Liar."

Heat flooded everywhere and I tried to fight back a whimper. He was climbing my list and fast. The only two things he hadn't overtaken were coffee and a puppy.

"Stairs are over there," he dragged his teeth down the column of my neck and I reached behind me for...

"Fu-!" He let go and doubled over. Winnie's head was where his manhood had just been. Not for the first time, I had to respect the dog's aim. Not having ever been a man, I had to wonder if it was a scent or intuition that drove her to the man's goods.

"Good girl," I tossed her a treat from my pocket and wrapped my arms around her neck. "Very good girl."

"Hey, I thought we were cool," Ian narrowed his eyes at her as he clutched himself and she walked over to lick his face before standing between us. A wiggle of eyebrows and a firm shake of her head said I was off limits to him and I sighed with relief.

I wasn't really ready to implode a future with Larry but I needed a little help saying no.

Because ninety percent of me did not want to say no.

"Winnie has spoken, lover boy. Get off your ass and let's go." I turned to go down the hall and stopped at the sight of the man impersonating my brother in the hall, hand resting on the doorknob. He had plain brown hair, plain brown eyes, and wore clothing that would look perfectly normal just about anywhere in the world. "Mr. Scott?"

He nodded, looking at the man on the floor and reflexively cupping himself.

"Your hand won't help you against her teeth," I smirked and his eyes widened. "For now though, she's good if you'll speak with us. If you run, you'll be speaking to us with a bruise in the shape of her jaw."

He nodded and reopened the door to his room. I hauled Cruz off the floor and we followed the man into a suite with a sitting area and large television. His blondish hair was more noticeable than it had been in the dimly lit photo, his face a bit older, and his midsection a bit fuller. All the room's curtains were drawn while every lamp illuminated the space. I walked to the picture window and tugged back a curtain… Cityscape and miles of farmland as far as the eye could see.

I heard Cruz and the man exchanging pleasantries, or personal identifying information.

It was hard to say because my eyes had caught on a treasure trove of spyware. There were fly-fishing lures, jewelry boxes, statues, and books, all laid out on a table. Beside them, Andrew had a laptop that was receiving feeds from the devices present, as I watched myself walk closer in the open split-screen window.

It was like receiving the Bond briefcase. All I needed was magnetic hooks and a laser beam lipstick. I started humming the Mission Impossible theme, not remembering any of the Bond anthems at the moment. There was no gun on the underside of the desk, I pulled open drawers to see blank plastic cards, but no stacks of cash or deboning knives.

"Where's all your money for secret, untraceable purchases?" I asked, reaching for one of the spy devices.

"Don't touch that!"

His voice was mildly shrill, but I continued to pick up the gold leaf edged copy of Alice in Wonderland. Flipping to the back, I took note of the small square cut into it, the popper style explosive, and the lens in the O of Wonderland. It was identical to the bible, and I set it back down on its edge carefully to not accidentally smolder another book.

Cruz muttered something, and I studied the fishing lure, this time wondering if it would also burn.

"Are all of these rigged?" I asked, picking up a small statue of Saint Anthony.

"No, just the books," Andrew sighed. A quick glance showed relief on his face. He'd been concerned about me dropping the copy of Alice... as if he didn't know that I was aware of the explosives.

"Why not the others?"

"People knock over statues and toss items that look like bugs in the trash. The device inside has a very limited battery life. It's really only good for single use," he shrugged and I ran a finger over the book's cover.

"Why are the books different?" I asked and watched him tense when my finger traced the spine.

"People keep books around for years. They hardly ever move or pay attention to them. When I was working abroad, I got insider intel using book cams. The explosives came later, when there was more to lose if I were found out. The smaller things, they can be remotely activated, but once the information is recorded, it can only activate when connected to a server."

Winnie sniffed at the table and alerted on the book. I moved that and had her search the surrounding area. She alerted on a box of rounds, two spots of carpet, and the man himself. When I studied the spots of carpet, I couldn't see or detect anything.

"I spilled gunpowder there," he said and gestured to the second spot. "Also there. Is that an explosives detection K-9?"

Without looking toward him, I nodded and had Winnie search the rest of the room. We found two more boxes of ammo, the box of lenses and batteries that had been stored near it, and a much larger box of arbitrary household items. Some had been prepped for camera installation; most looked unsuited to the purpose and were likely discarded.

None of them looked like something a person could wear as Carla had, and none looked set up for movement or multi-angle.

"How did you get the Bible in the senator's house?" I asked, giving Winnie a treat and letting her sprawl out on the hotel's couch.

"The Bible was in the senator's house?"

"Come on, I've already blown it up. What were you looking for?"

"I didn't put the Bible in the senator's house. I don't put any of these things anywhere. It's all about supply and demand. My surveillance supplies are legendary. I sell them to people, no questions asked, and then they do with them what they will. The pictures back up onto an external hard drive, but that's just an insurance policy. I've only needed it once, but it's gone now," he shifted nervously and I gestured for him to continue.

"Yvette Taylor, this woman who was big into gossip, she somehow got into my server, cloned it, then wiped it. Then she blackmailed me to get it back in exchange for that Bible, an inscribed keychain, and a water bottle."

"A water bottle?" Cruz looked pensive but I was more interested in why Yvette was a "woman who was big into gossip" and not "the dead lady" as everyone else called her.

"Yeah, one of those metal water bottles. She specifically wanted one with a Yankees logo on it. We'd done a little business in the past, but when I met up with her for the exchange, she was nervous and shaky. Usually we had a pretty friendly rapport, but she was snappy and jittery. Told me that she was recording the meeting and if I told anyone what I gave her, she would tell the world what I'd done," his mind caught up with his mouth and he slapped his hands over it. "Crap! Don't tell her! Please?"

"When was the last time you spoke to Ms. Taylor?" Cruz had clued in as well.

"A couple weeks. She said if it went according to plan, she'd make big news and I'd never hear from her again," he shrugged, apparently deciding that we would keep his secret.

"Why are you in Ohio?" I asked, again noting the closed blinds, the high-end tech, and the general sense that the man was ill-suited for the Midwest.

"What do you mean?" His eyes bounced nervously and I cut my gaze to him.

"You know what I mean. You could live anywhere. Stuff like this sells anywhere. DC and New York would be much more profitable than here. Why Ohio?"

He rubbed the bridge of his nose with his thumb and index fingers.

"My financing is here, OK? I was sued after those... test pictures came to light. I received an anonymous offer, set up business here and the financier would cover the bills until my operation was back at full strength. The guy even had the server and asked me to keep back-ups for all clients. It seemed a little underhanded to sell people something sneaky and keep copies for someone else, but I needed the money."

"So... the devices you gave Yvette backed up to the server under your control?" I started wondering who knew she was monitoring them.

"I uh... yeah? I guess..."

"Did you tell her that other people could see who she was monitoring?" He shifted and I rolled my eyes.

"It didn't seem important. I mean aren't people supposed to know inherently that data exists on servers so hosts can always access it? It might be wrong, but it's common knowledge technology," he was defensive and just this side of stamping his feet on the ground. His level of indignation said more than his actual words.

He was too stupid to realize his own shortcomings and I marveled at his success in espionage.

"You think it's wrong to keep back-ups, but giving people the power to record others and orchestrate revenge and blackmail is fine? You think keeping back-ups is wrong, but not telling people is fine?" I wanted to hit him, but his morally grey sense of justice reflected that of most, if not all, entitled white men.

"I mean... yeah? If the person went into the situation willingly, it's their fault if they get caught in it. Like I said, they should know data backs up to a server. I'm only selling the means of revelation, nothing sinister." Cruz looked inclined to agree with him, and I considered throwing an explosive book at both of them.

"You realize that's as bad as blaming the person your spouse cheated with instead of the person who did the cheating, right? Yeah, they both participated in whatever it was willingly, but only one person was responsible for damaging or hurting something they were supposed to value. Only one person went in doing it with the intention to cause harm, so realistically, you sold them the means to hurt someone else."

"Well... yeah. But it's not like anyone died. It was usually just used for fun, inconveniencing someone else, or leverage in tough situations."

"Someone did die! Yvette is dead, bludgeoned to death with boxes and boxes of pictures of people in compromising positions behind her crushed skull. Your pictures were hidden away and coated in her blood!"

His mouth fell open and I rolled my eyes.

"Are you kidding me? Have you been so busy getting blow jobs in the elevator that you haven't watched the news?" I crossed my arms, pissed that he didn't know and pissed that Cruz thought filming people at their worst was fine and pissed that I was once again nowhere on finding who killed Yvette. This guy was just a rotten voyeur with no sense of responsibility or integrity. "So you received the feed from the stupid fishing lure and blackmailed Amber to warn Chris... because?"

Andrew blinked at me twice and I sat down in the chair.

"Who did you sell the fishing lure in the blue canvas tote to? Who did you send the server footage to?" I asked and he scrunched his face and moved toward his laptop. Since I was sitting next to it, I got up again and sat beside Winnie. Andrew tapped his keyboard and scrunched his face.

"I don't have access to the server. It was either the buyer or the webmaster. Looks like I sold it to a town councilman... Burt Kielder."

Chapter Eighteen: Burt Kielder

"I'm waiting five more minutes, and then I'm going to find his home address and throw Winnie poop at his windows until he comes outside." My jaw was tired from clenching it. I spilled coffee down the front of my shirt when Mr. No Snacks in My Car tried to take the cup away, then I punched him and he drove up a curb. Now the car, my shirt, the man, and Winnie's left rear paw were wearing wasted toasted marshmallow latte. "Then I'm going to throw Winnie poop at you."

"I said no snacks in my car, chica." Cruz had a playful smile on his face. I was amusing him.

"I said take me home, that man is an asshole and I need coffee and a snack."

"It was too far of a drive to take you home," he slung an arm around my shoulders and I pinched his love handles... or where his love handles would be if he didn't have abs. "They feel even better under the shirt, do you want to explore?"

"No."

"Liar," he whispered as a car pulled into the lot.

We were standing in front of the newspaper building, watching evidence tape flap in the breeze when the Lincoln Continental arrived. It was shiny, black, and spotless. The man who stepped out of it was shiny, Mediterranean, and spotless. Neither looked like Winnie or I would be allowed to touch them.

I considered having her lean against his leg to transfer fur and slobber but the smell of his cologne had me taking a step back. Whatever he was wearing, he must have purchased it in bulk because he was clearly not using it sparingly. Winnie scented the air and let out a series of sneezes before pressing her face into my leg.

Mr. Keilder stood beside his car, waiting impatiently for an explanation.

Neither he nor his car looked impressed with my coffee stained T-Shirt and cargo pants. The car presumably because it was a car, the man because he was an elitist snob and I had a strong desire to throw glitter bombs at both of them. Probably the car didn't deserve a glitter bomb, but it was acceptable collateral damage for a man who didn't look to own a vacuum.

"Councilman Kielder, you're a hard man to track down," I said, trying to sound like an agent of justice in an action movie.

"Yet you seem to have managed anyway," he sniffed and I was immediately reminded of Senator Thompson's butler. Despite being economic and social classes apart, they both gave the distinct air of someone who needed to be taken down a peg or two. "Why have you forced my friends into doing your bidding?"

"Why did you murder Yvette?" I asked and he went deathly pale.

"Wh- what? You can't just.... I'm a councilman!"

I smiled, smugly crossing my arms. Cruz, for his part, did not try to smooth the man's ruffled feathers.

It had taken the entire trip from Dayton, plus two hours and three trips to the bathroom to get the small town council member to agree to meet with us. Despite compelling evidence and Cruz's government resources, the only way we'd gotten the contact info had been by contacting the senator and the dirt mogul to arrange the meeting. They were not surprised to learn Yvette had left the Bible, but they had no idea who would use the device after she was dead.

"You are a councilman of a town so small it is technically a village. Stop whining like you're Justin Bieber getting arrested for weed in an airport," I hooked a finger toward the newspaper building behind me. "Do you want to talk in there or in Derby's?"

Mr. Kielder balked at both.

"My office is right there."

He gestured vaguely toward a red brick building behind us.

"That's nice, but it wasn't an option," I snapped. Cruz shot me a warning look but this pompous jerk was asking to have his butt bit by Winnie. "Who knows what cameras and devices are in your office. Neutral private territory in that restaurant or loudly in this parking lot, Kielder. Those are your choices. If you don't pick one, I'll pick for you."

"What happened to the newspaper office?"

"Nothing, it's still sitting there. We just won't be going into it. You wanna keep pushing me, I'll take away another option."

"You can't just... Who the hell do you think you are?"

"A very annoyed woman who spent her whole day trying to track down a man who I can now see isn't worth the energy I spent looking for him! I've spilled coffee, been chased out of a dog park by a poodle, and there is a substance I can't identify on the bottom of my shoe. This man doesn't speak, and the radio in his car is disabled. Not broken, Mr. Kielder, disabled. He chose to deprive any and all passengers of an option besides silence. I gave you a damn option. Now make a choice!"

The man huffed, looking to Cruz for assistance but the Army sergeant wisely kept his mouth shut. He looked like he may want to defend his radio choices, but my stomach rumbled and reminded him that while he had given me coffee, he wouldn't let me eat Doritos in his car.

Burt opened and closed his mouth before sighing and gesturing to Derby's. It was where I hoped he would pick as they served coffee and ice cream... together. Instead of relenting, I mimicked Amber and stomped toward the restaurant dramatically. My leg hyperextended, rolling my ankle and I landed flat on my ass in the middle of the parking lot. Winnie licked my face and I buried my nose in her fur.

"Are you always so incompetent?"

Cruz cleared his throat in warning before I could get to my feet and remove the councilman's limbs. I was so over male egos, gravity, and Republicans.

The man had had sex with a married woman. He'd put a surveillance device in a purse and given it to Amber. The man was clearly self-important and arrogant and dismembering him could be as much of a public service as my accidental attempt to blow up Florida.

I bet the community would give me a medal.

Cruz helped me up and guided us toward the front of the building.

We walked into the bar, immediately pausing so my eyes could adjust to the darkness while my ears were assaulted. A glance down at Winnie showed she had flattened her ears and was considering placing her paws over them. Pat appeared and gestured us toward a back patio, removing purple ear plugs as the door closed.

"I hate bachelorette parties," Pat grumbled and I shuddered.

"Is that what that was?"

The owner nodded and we both shuddered while the councilman tried to peek back in through the window.

"Seriously? What the hell is wrong with you?" I asked him and Pat looked equally smug, blocking Burt's view.

"What? They are part of my constituency. It's my obligation to press the flesh and garner voter approval."

"Sit," Cruz ordered and the man's eyes widened at hearing Ian's voice for the first time. "Only time I ask."

Kielder sat and Pat exchanged an eye roll with me. Misogynistic jerkwad needed a Winnie head-butt to his testicles. I exchanged a look with the dog in question and she moved her brows, an impression of sportsball fans doing a wave in the stands.

She was game.

Pat went inside and returned with three cups of water, a coffee, and two sodas.

"I love you," I declared, taking a drink of the coffee and nearly choking. Pat gave me a wink, and I smiled at the unexpected Irish in my coffee. "Thank you."

"Give 'em hell," Pat waved before going back inside. A round of "Woohoo!" filled the night air and I drained the rest of my cup. Drinking was how I intended to survive the rest of my day. Drinking and imagining all the different methods of torture I could subject the councilman to with nothing more than the items on the table.

Decapitation by menu and finger removal with a fork were both immediately promising as options.

"Why is it looking at me like that?" Burt whined, and Ian looked down at Winnie who had her head resting on her paws beneath the table.

"The dog is resting, councilman," his response was curt, but far more diplomatic than I liked.

Scooping out his eyeballs with the spoon... slicing his finger with a butter knife and pouring a salt packet into it...

"Not the dog, the thing beside the dog!"

Cruz looked mildly amused, and I caught on to the accusation.

"Call me or my dog an *it* again, and I will cut your tongue out with a steak knife and grill it into lengua for tacos," I growled, and Pat brought me a replacement coffee.

"This one is stronger. Do not commit mutilation in my bar, please."

"He deserves it," I whined and Pat put a shot next to the coffee.

"I don't want to testify against you. Chill and let Sgt. Hottie do the questioning. Just get really relaxed and happy," Pat winked and disappeared again. I took the shot, chugged my water and then tried to slowly sip my coffee.

"Why is she the only one who gets alcohol? I've had a very challenging day. My golf game was cut short by you people," he puffed out his chest and I looked at my fork. If I poked him in the chest he would spring a leak and fly away into the setting sun. Never to be seen again as he burned up in the atmosphere, me and Winnie doing the Linus and Lucy dance on his empty grave. "Why is she looking at me like that?"

"She's imagining scenarios where she kills you in gruesome and possibly disgusting ways. That particular face indicates the presence of fire," Cruz said, taking a sip of his water. "How do you know Andrew Scott?"

"I don't *know* him. He was a legend in school though. He'd managed to rig a camera in the girl's shower, recording all the juicy moments and secrets. It's how we learned who put out and who to kick out. He hid this small video camera in this air freshener mounted to the wall. Nowadays, it's probably not that impressive, but in the late nineties that was the literal cutting edge of technology. When the school found him taking out the old film and putting in the replacement, he got sent to military school. It's how he ended up a foreign correspondent until he got busted watching babes, again."

Burt Kielder was weaving in small circles, and splitting himself in two while my head slowly floated away.

Crap, I was drunk.

"So you reconnected with him at a high school reunion?" Cruz asked and the man chugged his soda, snapping his fingers to summon Pat and ask for a beer. When Pat arrived, it was with another soda and a stern reminder that he was not permitted to drink on the premises after "the incident".

It seemed relevant to follow the conversation, but I was suddenly very aware of how soft and fluffy Winnie's head felt under my fingers. I pinched her ear between my fingers, folding and flipping it while her whiskers tickled my palm and she licked something from the leg of my pants.

"You're so pretty, good girl," I cooed, and Cruz appeared above me. "My, what long legs you have."

Giant Cruz shrank himself to my size, but now the table was giant and Winnie was a nice overstuffed pillow. He wrapped an arm around my waist and we were suddenly flying, landing as I grew to table size.

"You're a sorcerer!" I slurred and he held me steady in the chair.

"Chica, you are the world's worst lightweight. We need to ask this man questions so I can take you home," his voice vibrated against my skin and I fell against him.

"You're pretty. Amber thinks you're hot and wants you to arrest her. She told me at the body shop... though she didn't mention shopping your body *specifically*, I think she wants you. That man..." I gestured across the table but it was falling over even as Cruz held me in the chair. "He can show you pictures of her naked! Don't you want to know what she looks like naked?"

"What are you rambling about?" Burt tisked into his soda and I reached my finger out to cover his mouth, but poked him in the eye instead.

"Not rambles. Andrew sold you the canvas tote with the fishing lure that you gave to Amber. I don't know why, but you caught Chris and Mo naked and then blackmailed her to tell him to tell me to leave this whole thing alone so the world wouldn't know that you had sex with Carla... and her husband... probably. It wasn't in the pictures but you seem confused and entitled enough to use people of all genders, and I don't like you."

"What tote camera? Who the hell is Amber?" He smacked his hands on the table and I opened my mouth to shout back at him.

Then I fell all the way out of the chair into Cruz's arms, who tried to carry me back to the car.

"Wait! I have to pee!" I cried and he rubbed his temples, leading me into the bar and allowing me access to the bathroom. It took a few tries, but after I finally peed, I walked back into the insanely loud bar where the bridal party let out a solid whoop and I joined them.

"Shots!" I shouted and they agreed. A waitress was carrying around a tray of something amber colored that I took without question before trying to stuff $20 into her bra.

Twenty dollars that Cruz took from my hand, placed in her hand, and then carried me outside with a head incline toward Pat. The owner and Burt waited a respectable distance as Cruz sat me in the passenger seat.

"Chica, don't throw up in my car," he whispered, kissing my temple and straightening himself to speak to the man who had followed us to the lot. They were both gesturing, when Pat ventured over to interject and Cruz handed over money. Expectantly, Pat held out a hand to Burt who tried to stiff the owner and received some sort of warning before throwing his hands in the air, passing over a twenty and stalking off back toward his car. Pat shook hands with Cruz, handed him a few water bottles and appeared to tell him something about ice cream or wanting to play Sorry.

Cruz smiled at me in the car with a wolfish grin, and Pat came to the window.

"Girl, if you are going to get wasted that fast, let me know. I'd have brought you French fries."

"His fault. He wouldn't let me have French fries, or chips, or candy, or beef jerky in his stupid car, and he stole my pants cookies!" A bit of spit flew out of my mouth and landed on the window. Pat looked to Cruz and gestured for him to follow. They drew even with the bar, Pat gesturing wildly and Cruz staring guiltily between the car and his shoes. With a warning finger, Pat went into the bar and came out a few moments later with a bag. Another threat and Ian headed back to the car with the bag.

"French fries!" I squealed when he opened the door and I was hit with the scent. Wincing, he watched me stick my hands in and shove the potatoes in my mouth. "You were in so much trouble for not feeding me. Pat's gonna report you to the authorities and Cyn Protective Services are going to get you."

"So I was informed," he said, watching me eat with a look of amused horror. "If I'd known watching you eat was this hot, I'd probably have changed my mind and let you have the chips. Maybe that Go-Gurt too, so long as a responsible adult opened it."

He reached for the bag and I jerked it away.

"Mine! Now Pat gets all the credit and you get nothing," I declared, polishing off the fries. I climbed out of the car, staggering to the trash can that had previously been just inside the doorway. Inside it was empty, no gloves or crime scene booties. Nothing at all and I threw the French fry bag in. Then, with a sudden burst of inspiration, I pulled the trash bag out and tried to tie it around my neck.

"Eww!" I gagged as something dripped from the bag onto my pants and Cruz appeared to hold me steady. "It's sticky!"

"Why do you want it?" he asked, putting the bag back in the can.

"To be a superhero cape! For when I save the world!" I executed a pirouette, landed on my ass and stared up at Cruz. "You're tall again. Do you have Alice in Wonderland bottles? Could you give me the shrink one? I want to ride on Winnie like a beast of war."

Instead of trying to get me to walk, Cruz scooped me into a fireman's carry and started back toward the car.

"I'm all out of shrinking tonics, but I'll get you a GoPro for Winnie and you can pretend."

"That's not the same! I want to be a superhero! Or a tiny rider on a dog! Being me is boring! I can't even find a murderer! Or a webhost! Or a host of Yeerks who want to kill the Animorphs!"

"I believe in you," he said, balancing me on his knee to open the car door and set me inside. He grabbed a sweatshirt from somewhere and put it between my head and the frame of the car. He reached around and buckled me in, hands not straying from the most direct path.

"Not feeling friendly?" I slurred and he squeezed my hand.

"Sleep it off, Super Cyn. The yeerk in my brain would feel better if you didn't throw up on me."

"What did Burt say about the bag?" I asked, nuzzling the fabric and taking a long inhale of Ian Cruz.

"I'll tell you tomorrow," he answered, kissing my forehead before gently shutting the door.

Chapter Nineteen: No Peeking

My eyes weren't open yet, but something was wrong.

I held perfectly still, listening, while angry men with hammers played timpani in my skull. There were no sounds, no light coming through my lids, and around me was cool air and a smooth blanket. The hum of a fan tried to lull me back to sleep, but I stiffened trying to remember where I was last and if it was here.

"Winnie?" I asked softly, and a cold nose pressed to my face. If Winnie was here and not barking, probably we were OK.

"Where are we, girl?"

The blanket moved and I screamed, throwing out an arm that was promptly caught and pinned against me.

"Shh... Chica," the blanket stroked my arm and the smell of pine filled my nostrils.

"Dead?"

"Not yet. You are officially cut off though," Ian moved my hair and tilted my chin to him. Opening my eyes seemed like a terrible idea so I tried to glare at him with my lids closed. "If you open your eyes, I'll give you water and pain medicine."

"What kind of pain medicine?" Glaring with my eyes closed was painful.

"No idea. Whatever is in the bathroom."

"You don't know what's in your bathroom?" I opened my eyes to look at him and the timpani turned into a Southern drumline. "Ow!"

My eyes closed again and the blanket abandoned me.

"It's not my bathroom," he walked away. A jingle, soft thud and the bed dipped beside me.

Winnie had taken his spot, and I wrapped an arm around her. I peeled an eyelid half open and tried to see the room. There was a bed, three doors, and sparse walls. The actual blanket was some shade of grey, as was one of the walls that may or may not have been blackout curtains.

"Are we in a bomb shelter?" I asked Winnie, and Cruz set water and a plastic bottle of medicine beside me.

"No. Safe house. It's on loan."

I gulped water, fumbled with the pill bottle, and dumped a hundred blue pills onto the smooth wooden floors.

"Chica," he groaned, picking up two and handing them to me. I promptly swallowed them with the rest of the water and laid back down. I listened as Cruz dropped the pills back into the plastic bottle, each little click magnified in the agony of my skull.

"Stop?" I whined and he let out a soft laugh.

"Can't. The furry vacuum could get sick."

I groaned and rolled to the edge of the bed to help him. My hand flopped toward the floor and I patted the air, feeling for pills or the floor. Nothing, nothing... warm... rigid...

My eyes shot open and I met Cruz's heated gaze.

"Eep!" I squeaked, seeing my hand on his... "Oh my dog, you're naked!"

I slammed my hands over my eyes and he chuckled, prying my hand from my face.

"You've already stared, no need to be shy now."

"I didn't stare!" I hissed.

"Liar," he said back and stood up in one fluid movement. Nothing creaked or popped as he turned to walk back to the bathroom, and I had to admire the government's property.

It was absolutely flawless, down to the dimple in his butt cheek.

Larry's ass flashed in my mind's eye and I sighed.

"Are you comparing or appreciating?" He was beside the bed again and I cracked a lid. Cruz had put on boxers.

"Little of both. You put on pants."

"Would you like me to take them off?"

"For... comparison purposes or actual use?"

He flashed a wicked grin and Winnie licked my ear. I turned toward her and she let out a small whimper.

235

"What are Sgt. Pupperson's thoughts?" He asked, moving closer so the heat radiating off of him warmed my arms.

"Either she thinks I'm moving in on her turf, or she's reminding me Larry would be hurt," at the mention of Larry's name she put her head on my chest and gazed at me from under raised eyebrows. I tried to convey to my partner that Larry had no claim and Cruz is hot.

She put her paw on my hand, and I sighed in frustration.

"Did I just get cock blocked by a dog? Again?"

"Yeah. Put on pants, sex machine. I need coffee and we need to solve a murder."

"OK, but for the record, I'm going to think about you fondling me when I'm in the shower," he whispered, dragging his lips across my cheek.

"Me too," I whispered and heard him choke, just before the boxers landed on my face. They were still warm and smelled like him, but by the time I pulled them off, he was closing the door to the bathroom.

"Probably for the best," I said to Winnie who wagged her tail in agreement. "But I'm totally thinking about that in the shower later."

"Let's recap," I said, taking a long drink of coffee that killed the contents of the dinky cup. Whoever regularly stayed in the safehouse liked making repeated trips to the coffee pot to get their steps in for the day.

That or they were superhuman like Cruz, who claimed he "didn't need any coffee". The freak of nature in question was seated across from me at a two-person table. As this was his safe house, he was properly clothed.

Clothed and not drinking coffee.

I was wearing his Army PT clothes that hugged every single curve of my body and left nothing to the imagination.

Cruz had practically drooled and refused to let me borrow any other clothes.

Now, he was eating some sort of gruel that was called "instant oatmeal", while I had opted for an ancient package of pop tarts that might be older than Winnie. They had stale trims, crushed sprinkles and half of it was discolored.

Still better than oatmeal.

"Because that's helpful," he grumbled and I raised a warning finger.

"Look, you either need to drink coffee or get back in the shower, grumpy pants. Your attitude this morning is not helpful. Where is the perfectly prim and proper Stepford Soldier?"

"He's taking a nap. You have Crabby Man You Groped All Night and then Turned Down."

"Sucks doesn't it? To be left hot, bothered, and wanting after being promised so much?" I smirked and he sighed into his oatmeal.

"Can we switch to talking about murder?"

"Absolutely. Yvette Taylor was blackmailing a man who sold people spy equipment in exchange for some spy equipment of her own and access to his servers. Servers he doesn't control but she has somehow printed the contents of. We have a gay senator and gravel man who were being spied on with an exploding bible planted by Amber and abused by the webmaster... webhost? Server man? And... What was the deal with Amber's tote?"

Some of the post-hangover cobwebs were clearing and I realized I still didn't have all the information.

"He thought his side chick was cheating. Got the bag to call her out on it, he has no idea how it ended up with Amber."

"Who's his side chick?"

Cruz looked uncomfortable and I made the "keep going" gesture.

Instead of answering, he pulled out his phone and worked the keys. My coffee shot glass was empty, so I made my fourth trip to the pot, adding sugar because that was the only option available in this bunker. In a similar vein, the coffee was bulk freeze dried garbage and the powdered milk was empty.

This place made Afghanistan look like The Ritz-Carlton without all the delightful eye candy and random drive-by shootings.

"Her," I nearly jumped out of my skin when Cruz spoke from directly beside me. His phone was beside my sad, boring coffee and his hand was on my hip. I looked down at a small twig of a woman with inflated lips, inflated breasts, and an advertising campaign for silicone ass injections.

"Send me that?" I asked, and he texted the picture to me. I immediately sent it to Mo.

Me: *Do we know her? By we I mean you. Because I refuse to talk to anyone who isn't you.*

Cruz laughed beside me and I resisted the urge to elbow him by taking my prepared coffee shot.

"If you don't talk to anyone but Ms. Mary O'Connor, what are Larry and I?"

"Eye candy and distractions," I shrugged and read the response. "I guess she's one of Amber's cliques. She was in the woman's fake wedding we demolished."

I put the phone away and drank more coffee.

"So, assuming she gave the bag to Amber, the bag didn't sync until it connected to the Wi-Fi when she brought it inside and then... why would the webhost send the pictures to her?"

"What?" Cruz tilted his head like Winnie and I looked to the dog in question, sprawled in a sun spot. Thankfully, there had been dog food here. That or Cruz stopped for some while I was passed out.

"Whoever sent it knew Chris is a Firefighter, knew that he and I were friends enough that threatening him would get my attention to stop investigating... Why not send them to Chris? Or Mo even? Why send them to Amber?"

I paced the kitchen, Winnie wiggling her brows to follow my path back and forth across the room.

"Why do we assume she gave it to Amber?"

"Gave it to her, forgot it at her house and she thought it was hers... does it matter?" I was studying his face, but he was blank. "What?"

"Nothing."

"Don't nothing me, Stepford Soldier. What?"

"What makes you so sure it wasn't on purpose?" He asked, crossing his arms and studying me.

"You think Burt wanted her to spy on Amber?"

"I think Burt is an idiot, but Andrew is an expensive resource for an idiot. I think someone convinced him to seek out Andrew and then arranged the transfer of the bag... directly or indirectly," he leaned against the counter and I tried to think through his suggestion.

Convince Burt to buy the over-priced bag. Give it to the girlfriend to get it to Amber. Then hope Amber takes it somewhere or leaves it somewhere? It was over a month ago when she got it. What was happening a month ago? Amber didn't go anywhere. She and her posse haunted the town, sneering and causing drama to any and all they encountered.

Last month... last month she was dealing with...

"What happened with Amber's Shoe Ambrosia?" I asked, referencing the shop she'd purchased. It was the only shoe store in Sweet Pea and unfortunately, I'd needed a lot of shoes in January. Ian looked confused and I furrowed my brow. He hadn't been here, but someone had to have been here. The FBI agent who had been trying to get her brother out of a life of crime was temporarily unavailable... her husband was an enigma and also I'd seen him basically naked so avoiding him was ideal. That only left one person to ask and I groaned as I picked up the phone again.

"Hey loser," Daniel said into the phone and I ground my back teeth together.

Keep your cool, I talked myself down, *you need answers.*

"Daniel," forced calm. "Is Amber's Shoe Ambrosia still in business?"

"Yeah, but there are some complications and she's on probation for tax evasion," he shifted something on his end and I waited for him to continue.

He did not.

"And?"

"And what? Gretchen Harpole spoke to some real IRS agents after Amber freaked about the fake one. They didn't do anything for a couple weeks and now she's paying back taxes. The shop does an OK amount of business, so she should be fine. There was an unsavory character floating around at the time. Can't remember his name..."

"Would anyone remember the name?" I asked when he thought for too long.

"Chief Jones probably would. His retirement party is tonight at Casey's Bar, you can probably drop in no problem. I think Chief has a little thing for you. He kept bringing you up randomly since Amber was arrested."

"Eww," I said and I could hear him roll his eyes.

"Not that kind of thing, you sicko."

"Sicko? Seriously? Are you ten?" I heard a child screaming and something loud hitting the ground in the background of his end. "Never mind, good luck with the Satan you spawned."

"Are we going to a retirement party?" Cruz asked and I nodded.

"Also, I guess we should talk to the girlfriend and..." I shuddered. "Amber... again."

Chapter Twenty: Rules of Retirement

My headache was back and I had twenty minutes to get ready and across the street. After speaking to Amber, her friend, and Daniel... again, I needed a shot and a nap. Winnie had a chew stick and was happily chomping away beside the coffee table, officially off the clock.

"Why don't you have to go?" I asked her as I stared at the tension rod that served as my closet. It was as sorely lacking as it had always been. "What do you wear to a chief's retirement?"

Chomp. Chomp.

Winnie had no thoughts or opinions on the subject.

She also didn't have to go because health code regulations do not permit dogs in a bar. She could go to war, defend the country, but she couldn't walk into an establishment that sold food; a fact at least four people called to remind me of, and none of them would allow me to dress her up and pretend she was my child.

Apparently children aren't allowed in bars either.

"Seriously, Winnie, I need help! What do I wear!"

"Clothes are considered preferable over not clothes," Larry said and I looked back as he reached the landing. He was wearing black slacks and a collared shirt. His hair was combed, shoes clean, and he was holding a cup of coffee.

"Ugh," I groaned and flopped back on my bed. "I've already had a full day of morons and now I have to cross the street and talk to drunk strangers. What did I do to deserve this?"

"What morons were you talking to?" He sat beside my head and lifted it into his lap, stroking my hair. I sat up, downed the coffee in one, and handed back the empty cup before settling into his lap.

"Amber and her friend Cindy," I choked on the last. The woman had introduced herself as Silicone Cindy, an injection model. Between unnecessary words and even more unnecessary pouting, I gleaned that the woman had forgotten the bag while visiting Amber's house for a party. Burt had encouraged her to go, stating it was good for her to spend time with friends. She and Amber had the same bag and she'd taken the other by mistake, but since they were both new, it hadn't seemed important.

Neither was especially helpful on details from the evening. Either there was so much alcohol they didn't remember, or Amber was afraid I'd reveal her cosmetic secrets. Both options, however, did not equate to murder. After a look at Cindy's bag, I confirmed there was nothing special or interesting about it, so I handed it back and left.

"Cindy is a gold digger, but Burt kind of deserves it because he's a cradle robber. No one that age 'falls in love' with someone of his age. It's all about money, status, and power. If neither party has any of those things, then it's probably a carryover childhood trauma and the person needs therapy," Larry scratched my scalp and I nearly purred. "I never pegged Amber for the smart one of her friends, but I'm starting to think she might be."

"What did Amber say?"

"That her restitution is nearly paid, and that's why lawyers exist."

"So... fruitful day?" He teased and I raised my upper lip.

"If the fruit is plastic and deceptively placed somewhere one might try to eat it... and filled with poison."

"That sounds far more dangerous than the women you described," he propped me to a seated position and I barely refrained from whimpering. "Why don't you grab some pants and a shirt so we can get this over with."

"We? You're coming?"

Giddy elation filled me and he kissed my cheek.

"Yes. My brother asked me to babysit you."

The elation faded. We were once again at an impasse on the topic of friend, obligation, girlfriend, and lover. He wrapped his arms around me and pressed his nose into my hair.

"I'd have gone with you if you asked me, but you didn't ask. Why don't you ever ask, Cyn?"

"Because of all the times you said no before," I answered honestly and shrugged out of his arms. "I need to go to Marvin's and get back my no longer hideous Jeep before this party gets underway."

I did a little happy shimmy.

"Yeah... I saw it," he sighed and the look on his face said there was more.

"It's a nice color right?"

"You... picked it?"

"Yeah! I mean there weren't a lot of great options in my price range, but it was the least offensive."

Larry just stared at me and his frown deepened when my phone rang.

"You can have your Jeep back, but I'm going to need it again in a week. Sal screwed up."

"What do you mean Sal screwed up?" Larry's eyes were transitioning from concern to humor and a sinking feeling filled my gut.

"He ordered the wrong color."

"But I wrote the color code." Larry's amusement grew and visions of horrific shades from the rainbow filled my imagination.

"Post-it blew away. Told him it was open to the color page and it was marked in your price range."

"And?"

"Apparently the breeze turned the page when it blew away the post-it."

Larry came up and turned his phone toward me.

"It's orange!" I shrieked, looking in horror at the rust orange Jeep in Larry's picture.

"It was an accident. You can get your Jeep back some other time, just make sure I get it back in a week."

The man hung up and I gawked at Larry's phone. My Jeep, my poor abused Jeep, was now the color of rotted pumpkins. Not only was it orange, an unattractive orange, there were still gouge marks in the side from raccoons and what looked like a puddle under one of the doors. I tried to zoom in on Larry's picture, but he took the phone back.

"You don't want to do that.," he said, putting the phone back in his pocket.

"What? Why?" I asked, considering stealing his phone just to grope him.

"No point in seeing the inside before you have to..." he shifted and I gaped.

"What does the inside look like?" I whispered in horror and he gave me a hug.

"Let's not talk about that right now," he turned me toward my clothes and I turned back.

"Did he let more raccoons in?"

"No idea. But I'm guessing that call for a pregnant dog giving birth at his shop that I was summoned for... may have happened in there. Mostly because when I arrived, I was led to your Jeep to get out a dog and four puppies and the seat was... in need of sanitation."

"Puppies... were born in my car?" It was sweet as a thought, but probably the smell would linger.

Afterbirth looked like something that would smell awful... Also pregnancy looked like a horrifying and uncomfortable experience. Every calf I'd birthed had come out all elbows, knees and slime.

Pretty sure multiple babies meant multiple slimes.

I sighed and went back to looking at my clothes.

"If it was anything but an animal birth, I'd be so pissed."

Larry rubbed my back and handed me a long sleeve top from a hanger and a pair of jeans.

"What's with the sexy Army woman outfit?"

"It was all Cruz would let me borrow and the man is freakishly fit."

"Why were you borrowing clothes from Cruz?"

"Because I got drunk, passed out in his car and he took us to a safehouse." Winnie came over to poke me in the butt with her cold wet nose, reminding me that there had been no underwear in Cruz's house... besides the pair he threw at my head. "Can I meet you downstairs?"

"Why?" Larry's voice was hard and I whipped my head around to look at him.

"Because I'm not wearing any underwear and I forgot!"

"Where are your underwear?" An angry glare joined the harsh tone of voice.

"In the laundry. Have you ever been drunk? You pee fifty million times and get worse and worse at wiping until your underwear is disgusting! Not to mention the goo that dripped on my pants from the trash can."

His face broke into a round of laughter that forced him to double over.

"Stop laughing! That trash bag would have been the perfect cape if it didn't have goo!" I stomped across my apartment and pulled the pants out of the hamper. "Look!"

Larry walked over and studied the stain on my cargo pants as I looked at it properly for the first time.

"It kind of looks like blood, doesn't it?" I sniffed and pulled it away from my face.

"What does it smell like?" Larry asked, sticking his face against the pants. "What is that? Basil?"

We both sniffed again and studied each other over the pants.

"Maybe?"

"Why would something look like blood and smell like food?" Larry asked and something in the back of my mind pinged. Winnie shoved her nose up the too small shorts and I screamed.

"Cold! Cold nose!" Larry moved behind me, pressing my butt against his... "That's not cold..."

"It could be warmer though..." he whispered and my good spots warmed.

"Yeah?" I whispered and my shirt was gone.

"Definitely."

Oh thank dog.

We arrived at the bar about an hour into the party. My limbs were loose, my body sated, and my underwear... were still missing. Larry had my hand in his and when I leaned into his shoulder, I forgot why I was wearing pants.

"What are we doing here?" I whispered, and Larry kissed my nose.

"Questioning the retiring chief."

Oh right, I thought.

There were easily ten empty pitchers of beer per table and two-dozen empty shot glasses beside each. Every person present had started removing layers. Ties sat in a pile beside suit jackets, women's heels were piled willy-nilly, and the outgoing chief... was aloft.

"If you wish to join, you must pay the toll!" A man declared and I studied his face.

"Opie?" He laughed and passed me a shot.

"Every person who calls me that is required to take one and give one," he passed a glass to the man being carried in a chair above our heads. Despite not being in the chair, watching the buff men flex beneath it after what I was just doing had me wondering again if I really *needed* to solve a murder. Larry and I could just get back to... reconciling.

We could maybe even bring a friend.

"Cyn!" The older man bellowed and I waved as he issued a command to be lowered. The men holding the chair were wearing sexy cop uniforms, and I wondered if they were rented or supplied by Mrs. Charles. That woman might have been married, but she knew the value of muscle. Chief Jones smiled wide.

"I've been meaning to talk to you."

The four men lowered the chair, and I felt as though the Horah had just ended and we should be toasting the bride and groom. As though sensing my concern, he looked around and pointed toward the secret speakeasy door to the upper balcony. I followed and felt, more than saw, Larry bring up the rear. Chief Jones opened the door, shooed two necking officers, and closed the door. Though dimly lit, I could make out a fourth figure who was easy to identify by the scent.

"Cyn, Larry, you probably know Ian Cruz with... whatever he's with."

The jovial drunk was gone. Dave Jones was all business, and I looked between him and Cruz. Both men had that sense of contained secrets and an undercurrent of danger. Jones was Cruz's future and as I watched him chug a beer he scooped from a table, I wondered if he was a functional alcoholic.

What had he done to get here?

"Daniel said you had some questions, and I've been looking into it since we talked this morning," he pulled an envelope out of his pocket and handed it to me. "He said you wanted to know how Amber came to be on probation. Gretchen did her thing, but we had grounds to look into her after we got that."

He tapped the envelope and I noted that it wasn't sent through the mail. Just like the photos and envelope Amber got, it just said "Chief Jones" and inside was a generic piece of printer paper with a typed message summarizing Amber's suspected crime. Though not as rhyming, it had the same childish, "I'm telling mom" tone contained in every threat we've seen thus far.

"When I confronted her with the evidence, she folded. Said that she was struggling to make the payments and she saw online how to fix it so everything was cheaper. Never occurred to her that the solutions were illegal. She gave me the threats. They were more of the same, give me money or I'm turning you in. Though I still get the impression she's not completely sure what she's on probation for... or really what she was being threatened with."

"You think she saw the threat as like... they were going to share her secret to success with the world and she wouldn't be special anymore?"

"Maybe..." Dave Jones said, rubbing the grey scruff on his face. "Honestly, she got three letters. The last one dated around that time the business with the caskets went down. I think that was when she started to realize she'd done something wrong." He stared into his beer glass... puzzling while Ian worked through scenarios and Larry leaned against the wall. His eyes were fixed on the envelope, a head nod encouraging me to focus on the tangible.

Cruz gestured with his eyes at the paper and I sighed.

I flipped the envelope over. Unlike the paper, it wasn't generic. There was a crest embedded in the paper and though it was too dark and faded to see, I traced the lines and tried to picture the shape in my mind.

"I know what this is..." I said, tracing the edge of an open book. Beside it was an old-fashioned camera. "It's... from a newspaper."

My fingers found the YS as I suspected and I studied Chief Jones for a long moment. He'd seen the envelope, seen the mark, and suspected someone was giving him the information... Then what?

"You think Yvette was trying to get a story by having Amber arrested?"

"She'd already taken Amber down at that point," he shrugged and I tilted my head.

"So then... who from the newspaper did you suspect of sending it?" I asked and he took another long drink.

"Honestly? I looked into the possibility it was just the envelope and someone elsewhere in the building had tactically acquired it, but when Yvette turned up dead... I started to wonder..."

"Wonder about what?" I prompted when he was quiet for too long.

"Wonder if maybe there was something bigger going on there. People were complaining about strange charges, subscription fees they hadn't agreed to. It wasn't anything major, and certainly there wasn't anyone willing to make a case... I just got a feeling..."

"You got a feeling that maybe the newspaper was scamming people? Did you look into it?"

Again, he was silent a moment longer than I found comfortable.

"I did... which is why I'm retiring and giving this over to you."

"Are you serious? Why?"

With a sigh he pulled out another paper, a printed picture on copy paper. The creases matched those of the other letter. I unfolded it, expecting more taunts and triviality.

It was a picture of the chief in drag.

He had on fishnets, a big blonde wig and a five o'clock shadow in four-inch heels and a teddy. Beneath the image was a simple line, "Expose her or I expose you".

"Why did you give into this?" I asked, noting that the man had shapely calves and was crushing the look in his wig.

"Because this town isn't progressive enough to accept this if it got out, and my kids would suffer. I retired to get out of the line of fire after giving in to the threat. Then... I arranged to move you in front of the problem with Daniel. I'm sorry, Cyn, but you're the only person in this town that can't be blackmailed."

"I can be blackmailed," I muttered and all three men laughed. "What?"

"Chica, every incident you're involved in makes national news. There is nothing to hold over your head. Literally or figuratively."

"Getting that guy's arm out of that horse has over a million views on YouTube," Larry added and I gaped at them before looking at Dave .

"Really?"

The chief nodded his agreement and shifted.

"I don't like doing this to you, Cyn. If there'd been another way..." He looked depressed toward the bottom of his cup. "You're the last option for justice. Well, you and them."

Chugging the rest of his beer, he raised the glass in salute and left the three of us standing in the concealed room.

Chapter Twenty-One: Empty Shelves

"Oh my dog, it's even worse than the picture," I physically recoiled, looking at the Jeep. In the light of the sun, the orange was somehow more orange, the scratches deeper and the stupid smiley face was forcing its way through the orange. My poor, sad Jeep was now a Jack O' Lantern in a horror film.

Which meant there was, in fact, a worse color than yellow. I owed yellow an apology.

"I told you about the puppies," Larry said and I shook my head at him.

"The inside is beautiful compared to this!" I spread my arms wide.

"It's not that bad."

My lip went up and I let out a growl. Larry handed me a coffee and I drank until the urge to commit murder faded. Then I handed him back the empty cup and he passed me the one I'd poured for him. Winnie sniffed at the side of her transport, nosing the handle until I popped open the door. She put her front paws on the rear floorboard, craned her neck and tried to sniff the whole thing at once. She looked at me over her shoulder and I shrugged.

A few more cursory sniffs, a lick and she... peed on the side of the car.

"Girl dogs aren't supposed to do that," I scolded her and she lifted her chin as she took her paws off the car and seated herself beside me. "I'm just saying."

The back seat had a discoloration, and a pair of hoodies I kept in the car were now only suitable for the garbage. On the floorboard was Amber's bag, and I picked it up, noticing that while the raccoons and the dog afterbirth had soaked into my hoodies and the seat, her bag was still spotless. I rotated it, noting that it wasn't that nice of a bag.

"Why are you holding that garbage?" Mrs. Margot called from behind me. I turned to see my first client standing with her walker, disdain on her face. Though not an overly jolly woman, her choice of stark black dress and blood red accents made her more suited to drive my Jeep than I was.

"Hey, Mrs. Margot. What's wrong with this bag?"

"The bag is cheap, I'm talking about the rubbish stuck to the bottom," she huffed and I tilted my head. There was a copy of the Yellow Springs Newspaper stuck to the bottom. I pulled on it, but it stayed put and I realized my fingers had gripped a seam. Flipping the whole bag over, I studied the base. The canvas tote had a flat bottom, nothing remarkable, but in lieu of contrasting fabric, someone had created a fabric out of one of the issues.

"Who makes fabric out of a small town newspaper?"

Mrs. Margot tutted and came over to the car. She took a sniff, somehow taking in the car in a single sweep of her eyes.

"That is hideous."

Larry sighed and shook his head.

"Don't encourage her, Mrs. Margot," he grumbled and she shot him a look that threatened death and dismemberment. Winnie moved closer, and she got a similar look when she placed her nose near the tennis ball on the bottom of her walker.

"Winnie," I warned and the dog whined before moving back beside me. Mrs. Margot looked me up and down, then Larry, and I checked that we had both remembered pants. I was wearing khaki colored cargos, Larry had on jeans. My long sleeve T-shirt was green; he'd opted for a brown hoodie.

We were definitely suitable to be out in public, but Mrs. Margot was giving us both a hard look.

"I see you two have made up," she sniffed and I dropped my chin to my chest to sniff. I smelled like soap, deodorant, and coffee. Larry looked to be doing the same, and we exchanged a look before he mouthed "witchcraft" and we decided that must be it.

After the bombs Chief Jones had dropped, we'd gone back to my apartment. Cruz, Larry, and I had ordered a pizza, looked at the notes, pictures, and evidence, but we had nothing. Amber's bag was forgotten in my Jeep and I'd lost Yvette's job offer somewhere. After an hour of conversation and pizza, we had nothing new and Cruz went back to his bomb shelter. Larry stayed and reminded me why pants and underwear really were the most unnecessary clothing.

Twice.

Then again this morning.

"Don't wear that look looking at him, or I will tell your mother," Mrs. Margot warned and I raised a brow at her.

"It was her idea!"

She sniffed and muttered something about children of the seventies.

"It's not fabric, dear," she said, flipping the bag and balancing it on her walker. Yvette's job offer fell out and I picked it up while Mrs. Margot studied the bag. I couldn't remember putting it in the bag, maybe I'd slid it in when I checked my Jeep after searching her Mini Cooper. I studied the newspaper chosen to grace the bottom beside Mrs. Margot. The creator had memorialized one of Yvette's gossip articles, but the print beneath the by-line was obscured and I couldn't make out which had been chosen.

Winnie whimpered and gave the tennis balls a longing look.

"No," I corrected and she huffed out a breath to flop onto the ground.

"That dog gets more dramatic every day you're out of the Army," Mrs. Margot commented as the dog in question let out a wide yawn and a fart. Her head whipped around to sniff her gas and, disinterested, she went back to staring at the tennis ball and letting out small pleading whimpers.

"Mrs. Margot, what were you saying about the bag?" I prompted and she shook off her annoyance at my partner.

"It's not fabric, it's vinyl printed with the image on it and attached to a cheap bag. Probably screen print or iron on," she ran a nail across the bottom, making a scratching sound and I tilted my head as she flipped the bag back over and let out a humph. "These were on special at the Tractor Supply for a month last year. I'm delighted to see that my plan was a success though. I wonder how much they paid for them over at Betty's. That one was Amber's?"

I nodded.

"This one has a little extra in it... It was given to Cindy but somehow Amber had the same one and they got mixed up. If these are just cheap bags, how did they both get one as gifts?"

Mrs. Margot let out a bark of laughter.

"Now, don't go spreading this around, but I like to have fun," her eyes twinkled and she gave a conspiratorial look. "Back in January, I was carrying one of these bags filled with recycling when I saw Amber and her posse going on about designer this and quality that. So I told my friend who owns Betty's Boutique, Monica, to get a bunch of the totes from Tractor Supply, mark up the price and add a scarf to the handle."

Mrs. Margot snickered as she ran her hand along the green scarf.

"She got these on the Internet for a couple dollars and she must have sold dozens. There was a man who worked over at the government buildings who bought two and she remembered thinking he was probably getting one for his wife and one for his girlfriend. So Monica raised the price by a hundred percent, claiming it was the customization on the bottom. Smug little prick paid it and tried to sell her a newspaper subscription."

"Brown hair, brown eyes? The most unremarkable man on the planet?" I wasn't especially concerned with her answer, until she disagreed with my statement.

"No, that blonde bozo. Fairly certain he runs the newspaper but he doesn't sit with them so maybe I'm mistaken, but I've certainly given him an ear full. What's his name? Corn Head... Elle Woods..." she pulled her dentures away from her gums letting them pop back into place as she thought. While Corn Head was a cool slasher movie name and Elle Woods was the smartest blonde in the history of Hollywood, I had no idea who she was talking about.

Winnie made a yawn that sounded like a dinosaur calling for its mate and I laughed.

"Elliot Maize," she snapped her fingers with the declaration and I tilted my head. "The editor in chief at the newspaper?"

My mind came up blank, and I looked to Larry who shook his head.

We had nothing.

"Oh, come on. I saw him in front of your building a few days ago. Went right up to him and gave him a piece of my mind about his billing department. They charged me three times the approved rate until I cancelled all my cards and my subscription. My niece, the computer cracker, said my information was on the night web. She scrubbed it and now I'm safe shielded, she said, but it was a trying few weeks. No one over there was helpful, least of all that former baseball idiot assuming he works there. How he became friends with a council member I'll never know, but that Burt wasn't always the brightest bulb in the shed. Perfect for politics but mind you I wouldn't want him setting my policies."

My head throbbed as I tried to piece together her statement. The "cracker" was a hacker who had left breadcrumbs to a killer before. One day, I hoped to meet the woman and find out how many times she'd corrected Mrs. Margot about being a cracker before she just gave up. Night web was probably the dark web... not something I was familiar with but I trusted the "cracker" to have handled it. Safe shield was probably identity monitoring or her niece was an Avenger. Elliot Maize... who the hell was Elliot...

"Crap! I know him. He was here?" I asked, bewildered at the thought someone so idiotic had been seen near my building during walk of shame hours. Winnie let out another dinosaur sound and I nodded at her. "Yeah, I know, you remembered first."

"Said he was refilling the newspaper boxes, only he didn't have any papers. His hands were filthy though," she frowned at the memory. "He tried to stuff them in his pockets, but I told him he shouldn't ruin his pants that way."

I nodded but my mind wandered. I'd dismissed Elliot. The man couldn't identify a dog, but maybe he knew more than I gave him credit for. My goal had been to distract him and then find my brother, maybe he'd come to tell me something and I missed it. I really needed to answer unknown numbers on my phone.

"Thanks for your help, Mrs. Margot. I'm going to go talk to Elliot. Anyone else you know have a billing issue?"

"Damn near every citizen in Sweet Pea, Yellow Springs, and Deer Hook over the age of fifty. Like whoever did it thought we wouldn't keep tabs on our accounts. My check register is better balanced than most of the town's finances," I raised a brow at "check register" and she rolled her eyes. "You young people and your technology is why these jerks think they can get away with this nonsense."

Annoyed with us, she ambled away with irritated clicks of her dentures.

"Back to Yellow Springs?" Larry asked and I nodded.

"Maybe someone knows where Corn Head lives," I texted Cruz and he recommended we meet at the scene.

Cruz met us at the newspaper office and I noticed the cooked blood was still in the parking space beside the planter. Carla's Jaguar remained where it was, and a flashy new sports car sat angled across four spaces and I rolled my eyes. It was such an entitled jerk thing to do that I parked the Jeep half in two of the spots the car was in.

I climbed out and my former training sergeant gave me a strange look. His eyes wandered over to Larry, flashed something

I couldn't identify and went blank. Larry didn't notice but when his eyes shifted back to me, I saw nothing.

Ian Cruz had shut down, and I tried to shrug it off and looked at the monstrosity beside my own vehicular nightmare. It was a bright red Chevrolet Corvette with black leather interior and permanently illuminated red-hot lights. The eerie red glow combined with the dark interior made it a convenient place to murder someone, but no one looked to have been murdered inside. Just a trash bag in the back and a vanity plate reading MJRLGER.

"Major leaguer?" I guessed and Cruz half-nodded agreement. He was still upset about something he'd yet to clue me in to.

"Do you still have keys?" I asked and he nodded again, leading us to the fire door. Standing beside it was the trashcan where I'd found my perfect cape that betrayed me. My eyes flashed from the can to the stain in the parking space.

"Don't play with trash, chica," Ian said, holding open the door.

"I wasn't playing with trash," I stomped through the open door and crossed my arms. "I was acquiring a cape for my vigilante alter ego. Also, I think I know how that got there."

I pointed to the parking lot and Cruz raised his brow.

Larry's phone went off and he stopped to answer, Cruz and I waiting just inside the door. I heard him ask a bunch of questions that meant nothing to me before he checked his watch. Concern and fear colored his face, and when the call ended he gave me a pleading look.

"Can I borrow your Jeep?" He asked and I tossed him the keys.

"What's wrong?"

"Someone brought in a dog, looks like it was hit by a car. I need to go," he walked over and kissed me before giving Cruz a look and jogging to the orange monstrosity.

Cruz chuckled and I raised a brow at him.

"He just marked you, chica."

"No...." I started and then let out a breath. "Yeah. That was definitely a 'hands off' look. I'd be mad, but I'm too satisfied to care."

"So you two made up?"

"I guess..."

He nodded and studied me, then the spot where Larry had disappeared, and finally the parking space.

"You think someone removed the trash bag and the blood dripped from the bag into the spot?"

"While being bumped against the ground. Maybe the murder weapon? I just don't know how it got from here to there without getting any in between. You're wearing your Stepford Soldier face, what is it now?"

"Nothing," he started to turn away and I grabbed his hand.

"Damnit, if you got beef let it out!" Winnie whined at the mention of one of her favorite foods, but I kept my eyes on Cruz. He took the hand I grabbed him with and used it to bring me closer.

"You're going to get bored. With him, that town... everyone but Winnie, and then we'll finish what we started," he pulled me against him, and kissed me. Our tongues touched and heat coursed through me, fisting my fingers into his shirt, I lost control and when we broke apart I was breathless. Winnie let out a soft growl and moved between us, giving Cruz the stink eye.

"Winnie knows it too. But she doesn't want this life... not like we do."

Scared of what might come out of my mouth, I stayed quiet and studied the directory.

Elliot Maize was on the second floor. Surprising since the entire rest of the newspaper staff was on the first floor, but maybe it was a managerial separation deal.

Or he was a jerk who thought he was better than everyone else.

We started in the downstairs offices, and I skipped Yvette's to look in Carla's while Cruz detoured to the copy room. Carla's door was locked, but the doors and locks were cheap and I jimmied it open with a credit card. The wooden door swung open to reveal an impersonal and sterile office of wood tones and beige. There was nothing on her desk, no shelves of books or personal items, and her trash bin was empty. I ran my finger along the desk and came away with a layer of dust and something... sticky? Tacky?

I leaned into the surface and sniffed.

Paint?

Her desk drawers weren't locked and the contents were as uninteresting as the rest of her office. She'd either cleaned it or someone had emptied it in her absence and I made a mental note to check her car for signs of life. If she was going to be with my brother, she was going to need to get comfortable with messes.

My partner sniffed the desk, the floor and the file cabinet, but nothing piqued her interest so we moved on. Winnie and I left the office and she sniffed at the base of Yvette's door. Curious, I gripped the handle and prepared to get the credit card out again. It wasn't locked and swung open soundlessly.

I braced myself for the smell and sight that had been here before, but there was no carnage. The blood had been cleaned and the furniture removed. While I knew the books and photos were in police custody, I had to wonder what someone did with a cracked glass desk someone was murdered on. The shelves behind the desk weren't completely bare, I noted, as a few of the books had been real and were lying flat haphazardly. I picked one up and flipped through it, nothing but the words of Mr. Edgar Allen Poe. Same with the one written by Ms. Jane Austin and I looked at the remaining books. All of them literary classics with the exception of The Last Coyote by Michael Connolly, a book mid-series about an LAPD detective who played by his own rules.

It was hardcover, and I picked it up. The spine was well worn and the pages were a little discolored from either age or use. I flipped it open and an envelope fell out of the middle of the book. It wasn't postmarked, addressed, or labeled on the outside, but it was a medium sized yellow with a pretty hefty volume to it.

The metal tabs moved easily, the sticky surface not sealed. I pulled out the stack of papers and unfolded them to see line after line of numbers. They were arranged in four columns of four then a column of three, two and then another four. Flipping through the stack there were over a dozen pages. On the third to last, a small handwritten note in purple ink underlined one of the rows and drew an arrow.

Busted

Winnie let out a grumble and I turned my head, Mr. Elliot Maize was standing in the doorway.

"Velociraptor?" he held out his hand to Winnie and she flattened her ears. His wide eyes and toothy grin were unnerving and I wondered again whether or not his hair was real and if he abused substances. "No need for alarm. What have you got there?"

He rocked on his toes, moving multiple directions and still remaining in the doorway.

"Just... a job offer," I said, carefully pulling the job offer envelope from my pocket while keeping my hips squared to the shelf. I slid the envelope into the book and tucked the stack of papers beneath the dust jacket of the book before closing it. "Looks like Yvette was leaving."

Elliot's eyes flashed to the paper and anger mixed with accusation.

"Can I see that?" He stammered and I nodded, walking it over to him. He reached for the book but I only gave him the letter. We stood for a moment, waiting to see what the other would do. Resigned, he scanned the page and feigned interest before looking at me, the book, and back to Winnie. He folded the letter and stuffed it in his pocket, eyes calculating his next move.

He definitely wanted the book.

"I... I think we should talk. Maybe you can help me out with a problem we've been having. Could you meet me in my office, without the uh... dinosaur?"

"Sure. Give me a minute," I said and he nodded repeatedly before leaving down the hallway with a last look at the book in my hand. A figure was silhouetted against a doorway in the opposite direction and Ian held a finger to his lips, encouraging quiet until the door clicked closed at the end of the hall.

Ian moved into the doorway and offered me a brow raise. Silently, I passed him the book, removing a flap of the dust jacket and tapping the papers. My eyes were searching for something that would indicate we were safe, but I had a sense we were being watched. Cruz unfolded the papers, eyes scanning the page and offering me a knowing nod. I gestured to Winnie and he pulled a leash from his pocket, clipping it to her.

"Fifteen?" He asked and I nodded, starting to move past him and pausing.

There were black smudges on the door handle. I leaned in and sniffed... paint?

"Be good, good girl," I said, ruffling Winnie's ears and going down the hall. The drips of blood had been cleaned, but the spots were cleaner than the normal carpet. It was a nearly straight line to the door and out into the stairwell. This floor had also been cleaned, but I paused at the fire door.

It was sitting slightly ajar and in the metal track was a single drop of blood that was mirrored on the wall beside it. How had the weapon gotten to the parking space before dripping?

"Ms. Sharp?" Elliot's voice carried down the stairs and I trudged up the two flights, studying each step for blood. There was none in the uneven rock and cement surface. Knowing how hard grout was to clean, I leaned closer but there was nothing. Whatever the weapon was, it hadn't come up this way. My eyes went back to the door and the wall... It had gone in the trash bag, been bounced in the parking lot and...

"Ms. Sharp!" He called again and I rolled my eyes.

"Hold your damn horses," I shouted back, studying the corners of the room. There were no obvious cameras, but that meant nothing now that I'd seen what Andrew Scott could do.

Andrew Scott, canvas bags, two purchased by Elliot...

I rubbed the bridge of my nose and finished climbing the stairs.

It all pointed to Elliot except the weapon. If he was a pitcher, he wouldn't have a bat. That much I'd gleaned from Google.

The stairs ended at a glass door that led into a hallway for the medical and police staff. There was a small landing before the door, and off to the left a wooden door stood open with the blonde man at an oversized wooden desk. He was staring at a computer screen, fingers working the mouse, and I walked forward.

His sharp gaze cut to me, he rubbed his nose and smeared black paint on the tip.

"What do you want to talk about?" I asked, leaning against the doorway and looking around the office. Every wall was covered in sport's memorabilia, as was every surface. Signed baseballs, baseball cards, and jerseys were displayed with no rhyme or reason. Behind him was a large picture of him with...

"You know Burt, right?" He asked, following my line of sight to the picture.

"Yeah, we've met. How do you..." my eyes stopped on a pair of wooden hooks that ended in a curve with a small plaque. I moved closer to read it and saw that it was the game winning bat for a world series game ten years ago, but there was no bat.

The door clicked shut behind me and I turned to see Elliot Maize pointing a gun at me

"Have a seat, Ms. Sharp."

Chapter Twenty-Two: Batting a Thousand

"Huh," I said, staring at the man with a small revolver.

"I said sit! First you don't listen to the warnings, you, Yvette, Carla, the Senator... You're all a pain in my ass! Sit!"

He jabbed the gun toward me and I half raised my hands. It was a Derringer of some sort. Either it was a single shot or a two shot, and the man in question didn't look skilled in the use of firearms. I slowly walked toward the chair on the visitor side of his desk, hooked an ankle in the leg, and faced it toward him.

His eyes were still too wide, his smile manic, and a dozen others now joined the bead of sweat I'd seen at his temple downstairs. Though not of immediate concern, his spray tan was dripping down with it, and I wondered whether or not he could get a refund for their crap work if he killed me and managed to walk away.

A few droplets of sweat rolled down my back.

If he killed me.

"What did you really find in that office?"

"The letter," I answered. He moved quicker than I anticipated, striking out and crushing his gun hand against my face.

My vision blurred and I tasted blood.

"Don't mess with me, Ms. Sharp. I may have used up my only bat, but you've seen my work. I'm still strong enough to crush your skull," he laughed, his voice too loud and too high pitched. "Now, tell me what I want to know, and we can walk out of here. As soon as we're clear of the authorities, I'll let you go. What was in the book?"

I spat blood on his carpet, leaving a trace of myself in the room.

"Bitch!" He shouted, and smashed the gun into my face again. A sharp bite into my flesh and warmth rolled down my cheek. I swiped a hand on my face and it came away with blood and black paint.

"If you hit me again, I'm going to make you sterile," I warned through gritted teeth. Elliot's eyes shifted, uncertain and alarmed.

"I have a gun!" He thrust it out in emphasis and I shrugged.

"I don't care. Hit me again and you lose your balls, man. First and only warning."

He rubbed his hand over his face, swiping up the orange drips into his bleached blonde hair. The whole thing shifted on his head and confirmed it was either a piece or a wig. Rather than dwell on the man having a meltdown, I scanned his office again. Noting that the computer screen was angled in such a way that if I moved back a foot, I could see it. A black personal sized shredder sat beside the desk with the full bin light illuminated. He had a backpack beside it, a stack of paper bags, two cans of spray paint and a can of lighter fluid.

A wave of nausea jolted through me.

"What was in the book?"

"Pages of numbers," I said and he raised his fist at the truth. This time I was ready, pushing the chair back a foot so he'd miss and connected my knee with his crotch. I misjudged the force and the chair toppled, sending me sliding half under the desk. My arm caught on the monitor cord and it crashed to the floor. Quickly, I crawled under the desk and tried to view the monitor but it had cracked. There was only a series of lines and colors. It smelled like paint under here and I toppled the trashcan to see the paper bags stained with spray paint.

"Seriously?" I grumbled, wondering what sort of grown man would huff paint while also stealing money from old ladies and blackmailing voyeurs. It explained the crazed look and the smears of paint everywhere, but how do you go from stealing money to murder?

Fingers fisted into my hair and I was hauled roughly from the ground.

"You bitch!" He landed a punch into my kidneys and I held back bile as the pain tore through my ribs. "You broke my damn monitor! Now how am I supposed to know when to detonate!"

"Detonate what?" I choked out and his maniacal gleam sent a shiver through my core.

"The decoy. When the cops show up, that Corvette goes ka-boom and we drive off into the sunset."

"It's nine in the morning," I heaved and his nails bit my scalp as he dragged me up by my hair a second time.

"If you keep this up, bitch, I'm going to take my chances getting away without a hostage. You and that nosy gossip bitch thinking she could spy on me. I'm the webhost, dammit. Just because she hacked my server..."

Elliot threw me roughly into the desk chair, pacing to the window and back to the door as he looked at the memorabilia scattered around his office. A metal water bottle with a Yankee logo clattered to the floor and I saw a small lens in the O of New York.

Was it still active?

"It was perfect, you know," he jostled the blinds to look below. "It went flawlessly for years. Most old people don't know how much money they have or what they pay for anything. Two decades I've run this business, taking a little extra from the subscribers. Then the assholes start noticing, print is dead, and it's available online for free. What can I give them that the Internet can't?"

He was back to looking out of the window.

"Then I had to hire that damn gossip reporter. She was my ace in the hole, with her I could pretend I'm charging more for the new talent. People were so interested in reading her scandal coverage that I got the idea to look into scandals of my own. But she was too brazen. Too willing to draw attention to her crimes... and mine. I tried blackmail, but everyone puts their business on the internet. No one cares if the world sees their flaws."

My phone buzzed in my pocket but I didn't reach for it. Elliot had come to a stop in front of me, spray tan completely streaked over his face, his shirt, and his toupee had slid halfway back on his head.

"I was supposed to play in the MLB, Ms. Sharp. I was the best! The only pitcher who could pitch and hit with enough force to take out a man and never get injured."

"Until you got injured?" I offered when he stared silently a beat too long. Elliot had gone off the rails. "Or until they discovered your addiction to huffing?"

"Until I injured one too many opponents, Ms. Sharp."

I watched his eyes light up in pleasure.

"Nothing as thrilling as crushing a woman's skull with a world series bat, just a ball to the ribs here and a bat to a runner there. The pain in their eyes, the ease with which they'd believe it was an accident. The whole industry was so easy to manipulate I nearly cried... until they started to look for patterns. So I played sick, got their sympathy, weaseled into their hearts so I could suck every last bit of humanity out of them and turn them into pawns," his fists were clenched at his sides and I watched his trigger finger.

He was dangerously close to pulling it and with every declaration he'd lift his hands again, aiming it at me, the window... the lighter fluid.

"No one even suspected me! I started getting money, access, jobs... hell I only work here because I worked every connection I had and bled them dry. I was the nice guy, the genuinely sweet person who made friends with everyone and insulated myself in a cocoon of lies and security. Then I had to hire a damn gossip blogger."

He kicked the shredder and sent the tiny shreds of paper raining around the room. I seized the opportunity and lunged, catching his waist and sending him to the ground. The Derringer cracked, splitting my skull in two with the sound as the projectile lodged itself in the neighboring wall. I shoved Elliot back, scrambled to my feet and ran for the door.

Hand on the doorknob, it slipped from my grip as the sticky black paint transferred to my hand.

He's high as a kite right now.

I got the door open and staggered toward the staircase as another shot rang out from behind me. Throwing myself to the ground, I felt the impact and the rain of glass as the door to the government administration offices shattered.

"I'm going to kill you, bitch!" Elliot called from behind me and I scrambled to my feet as a weight collided against me and sent us both through the glass wall of the administration reception area.

A scream slipped from my mouth, burning my throat as I rolled in broken glass. My knee collided with something soft and

I struck out again, this time coming up with nothing. Fighting pain and nausea, I staggered to my feet, trying to force open my eyes as the ringing in my ears continued. A brick wall barreled into me, sending me staggering back to land in a pile of broken glass on the floor, blood dripping into my eyes.

"I'm going to rip off your limbs and carry them out in a trash bag like I did the baseball bat!"

His voice was the same volume as the ringing in my ears. Everything was too loud and the sticky sensation of blood came from a gap between my T-shirt and jeans.

A heavy boot collided with my ribs and I wretched up the morning's coffee onto the floor.

"That's disgusting!" His boot connected again and I rolled away with the impact. I fought the pain and vertigo, staggered to my feet and wiped the blood out of my eyes. Elliot was staggering around the room, kicking at air and trying to connect. His face flashed toward me, his eyes were squeezed shut as more of the spray tan dripped down his face.

Quietly as possible, I moved away from him, deeper into the office space. The air was still, air conditioning causing the sweat to dry and I shivered. My eyes stayed on the large man, he was moving more normally and I had a bad feeling he'd be able to see soon.

I ran to the nearest door, threw it open and locked it behind me.

"You think that door will stop me?" He howled and the whole wall shook as he flung himself against the door. "You think sending the cops sniffing around my business will stop me? You think getting proof I was stealing from old ladies will stop me?"

His body being thrown against the wall, shaking the framed certificates hanging behind the desk, punctuated each of his accusations. I backed away from the door, grabbing desk drawers that my bloody hands couldn't open.

Once, twice, the top drawer slid open as the door splintered.

I froze as with another slam, the door shattered completely and he barreled through. My eyes dropped to the drawer, and I picked up the black semi-auto inside, firing three rounds at the man in front of me. He crumbled to the ground just as a series of explosions shook the entire building.

Chapter Twenty-Three: Back on the Farm

My phone was ringing, everything hurt, and Winnie was lying across my chest. A hand reached around me and a male voice answered the device. I closed my eyes and tried to go back to sleep when the phone was pressed against my ear.

"Vacation is over Cynthia. I need you here this afternoon to help with the goat milk."

"Goats are jerks, Joseph," I grumbled and Larry took the phone back.

"She'll be there when she can stand up," he said and hung up. "No!"

He kissed my cheek softly and climbed out around me.

"It's been two weeks, Cyn. You can't stay in my bed forever."

"Why not? I was shot at, kicked, and I still have stitches!"

He ran a finger over the cut on my cheek and flipped back the blanket to check out my discolored ribs. Concern and sadness filled his eyes and he left the room. I snuggled back into the bed only to have my blanket stolen and coffee placed in my hand.

"Out, you little bed bug," he commanded, and Winnie joined me in growling at him.

Larry reached to take my coffee back, and I sobered enough to down it in three gulps. His eyes heated.

"That was hot," he whispered, moving in for a kiss and taking the cup back. I nearly had him back to horizontal when a throat cleared in the doorway and I groaned.

"Go away!"

Winnie grumbled her agreement, and Larry flipped his brother off behind his back.

"We need to get your statement on record," I shifted around Larry to look at him and saw that he was staring pointedly at his shoes.

"My statement is on record." Larry let out a sigh and moved off of the bed to my horror and dismay. "Damn you, Daniel! First that damn video of me getting my ass kicked goes viral, and now this?"

"I pinned that video to the top of all my social media feeds."

"Shouldn't you be trying to figure out who leaked the damn video instead of sharing it, deputy?" I snarled.

He smirked and I grabbed a pillow to chuck at his head. Daniel batted it away easily and Larry helped me stand up. Though I was wearing pajamas, they were a bit catawampus, and Daniel's eyes went wide at the sight of my bruises. I adjusted my shirt and also discovered most of my left boob had fallen out of the shirt's armhole.

"My eyes are up here, Kirby." It came out as a growl and he barked out a laugh. "This going on the internet too?"

"I've seen your eyes, haven't seen that before," Larry adjusted my shirt and helped me to the door before letting go and punching his brother in the gut.

The older Kirby laughed again.

"Bro, your girlfriend hits harder than you. This, though, is just for us, man. No internet involved."

"Winnie," I called and she got to her feet. Ears and eyes at the ready, she waited for my next command as I stared evenly at Daniel. "I shot a man, was evacuated from a burning building, and had the crap beat out of me, footage of which was then published on the internet. Can the snark or get a tooth hug? I'm not in the mood today."

Daniel's face sobered and he tried to exchange a look with Larry, but the good animal doctor was focusing on trying to get me to the living room.

"His body is still unclaimed in the morgue." Daniel's fingers knotted together nervously. "No one is answering their contact requests, and Burt is pretending they've never met."

I felt my shoulders shrug, the horror of taking a life not quite extending to sympathy for the man I'd killed.

"New chief gets sworn in today," he shifted and I didn't have any thoughts on that either. Whoever it was would have had to investigate my self-defense claim... if the whole world hadn't seen me hit, kicked and thrown through a window.

"I uh... picked up your Jeep for you," Daniel changed the subject and I held my breath.

"What color is it?"

"Grey. They also changed out the seats and the steering wheel as an apology for the orange... and the puppies. Kinda looks exactly like your old one."

I nodded in relief.

Grey was a perfectly acceptable color. I could handle grey.

"So what statement do you need from me?"

"Are you Larry's girlfriend?" I felt Larry freeze beside me. It was his turn to hold his breath for an answer.

"Yeah," I answered and Winnie wagged her tail. "As long as he kicks you out of this house in the next fifteen minutes and refills my coffee."

Showered and caffeinated, I pulled the newly grey Jeep into the dirt lot of the dairy and climbed out. A line of people was assembled outside the ice cream parlor and Winnie gave it a hopeful look before turning back to me.

"No," I warned and she flattened her ears.

"Nice of you to show up," Joseph declared from behind me and I jumped before clutching my ribs. The jolt of pain was intense and I again marveled that anyone recovered from broken ribs. Every movement of my arm was agony. All minor twists and adjustments were literal hell and sudden movements sent me curling into a ball on the ground.

"Where are the jerk goats, Joseph?" It was too much work to turn so I projected my voice and startled a flock of crows on a nearby fence post.

"No need to yell," he said, coming even with me and then leading me toward the barn. While not a tall man, Joseph moved around at a pretty good clip, a fact that was reiterated when he kept turning around to wait for me as every movement jostled my injuries. Joseph checked his watch three times before we made it to the horse pens and was sighing more than he was exhaling.

"Don't get pissy with me, this was your damn idea," I grumbled, slightly winded from the effort of walking fifty yards. Dust bloomed and I checked that my stitches were covered before continuing. I hadn't been as careful last time I had stitches. That set got infected, and Winnie had been assigned the task of wound cleaning.

By herself.

We trooped forward, and when we got to a fork, he turned away from the goat enclosures.

"Did you move the goats?"

Joseph didn't answer and I looked at Winnie. She scented the air, wagged her tail and took off past Joseph.

"Winnie!"

I heard a thud, squeals of laughter and a bark. Fighting the pain, I ran after my dog, prepared to defend her against accusations of attack. In the last stall was Seth, Carla, and his kids, standing beside a dog nursing four puppies in a whelping bed. Winnie had sniffed mama, the puppies, and was now tackling my niece and nephew to the ground for whatever they had smeared on their clothes.

"Hey sis," Seth came over and gave me a bear hug that forced a scream from my throat. "You look like crap."

"Can it, Sethany."

"Auntie Cyn!" Sylvia screamed and jumped toward me. I caught her, spun in a circle before falling on my ass beside the puppies. "What happened to you? Did you hear about the 'splosion at daddy's friend's office?"

I nodded and my eyes tracked to "daddy's friend". Carla was relaxed, wearing clothes that were both elegant and comfortable while gazing adoringly at the kids and the puppies. Erich stood to the side, petting Winnie and waiting for the room to quiet down. He wasn't big on loud noises, and I wished I'd known he would be here so I could bring him headphones.

This family was always loud.

Especially his sister.

Sylvia waved me closer and I leaned in so she could whisper in my ear.

"I saw them kissing!" she hissed and slobber coated the side of my face. "We're getting a puppy!"

I jerked back. The kid had no concept of volume control based on proximity, and I tried not to search for duct tape to quiet her as my ear rang from having the second part shouted at me.

"Your kid's a jerk," I said to Seth as she bounded out of the pen and collided with someone who gruffed in surprise. Sylvia squealed her way back in, a man holding her aloft.

"Hey dad," I said and he smiled as my mom came in behind him.

"Cynthia, what happened to your face?"

"Hi mom," I said in lieu of explanation. I knew she'd already seen the video, her friends had all commented on the original post. Comments on my fighting, my weight, and whether or not I had had enough orgasms. They all only agreed on the last: no I had not and it was really fortunate I hadn't died.

Apparently

Larry came in next, and I tilted my head at his expression and the book in his hand.

"Are you all ready?" He asked and I stared at him bewildered.

"Yes," Seth and Carla said together, standing to hold hands before him. Sylvia squealed and Erich clutched my mom's hand, she pulled out some earplugs and placed them in his ears until he relaxed against her.

I remained on the floor, stroking a puppy as Larry married his ex-lover to my brother. They kissed to seal the deal and everyone tossed animal feed into the air.

My parent's exchanged misty eyed looks, and Carla's eyes brimmed with happy tears. She looked beautiful in a simple white sheath dress, a hat on her head, and a small silver band on her ring finger.

"What are you thinking?" Larry asked, coming up behind me to rest his head on my shoulder and press me against him.

"That Thanksgiving is going to be super awkward," I let out a breath, marveling at how simple and happy their family looked.

"Why would Thanksgiving be awkward?" Larry nuzzled my neck and I tried to hide my evil smile.

"Because my mom will probably be the only woman there you haven't seen naked up close and personal."

Larry returned my smile with one of his own and my heart skipped a beat. As he turned around to give me a long lingering kiss.

"That's what you think..."

I punched him in the arm and heard footsteps just outside the stall. Daniel rounded the corner, looking sweaty and a little pale.

"What's wrong, loser?"

"The new chief..." his eyes darted behind me and I heard Carla clear her throat.

"Problem, Officer?"

I turned to see a wicked gleam in her eye and felt an excitement build in my gut. She looked over at Seth and I looked at him as well. He smiled and pulled Erich against him in a hug. Sylvia launched herself onto his back in a choke hold he pretended was effective in a fake gagging gesture. Larry wrapped his arms around me again, contentment settled in and I felt Winnie leaned against my leg tail wagging as we all turned to stare at Daniel's pale sweating face.

"Ha ha, my sister-in-law is your boss!"

He swallowed hard and Larry slid his hands up my shirt, gently stroking the bruises on my ribs, kissing my neck and I forgot everything around me until my mom cleared her throat and Seth let out a wolf whistle. My face burned and I snuggled in closer.

"Get a room," Carla laughed and I looked at her over my shoulder.

"Anything you say, Chief Sharp."

Sneak Peek Book Three: Eating Up the Evidence

Chapter One: Heat Wave

It was eleven in the morning, I'd had a gallon of water, and I was still thirsty.

On the ground beside me, Winnie was half under a shrub trying desperately to get relief from the unrelenting sun. Despite four years in the Army together, the canine and I had never gotten used to the heat. Winnie, formerly Sgt. Winnifred Pupperson, was a German Shepherd Mallinois mix that was only a working dog by breed. In terms of personality, she could best be described as an occasionally competent demolitions expert. Since that could also be used to describe me, we were the perfect team.

The perfect team at completely destroying things people still wanted and or needed. We didn't just occasionally start small dumpster fires or accidents that could be cleaned with a mop and some elbow grease. Nope, we indirectly caused the burning of a sports car and a newspaper office just over a month ago. Before that, we had destroyed the church event space, several walking aids and B-32 at a game of Bingo gone terribly wrong.

We were never the bystanders of "little incidents". A fact that usually led us to getting assignments such as this: melting in the sun far away from people and buildings.

I sighed at Winnie and looked longingly at the barn.

There was a fan in the barn.

Despite only being the first week of May, it was over ninety degrees. The dairy was doing killer business at the ice cream shop and no one wanted to be outside. No one including me, but I didn't have much choice in that given it was my job. I looked around the dirt landscape, void of anything that could harm the animals that lived there.

Harm or offer shade to the unfortunate soul sent to check on them.

A goat bleated and I looked at the evil monster. It was grey, with normal-sized horns, and a beard that was rather unimpressive for his five years of age. Berry was the reason we were out here, checking all the goats for injuries after he barreled through a wooden fence and orchestrated a jail break into the horse enclosure.

The horses were not amused and a female goat who was actively lactating had nearly been trampled. Since this was a dairy farm, her milk was far more important than Berry and his need for freedom or an amorous encounter with a horse. As the farms animal technician, it was my job to make sure her milk was still suitable for consumption and none of the animals needed a visit from the local vet.

"I hate you," I muttered at Berry, stuffing my dishwater blonde hair back under my hat after wiping a gallon of sweat off my forehead. I squinted my lavender eyes at him, trying for menacing, but even towering over him, I could see he was unimpressed. "If we were in the middle east, I could cook you and serve you to a hungry Army base."

He bleated at me and I glared as he galloped away.

"Yeah, you better run!"

"Cyn! Aren't you done yet?" I winced at the voice of my boss, Joseph.

I glanced over and down at the short squat man in pristine work clothes. At six feet, I towered over his five something frame. He had on a cowboy hat in contrast to my ball cap, nearly new cowboy boots and a flannel shirt stretched tight over his belly, the buttons looked more likely to pop than our currently in labor cow. I was no super model at size fourteen, but I was definitely not in danger of bursting out of my clothes. The t-shirt and cargos were sweat stained and stuck to every inch of my flesh like a sticky second skin. Both were coated in dust, grass and what might be manure, but I wasn't bursting out of them.

In fact, it was going to take a pry bar to get these clothes off.

"Cynthia Sharp, I asked you a question!"

Another Army flashback to hearing my name shouted in *that tone*. Every time we'd blown up a marketplace, crushed a pretzel statue, or set Florida on fire, someone would use my full name. Usually they'd include my rank, but since my "accidental" retirement when no one noticed my contract was up, I didn't have any rank.

"Joseph, it's hotter than hell out here! I'm working on it!"

Winnie whimpered under the shrub and I gave her an apologetic look.

"It's only May, don't be a baby!" Joseph mopped sweat from his forehead as he shot daggers at me. I noted that much like the brim of his hat, his shirt was wilting fast and pools of sweat had formed in his pits. "The men are done fixing the fence, you can't check a few goats in the same time it takes them to replace a whole ten foot section of fence?"

"There are ten of them, they have tools! Also it's not a few goats, it's two dozen and they won't stop moving around. Also, they all look the same!" I shouted and grasped the scruff of a goat as it passed and looked it over. "I can't tell if I've checked this one and you won't let me draw on them, so this is where we are Joe!"

"Don't yell at me! I'm the boss!"

"Yeah, yeah," I grumbled and freed the goat. "They're all fine then I guess. Happy?"

"No!" He pulled his hat off to fan his face and his comb over fell into his eyes. "I want you to check the damn goats!"

"I did!"

Without a backward glance, I walked away from Joseph and the goats. Winnie's collar jingled behind me and I looked down to see her panting in a pink camouflage collar with her name stuck to it in Velcro. The jingle was a Christmas bell Joseph made her wear after an incident with some sheep and the seat of his pants.

It had been hilarious, but now Winnie's presence requires announcing.

We made it to the barn door, pausing to enjoy the blast of air from the fan. Winnie lifter her head and froze. Scenting the air, she let out an excited bark and took off toward the open-air paddock. My nose couldn't detect him, but I knew where she was going and a smile look over my face.

Larry had arrived to help birth the calf.

Larry, Dr. Lawrence Kirby, was the sexy commercial livestock vet. He was tall, muscled like a nerd who walked into a gym and was too embarrassed to leave without working out, and funny in a way that was rarely on purpose. I rounded the corner to see Winnie easily leap the enclosures fence, run up to Larry and shove her nose into his testicles.

Just as the calf started to emerge and he took hold of the legs.

Face pale, with a small but manly scream; he welcomed the calf into the world before collapsing in on himself in pain. For her part, Winnie licked his face and the arms as the hands arrived to remove the calf.

"Hey," I said, looking down at him. For the first time, he was the one coated in gunk and I... was coated in different gunk. So it was actually situation normal, all fluffed up.

"Your dog is a jerk," he grumbled, ruffling her fur with affection.

"Yup," I said, looking down at both of them. "She said you missed your annual health exam and wanted to make sure you saw a proctologist."

"She checked my cavities this morning!" He complained and I squatted beside him to kiss his nose.

"And you checked mine. What's your point?"

His smile was decidedly very male and I determined he would live, so I offered him a hand up. With a tug he was back upright and pressed against me.

"Should I check them again... just in case?" His face moved closer to mine, and he choked before taking a step back. "What is that smell?"

I sniffed the air and looked around.

"I don't smell anything."

Curious I lifted my shirt and took a cautious sniff and gagged.

"Goats. That smell is goats mixed with sweat and manure."

"Maybe I should help you check all your cavities in the shower, with soap," he waggled his eyebrows but didn't get any closer.

A man cleared his throat behind me and turned into my brother.

"Dude, I know you've had sex with my wife and everything, but don't remind me that you're doing my sister," Seth made a face and I punched him. He grabbed my arm, put me in a rear wristlock and held firm. Despite being nearly the same height, and his nerdy occupation as a structural engineer, Seth managed to maintain his grip while I struggled to get free.

"Geez you stink!"

I rolled my eyes and considered stomping on his foot or sending Winnie after his nuts, but smelling me was probably worse than both of those. It would also be embarrassing to admit that a trained soldier was incapable of freeing herself from a nerd.

A nerd who was my brother, meaning fighting dirty was definitely on the table and I was still losing.

"Carla and I need your help... with mom," he said and I shuddered. His wife Carla had been a honey trap government agent with an affinity for side gigs... including Larry. The one saving grace in this is that she hadn't had sex with my brother during the times she was hooking up with Larry or I'd have needed a lobotomy to recover from the second-hand incest. She'd retired from that after one final mission to expose a corrupt council member that lead to the death of a reporter, married Seth, and was now Sweet Pea, Ohio's chief of police. Despite the hate toward the way she got her experience, Carla was more than qualified to supervise Larry's brother Daniel and Barney Fife, no relation, who worked with him. My niece and nephew adored her and a few shots of tequila followed by a tell-all girls night had made the lingering animosity about her screwing Larry fade.

Carla was a hot redheaded bombshell and turning her down would be hard for anyone. Larry was just a man, and she promised me she was more than done with him. We shook on it, had two more shots, and made Larry and my brother drive us home while we loudly discussed our sex lives.

The woman was my new favorite sister.

My mom, on the other hand, was not exactly family friendly or easy on the feint of heart. While Lynn Sharp was not a drug user or an advocate of flag burning, the conservative community secretly wished she hadn't retired from academia and branched out into practical experimentation. Teaching sexual liberation and the historical repressions of female sensuality had been one thing, but insisting the senior citizens in the community explore theirs was another. No matter how hard Mrs. Kirby tried, she could not get the church to excommunicate my mom... or do more than suggest that she herself could benefit from one of Lynn's "meetings".

Her meetings were sex parties, where she encouraged swinging and sold pleasure toys. Toys that she was happy to demonstrate on herself and others, my dad included. The group had also hosted a live nude art in the park that featured my neighbor and her husband getting jiggy with it for the entire world to see. The basement was now the only bedroom in the house after Seth's was converted to a library for their ever growing collection of research and my bedroom became a "playroom" modeled after those Fifty Shades books.

Books my sister Heidi gave her. My sister Molly supported this by sending them tips and tools for pleasure from around the world. They also cohosted and researched half the "experiments" conducted in the house.

Hence, Carla was my new favorite sister.

"Not a chance, Sethany," I wriggled free and he let me go. "You are on your own with the Goddess of Giving."

I stuck my tongue out at him and he did it back.

"Let me re-phrase that. Carla needs your help keeping mom happy so that we don't tell her about the time you smashed every glass Christmas ornament in the shed for target practice," he crossed his arms and I hitched a shoulder.

"That was twenty years ago, she probably doesn't even remember the raccoon raid the shattered her family's Christmas Legacy collection."

"She will when I remind her," he countered and I narrowed my eyes.

"Then I'll tell her the real reason you were come late from school that day you had to go to the ER for getting your penis stuck in the pottery wheel trying to make an impression for Dana Cummings," I countered and he turned a little pink in the ears. "An artistic rendering so she could satisfy herself at band camp without needing to resort to a flute."

"She played the clarinet! I couldn't compete with a clarinet!"

"So, no one will know if you leave me out of this," I smiled in victory.

"If you tell her that, I'll tell her about the time you got drunk and taught a pole dancing class to junior high girls..."

"Enough," Larry said, coming up behind me but keeping his distance. "While hearing the end of that story sounds very promising for future blackmail, we do need to get back to work. What do you need help with?"

"Mom is pissed," he said and I felt the hairs on my neck stand up. He should have opened with her being mad at him. I had friends all over the world, probably Carla and I together could get him into some sort of Engineers Without Borders program.

"What did you do?" I whispered, trying to plan his evacuation to Canada or the Middle East. Revolutionaries with guns were less scary than our mom when she's angry.

"I got married!" He threw his hands in the air and my head dropped to the side. "I got married in a barn and there was no party or decorations or fanfare. She never met Carla until after the ceremony, she didn't get to pass her anything symbolic and there wasn't even a cake, Cyn. Mom is pissed! She wants to throw her a party, get to know her and introduce her to the family."

I relaxed.

"Then let Ma throw her a party. Dad can cook, Mo will make a cake, no big deal. If it'll make Ma happy, just..."

"No! Not a party, a *party*. A pleasure party, with her toys and her... methods of experimentation book."

"Has she met Carla? That woman is not a shrinking violet," Larry said and I gave him a warning look. We may have worked through my jealousy, but I did not need him to remind me all that he knew about my sister-in-law.

"Exactly! She said the reason Carla was so... diverse in her experiences was because she was exploring her pleasure. Ma said that if I want her to be happy, I needed to let her do a detailed analysis of the woman's pleasure and take excellent notes or some crap like that. She said it's a..." he shuddered and I bit back a laugh.

"She said it's an Outgoing Orgasm Party, and we all need to be there."

"What do you want me to do? Doesn't sound like you have a choice," I smirked and he shook his head.

"I need you to demolish it in a way that only you can: accidentally and completely."

"Why would I do that, big brother? I'd hate for your wife to go unsatisfied after all she's been through... marrying you."

"You weren't listening, Cyn, I said all of us. Carla, me, Heidi, her husband, Larry and you are all expected to attend. Molly might even Skype in with her wife. It's family sex education night," all the blood left my face and I looked between Larry and Seth in horror. One was laughing and trying to disguise it as a cough, and the other was pleading me to get our whole family out of this.

"I'll think of something," I swore but the dread building in my gut said nothing short of an apocalyptic event would get any of us out of this.

About the author

E. N. Crane is a fiction author writing humorous mysteries with plus-sized female leads and their furry friends. She is one of two authors under the Perry Dog Publishing Imprint, a one woman, two dog operation in Idaho... for now. My dogs are Perry and Padfoot, the furry beasts shown above. They are well-loved character inspiration in all things written and business.

If you are interested in joining my newsletter, please subscribe here: https://e-n-crane_perrydogpublishing.ck.page/578ed9ab 37or on my website, PerryDogPublishing.com

You will receive A Bite in Afghanistan, the prequel to the Sharp Investigations Series, as a thank-you for joining. I only have one newsletter for mental health reasons, so both romance and mystery are on there! If you only want one in your inbox, follow

Perry Dog Publishing on all socials to stay on top of the latest news... and pet pics.

Made in the USA
Las Vegas, NV
11 December 2024